THE
SLEEPER STREET
GANG

MARSHALL SEDDON

NFB
Buffalo, New York

NFB
NFB Publishing/Amelia Press
119 Dorchester Road
Buffalo, New York 14213

For more information visit Nfbpublishing.com

This book is dedicated to Uncle Jack and Dad –
the two greatest storytellers of my life

CHAPTER ONE

The first time I saw Uncle Walter's pistol I was surprised. It wasn't the pistol itself that surprised me, I'd seen pistols before, and even shot one a few times at my cousin's house back when I was about ten. It was Mike Sullivan's service revolver, he was the county Sheriff and was a friend of my uncle Charlie. He carried a snub-nosed .38 and, after a short lecture on gun safety and a demonstration, he let my cousin Joe and me fire a few shots at an empty beer can. I remember that it was heavy and had quite a kick.

What surprised me about Uncle Walter's pistol was that it was *Walter's*. He was not a hunter and didn't target shoot or even plink, plinking being a common practice in those days. Plinking involved walking through a woods or a field with a .22 rifle or a small pistol and shooting at targets of opportunity: a knothole in a tree, a turtle on a log, an old can, or an unlucky crow or woodchuck. Uncle Walter never did anything like that.

I never saw Uncle Walter cleaning his pistol. Most guys with pistols obsessively cleaned and oiled them, spinning the cylinder and checking the action. They all smelled of gun oil, those guys. It was a unique smell, and unmistakable. Walter didn't have that smell; he mostly smelled like witch hazel, which he used as a general tonic, and Middleton's #59 tobacco smoke, which he burned in an old charred corncob pipe.

The pistol had Japanese markings on it and I recognized it as a Nambu from a tattered copy of *Weapons of World War II* that I used to leaf through. It had a slanted pistol grip with a spring-loaded magazine in the handle and was usually carried by officers of the Japanese army during the war. The pistol slipped out of Walter's musette bag which he kept on the floor of my father's '63 Pontiac Catalina station wagon when traveling. I slept in a sleeping bag in the back of that wagon, on a leaky air mattress and kept my shaving kit in the front, next to Unlcle Walter's musette bag. A musette bag is a canvas GI issue knapsack, World War II vintage. Walter kept his after the war and rigged it with a single strap, so that it could be carried over his shoulder like a satchel. It was olive drab, faded and worn with "US" and his name on it: Walter Edwards. He called it his "possibles bag" named after a frontiersman's kit bag. Frontiersmen carried their black powder equipment, fire starting materials and personal items in a large handmade leather pouch. Walter considered himself an expert on the frontier, and spoke endlessly about it.

"They were out there, alone or in small groups," he would say. "The weather was uncertain, the trails un-mapped and there were dangerous wild animals: wolves, rattlesnakes, buffalo and bears. And the Indians were less than friendly. If a war party came upon you, you'd be finished; death by torture if you weren't lucky enough to die fighting.

"The frontiersman carried nothing but his flintlock rifle and black powder in a horn. He had shot, a knife, a blanket and his possibles bag. The bag usually contained a firestarting kit, needle and thread, a bullet mold, a few tools, a braid or two of tobacco and some jerky."

Walter's possibles bag contained his shaving gear, comb, toothbrush, an old, well-worn pair of binoculars and a few tattered books. The books were classics by Mark Twain, a book of poetry by Thomas Galvin, and a Peterson's Bird identification manual. And, it had suddenly become apparent, a pistol.

But the pistol wasn't the real surprise that morning; it was the musty, old leather-bound journal that slid out of his satchel when I tried to put the pistol back. It startled me. Like opening the door on an old shed and seeing a snake, I sucked my breath in and recoiled. I recognized the book immediately: It was my Grandfather's personal journal. My stomach did a flip as I pushed the book, the pistol and other items back into the bag with my handkerchief. I gagged as I walked swiftly away from the car.

It was early, still not yet dawn and the darkened site where we were camping smelled strongly of wood smoke, wet canvas and boiling coffee. A campfire flickered in the distance and I could hear muted voices and snatches of laughter. I stumbled towards it, my footing uncertain in the dark.

We were on a camping and fishing trip; my father, my cousins and my uncles. It was a long, roving adventure, based around Lake Erie and the Allegheny Valley. We would camp for a few days in a central location and rove around, fishing wherever there were fish.

"All the legendary fishing holes," Walter said when he presented the idea to the family. "The ones we've been to and the ones we've heard about. We'll hit 'em all."

Walter was the planner and the inspiration for the trip. Henry Motors, the big automobile plant in town, was closing. My father and all of my uncles and their friends either worked at the factory or in related businesses. The town was in an economic tailspin because of the closing, and families were leaving town in droves. For our own part, my father had accepted a job in San Diego. My mother was devastated.

"I can't imagine leaving my home town," she said. "All my friends and family live here. This is the only place I've ever lived."

I felt the same, at least to a certain extent. I'd grown up in the area, and never left it except for family camping trips. All of my friends were there. We'd grown up together. I'd gone to school with them and played sports with them. We'd been in the Scouts together. But another part of me yearned for something new, and the beaches of San Diego beckoned me. I imagined myself walking along a sun-drenched beach, carrying a surfboard and waving at the girls.

My father had a more simple philosophy about the move: "We've got to go where the jobs are," he said.

One cold winter night, Walter came up with the idea of going on a fishing trip, while the news of the factory closing was still sinking in.

"We'll never have the chance to do this again," he insisted. "We're all moving on. Besides, what else will we have to do between the time the factory closes and we all move away?"

The men spent the rest of the winter mapping out a route and arguing about the best fishing spots and campgrounds. The women, my mother, aunts and sisters, were not happy about the trip. It was their collective opinion that if a trip were to be planned, it should include nice hotels and excellent restaurants. Camping out and fishing was not their style.

"If you think for one minute that I would stick a squirmy worm onto a hook and try to catch a slimy fish and then eat it, you've got another think coming," my mother said to my father more than once. "And sleeping in a musty army tent? No thanks!"

"Don't worry, we'll take a hotel trip after we get back," my father replied. "I promise."

I was thinking about my grandfather's journal as I walked towards the campfire. I had never seen it up close, and the thought of it and how it had been gotten made me feel faint. I rounded a large army surplus squad tent and saw several silhouettes made red by a campfire and the morning mist. Voices murmured as a Coleman lantern sputtered and hissed, throwing a bright white light on a camp table located under a canvas dining fly. Three of my cousins, Calvin, Donnie and Joe, were sitting by the fire. They were not normally early risers and I concluded that they had stayed up all night, too excited about the first night of the trip to sleep.

"What's the matter with you Tommy?" My cousin Calvin asked as I came into the light. "You look like you seen a ghost." He was my age, seventeen, but shorter and he was puffing mightily on a corncob pipe that he could never manage to keep lit. Calvin tried desperately to imitate Walter, who always had a corncob pipe clenched in his teeth. Calvin was sitting by the smoky campfire, watching a large blue speckled enamel coffee pot boil over, causing the fire to hiss and spit.

I ignored his question and searched for a coffee cup. I was hoping that a little hot coffee might settle my stomach and my nerves. I rummaged around in the camp box and found an old, dented enamel cup that looked reasonably clean.

"Coffee ready?" I asked Calvin.

"How would I know?" Calvin said. He often adopted a surly tone when asked a question that he didn't immediately comprehend. He had asked me a question and hadn't expected a question in return, especially one on a completely different subject. He patted at his pocket for a fresh pack of matches. His pipe had gone out again.

"Calvin!" A voice said. We both turned to see my cousin Neil – Calvin's older brother— emerging from a darkened canvas tent. "You're letting the coffee boil over!"

"It's not my job," Calvin said defensively. "Walter put it on."

Neil walked over to the fire and slid the pot off to the side, burning his hand slightly as he did so.

"You're a moron Calvin," he said, clearly annoyed.

"What was I supposed to do?" Calvin said. "Walter put it on."

"Well, Walter's not here," Neil said. "You should have seen that it was boiling over." He looked around in the camp box, searching for a coffee cup.

"I *did* see that it was boiling over," Calvin retorted. "But I didn't put it *on*!"

Neil found a cup and a tattered and burned oven mitt. He lifted the scalding pot and poured himself a cup. He held the pot out for me.

"Thanks," I said.

Neil looked at me dubiously. "You OK? You look like you saw a ghost."

"Bad dream," I said, burning my mouth on the hot coffee. It was bitter and full of grounds, but it helped. I watched as Neil turned his attention to Calvin again.

"What are you doing with that pipe, Calvin?" He asked. Neil was nineteen and worked part time at a high-end clothing store while he finished college. He was tall, with a shock of wavy blonde hair and dimple in his chin. He got a deal on clothing from his store and dressed well, even when camping. Saving his money, he bought a car, a sweet looking '57 Chevy Bel-Air with a V-8 Turbo-Fire engine. The car was painted Matador Red. We all envied him and he enjoyed being envied. Neil was the oldest of all the cousins and never let any of us forget it.

"Lighting it," Calvin said in answer to Neil's question. He struck another match and puffed madly on his pipe.

"You've gone through a whole pack of matches and still can't get it lit," Neil persisted. Neil liked to taunt people, and Calvin was a favorite target.

"Shut up Neil," Calvin said. He struck another match, which sputtered out as he drew too hard on the pipe. "It's these damn matches!" He exclaimed. He threw the empty match pack towards the fire. "They won't stay lit!"

Neil snorted loudly into his hand, as if trying to suppress a laugh.

"Leave him alone, Damnit!" a voice from behind us demanded. We turned to see Uncle Pete silhouetted in the entrance of his tent by a Coleman lantern. He was a thin man with a high-pitched voice and an Adam's apple that bobbed when he talked. My Aunt Betty had married Pete shortly after the war and everyone had always wondered why. He was a man of strong opinion and questionable good sense and his opinions and schemes were a source of annoyance to nearly everyone except my Aunt Betty.

"Pete wasn't always like this," my father explained to me once. "He was lively and fun when we were growing up. But, early in the War, he was captured in the Philippines and forced to walk sixty- five miles in tropical heat to a Japanese prison camp. Anyone who fell out of the line was bayonetted. It was called the Bataan Death March. After spending the next three years in a filthy prison camp he came home a bitter man. Betty took pity on him. She somehow still sees the little kid in him that we all knew."

For some reason, Pete felt that our teasing of Calvin was abusive. He didn't like Calvin that much, he didn't like any of us kids that much. But, whenever we were having a little fun with Calvin and Pete was within earshot, he would come to Calvin's defense. We all looked away as he approached.

"What's the problem here?" He demanded.

"Well, ya see," Neil said in his best John Wayne voice. "Calvin here's been tryin' to light his pipe, and we... well, we were just tryin' to give him a little advice."

My cousin Joe snickered and I bit my lip to keep from laughing. Pete glared around at the group.

"Shut up Neil," he said. "Leave him alone for a change. And stop trying to smoke that stupid pipe Calvin. You can't keep it lit for a lick!"

Pete walked off towards his tent, muttering something about those

"Goddamn kids!" We all burst into laughter— including Calvin.

Walter, who had been watching the whole thing from off to the side in the shadows, walked up to the fire.

"Here's how to light a pipe," he said softly, addressing the group. He pulled his pipe out of his pocket, along with a yellow plastic tobacco pouch and began packing the bowl with tobacco. He smoked a corncob pipe with a plastic mouthpiece. "Missouri Meerschaums, they're called." He often said. "They smoke cooler than briar and aren't as fragile as clay." It was my father's opinion that Walter used them because they were cheap.

He gently packed the tobacco down with his forefinger.

"You don't want it too tight or too loose," he said. "Either way, it won't stay lit," He pulled a stick match from his pocket, an *Ohio Blue Tip*. He flicked it lit with his thumbnail and put the flame to the bowl, drawing gently. Soon a fragrant plume of smoke wafted into the air, mixing with the scent of pine, canvas, bacon and coffee. The aromas made me remember that I hadn't had breakfast yet.

Calvin tried to copy Walter's demonstration. He gently packed his pipe bowl and asked Walter for a stick match. But as he tried to flick the match lit with his thumbnail, a piece of the sulfur tip caught under his nail. Sulfur burns white-hot, and the little piece, caught under Calvin's nail, sizzled its way into his flesh. He yelped and danced around, fanning his hand in a desperate attempt to stop the burning.

The event caused my cousin Joe to laugh maniacally.

"You look like a chicken with its head cut off!" He crowed.

Joe was my cousin on my mother's side, but he could have been Calvin's twin brother. It wasn't so much that they looked alike. Calvin was short, while Joe was tall and broad and had a big space between his front teeth. Joe was a motor head, who liked nothing better than tinkering with engines. Calvin didn't know which end of a wrench was up. It was the constant bickering and snickering that they engaged in that made them seem similar, pranking, tripping, and making fun of each other.

As Calvin tried desperately to stop the burning match tip, he glared hotly at Joe, who was openly laughing at him. The sulfur was caught under the nail, and it kept burning until it finally burned itself out.

"Jeeze!" Calvin exclaimed as he examined his burned nail. "That match was faulty!"

"The only thing that's faulty around here is *you* Calvin," Neil said. The comment brought general laughter from the group.

Calvin's younger brother Donnie stepped forward to examine Calvin's thumb. Donnie was a skinny fourteen year old and the youngest of the group. He was starting to feel his oats and liked to test his wit on Calvin whenever he could.

"That looks bad," he said, looking at the burnt nail.

"It is," Calvin said, shooting a dirty look around at those of us still laughing. "It hurts like hell."

"Hey, I've got a match for you," Donnie said. "Your face and my butt."

Calvin forgot about his hurt thumb and lunged at Donnie. But Donnie was too quick for him and scampered away, laughing. Calvin pursued, issuing a series of threats and curses.

"Enough!" A man's voice barked. I instantly recognized it as my uncle Frank's. Frank was Neil, Calvin and Donnie's father. He was a foreman at the Henry Motors Company in the noisy grinding station where one had to yell to be heard. On top of that, he had lost a good part of his hearing during the war as an artilleryman in Patton's 3rd Army. As such, his voice had touch of the bellow to it. We all stopped laughing and looked at the ground. Walter slipped back into the shadows.

"What's going on here?" Frank demanded. No one spoke.

"Neil?" he said.

"Calvin burned his thumb with a match tip and Donnie made fun of him, so Calvin chased him."

"How did you burn your thumb with a match tip Calvin?" Frank asked. He raised his eyebrows a little in wonderment. Everyone relaxed a little.

"I was trying to light it with my thumbnail, like Walter showed me."

"Walter showed you how to do that?" Frank said, shaking his head and laughing a little. "And you fell for it?"

"How was I to know?" Calvin said. He had a hurt look on his face.

"He made it look easy," Calvin added.

"Made what look easy?" My uncle Charlie said, emerging from his tent. He had a cigarette in one hand and an empty coffee cup in the other. He headed towards the coffee pot.

"Lighting a match with your thumbnail," Neil said. "Einstein here tried it and got burning sulfur under his thumbnail."

Charlie gave Calvin a funny look and shook his head. Charlie was an uncle on my mother's side and was Joe's father. He worked the political beat for the hometown newspaper, the Lockton Gazette. His job, he told me once, was to hang around The James, a bar across the street from the courthouse where city officials, judges, lawmen and lawyers took their two martini lunches.

"I get all the dirt there," he said. "Who was under indictment for fraud, which councilman was cheating on his wife, which construction company was getting a fat city contract and which cases were going to a Grand Jury; But let me tell you something Bub, I never break a confidence or print something that the Mayor, or the Judge or the Sheriff doesn't want made public. That's how things work."

Charlie poured himself a cup of coffee and then produced a flask from an inside pocket of his jacket. He poured a liberal amount of its contents into the steaming coffee and raised the cup to no one in particular.

"Top o' the mornin,'" he said, affecting an Irish brogue. He blew on the coffee to cool it and took a long sip. "Ah, a little hair of the dog that bit me," he said with a wink and a smile.

Charlie was rarely without a cigarette and a glass of scotch after noon on any given day.

"It's because of his wartime experiences that he drinks," my mother often said in his defense. "His ship was sunk by a Japanese torpedo and the survivors floated in the hot sun for days under constant attack from sharks. He told me once that he still hears the men screaming."

She was referring to the sinking of the USS Indianapolis, which had been on a secret mission to deliver the atomic bomb to the U.S. airbase on Tinian Island in the Pacific. After the bomb was delivered the ship sailed away, only to be torpedoed by a Japanese submarine. The few survivors of the sinking languished in the ocean for four days, dying by the dozens from burns and wounds, exposure, thirst and shark attack, the largest in history.

Charlie had been a reporter for *The Stars and Stripes*, the official Armed Forces military publication. After the war he published an account of the ordeal called: *"Fire and Fins, The Sinking of the USS Indianapolis,"* which was serialized in the *Stars and Stripes*.

Women found Charlie irresistible. He was tall and thin, with thick, wavy brown hair and an easy smile. His face, slightly mottled and leathery because of the sunburn he had endured, gave him the look of a man who lived his life with his face to the wind. At the time of our fishing trip, Charlie had been twice divorced and three times married.

The excitement over, I made a sloppy sandwich of scrambled eggs, bacon and grape jam. I was halfway through it when my father stepped out of our tent.

"Saddle up," he barked. "Let's get down to the launch before everyone else gets all the boats!" My father was the commanding officer of the local National Guard unit and liked to use his command voice whenever he could, a mannerism that annoyed my uncles.

"Yes *sir*, General Confusion," Walter said. He made no attempt to rise from his chair and continued to smoke his pipe in a contented manner.

My Uncle Charlie, enjoying his Irish coffee in a lawn chair, jumped to his feet, stood smartly at attention, and clacked his heels together. "Jawohl, Herr Oberst!" he said in clipped German.

My father ignored the wisecracks. "Thomas," he said to me. "Get your gear and get in the car."

"I'm riding with Neil," I said, looking hopefully towards my cousin.

He looked over at me and nodded.

I grinned, everyone wanted to ride in his '57. I finished my sandwich, grabbed my gear and started towards the car.

Calvin jumped up, reaching for his gear. "Hold up," he said. "I'm coming too."

"Yeah, me too," Joe said.

"There's not room for you two," Neil said. "Walter's riding with me."

A bonus, I thought. Everyone wanted to ride with Walter. He was the type of person that made time pass quickly. He told stories, jokes, and dispensed commentary on whatever came to his mind. He noticed things that another person would not have ordinarily seen, like an unusual cloud formation, a strange looking tree or a rare bird. An old farmhouse might remind him of a battle fought during the Civil War. The sight of a river meandering through the hills could take him back to times when virgin forest covered the land, a home to wolves, bears, cougars, eagles and Indians. An old railroad trestle would bring to mind men "riding the rails" under a train during the Depression, traveling from town to town looking for work. He could make going to the store for groceries sound like an adventure.

I climbed into the cramped back seat of Neil's car and Walter got himself comfortable in the front. Neil fired up his V-8 and put the car in gear. Its headlights danced on the trees and bushes along the bumpy campground road as Walter began one of his stories.

"To the early colonists rivers and lakes were like highways," Walter said. "The French were the first in here. They didn't come to settle, they came to trade. Blankets, knives, guns, shot and powder for furs. The furs brought a fortune in Europe. They made hats out of them. Hat makers used a chemical to treat the fur before they pressed it into form. It affected their brains and made them crazy. That's where they got the expression "mad as a hatter.""

"The French fur traders would take big trade canoes all over their trading empire, loaded with trade goods and paddled by big, rough men called 'voyageurs'. They had to paddle all day, and carry the canoes and trade goods over portages around rapids and falls or to another river system. They carried big knives, sharpened to a razor's edge. If you looked cross-ways at a voyageur, you'd be liable to have your throat slit, or your liver pierced. Life was cheap on the frontier.

"The traders used tricks on the Indians to get more furs for the money. They convinced the Indians that the longer the musket, the better. The Indians would pile their furs to the height of the musket. 'Trade muskets,' they called them. They were made cheap and they often fell apart before long. But that didn't matter to the Indians. A musket was a status symbol. An Indian with a long musket would strut around, showing it off to everyone. The squaws admired a man with a long musket."

I saw Neil glance at me out of the corner of his eye and suppress a snicker, but I didn't rise to the joke.

"They traded brandy too," Walter said without missing a beat. "The Indians weren't used to drinking and would get *wasted*. But the best trade items were beads. Potters in Europe would make clay beads with a hole in each one so that they could be strung on a cord and worn like jewelry. They glazed them in different bright colors too. The beads hardly cost anything to make, and the Indians snapped them up like crazy."

"Pretty stupid, weren't they?" Neil said.

"Who?" Walter said.

"Well the Indians, of course," Neil said.

Walter laughed and relit his pipe. "To the Indians, furs didn't mean much. The hills were crawling with beaver, mink and muskrat, at least at first. But the beads the traders brought were like diamonds are to us. They used them as wampum— money. A young brave could get rich trapping."

Neil drove down a two-lane back road for a while, sticking reasonably close to the thirty mile an hour speed limit; not because of the rule but because of the ruts and holes in the road. The powerful engine in his Chevy grumbled and shook at the restraint, like a racehorse champing at the bit. He made a couple of turns and then took a ramp onto the interstate. The engine roared and whined as Neil jacked his way through the gears, finally coming up to a good cruising speed somewhere north of seventy.

As we drove up the Interstate, I looked at all the development around us: towns, cities, factories and housing complexes, only a couple hundred years removed from Indian times. I tried to imagine the huge trees, soaring eagles, Indian villages and trading outposts of a different world.

Walter liked to tell stories about his brothers and sisters when they were young. A favorite was the time someone dropped a lit pack of ladyfinger firecrackers down Uncle Frank's overalls, causing him to do a frantic dance as they went off. Walter liked to imitate the dance when he told the story; he would skitter around flapping his arms and squawking, his eyes bulging out in panic and surprise. My father liked to say that he looked like a chicken with its tail feathers on fire. I have always wondered how he knew what that would look like. Everyone would laugh, except Frank.

"That's not how it happened at all, Walter," Frank would say, the color rising in his neck. "It is true that someone did drop a pack of ladyfingers down my pants once though, and I know it was you! But I never did any dance. I did get burned though – I couldn't sit for a week!"

Walter would just laugh at the accusation and deny it.

"No, no, I wasn't the one," he would say. "I think you dropped them there yourself... by accident!"

My father, and uncles and aunts grew up in a small town on the Erie Canal called Littleport. They lived in a house on Sleeper Street, a little lane down by the Canal. Pop, their father, had been a coal miner in West Virginia. He had left the minefields during a miner's strike and there was much conjecture among the family as to why he had left so suddenly.

"He was in the Molly Maguires," my father contended. "They were a violent bunch; they destroyed company property, exacted revenge on company detectives and blew up bad mines to save the miners from having to go down in them. Once in the Molly Maguires there was no way out, except death."

"The Molly Maguires were Irish," Pete informed him. "Pop was Welsh. Besides, the Molly Maguires operated in eastern Pennsylvania during the 1800s. They hanged most of them in the 1870s."

"That doesn't mean they didn't live on in secret," my father retorted. "And they would have welcomed any Gaelic members, Irish or Welsh. You remember how Pop used to sing in Welsh, before he left."

Pop had unexpectedly disappeared during the dark days of the Great

Depression. He left no note or any explanation. When anyone asked my Grandmother about it, she would just smile and say: "Good riddance to bad rubbish."

The boys, my father Owen, Walter, and Frank, who was an orphan raised by my Grandmother as one of her own sons, liked to call themselves "The Sleeper Street Gang," or just "The Gang." They were joined by my mother's two brothers, Charlie and Doc, who lived just up the street. There was also Pete, who lived in a small apartment with his grandmother. He never told anyone what had happened to his parents and no one ever asked.

The Gang spent a lot of time at my mother's house, mainly because there was food, a scarce commodity during the Depression. My grandfather Karl worked in a tool and die factory that was still open, meaning that he still got a steady paycheck. My grandmother, "Doonie," was a hard German hausfrau with a soft heart. She seemed to be always in the kitchen cooking; bread, cakes, cookies, pork and kraut, roast beef and chicken. I still remember her pouring scalding water over a freshly killed chicken and then ripping the feathers out by hand. It made a sound like packing bubbles when you squeeze them.

She couldn't bear the thought of kids going hungry, or anybody else for that matter, so she always had table full of neighborhood kids and men down on their luck and willing to do odd jobs for a meal. The men would mark a notch in the fencepost of a house that would give a meal to a stranger. Doonie's fence had a lot of notches. Karl didn't mind as long as no one minded him smoking his big stogies and drinking his homemade beer. The only one who did was Doonie.

"Put that cigar out," she would say. "It's stinking up the house." But Karl would just laugh and keep on smoking.

Doonie was especially welcoming to my father and his two brothers and two sisters. She was shocked that their father had abandoned his family at such a desperate time.

"The father is bad," she would say in her thick German accent. "But the children, they shouldn't suffer for it. They can eat here any time they want."

The only problem with the kids eating at Doonie's was my other grandmother, Gram. By all accounts she was a kind, charitable person, but she was also stubborn and proud. She would turn away well-meaning church groups that would show up at her door with boxes of donated food and clothing.

"We're just fine," she would tell them. "Give it to someone who needs it." If they persisted, she would slam the door in their faces. She would not have liked her kids eating at someone else's house— "sponging," she called it, so everyone kept quiet about eating at Doonie's.

No one in the family knew the reason why Pop abruptly left his family. There was a lot of speculation about other women or money problems, but my father's guess was simple: "Cowardice," he would say whenever the topic came up. "Those were hard times and not everyone could keep his courage up. He just ran away."

I only saw Pop once a year, around New Years, when we would visit him for the holidays. He had gotten re-married to a hairdresser in Monroe named Margaret. He taught me how to wink and gave me a book of poetry by his favorite poet, Thomas Galvin. He died when I was nine – Black Lung Disease from the mines, I was told. He was not much grieved by my father and uncles, although my aunts cried a little at the service. Gram didn't attend.

The way I heard it, the Sleeper Street gang was a tight knit bunch that had each other's backs with outsiders. Walter, being the oldest, was the accepted leader. But it wasn't just his age that made him leader, it was that he had the best ideas. They dressed in long coats and goggles and had BB gun wars; they had huge bonfires down by the mill pond; they stole apples from local orchards, Walter organizing the lookouts, pickers and escape routes. He challenged other neighborhoods to baseball, basketball and football games. There wasn't much for kids to do during the Depression, but Walter always found something.

Once, when they were all camping at a place along Red Creek called Wheelman's Rest, Walter decided to have a little fun with the neighborhood bully, a big kid named Koot Whitmore. Koot liked to pick on the younger kids when no one else was around. Walter invited him down to the camp one night under the pretext of drinking some hard cider that Walter had filched from an old farmer's barn.

After Koot had several big swallows of cider, Walter began to talk.

"Koot," he said, "you're a big, powerful man, but I doubt you'd have made it in Indian times."

"Whaddaya mean?" Koot said, offended by the comment. "I've seen a lot of Indians over to the Reservation. They ain't so big."

"Indians may not be big, but bigness has nothing to do with bravery," Walter said. "Back in the day when the Indians ran this place every male Indian had to prove his courage in order to become a brave. Otherwise, he would become a squaw-boy and have to stay at home with the women and kids when the braves went out hunting or raiding."

"What would they have to do?" Koot asked. He took another long pull on the cider jug.

"Well," Walter said slowly. "Different tribes had different traditions. In one, a boy had to take a mouthful of water and run a long course in the hot sun. If he swallowed the water, he was *out!*"

"I could do that," Koot said confidently.

"I don't see any sun," Walter pointed out. "Plus, I've never seen you run even two feet!"

Koot gave him a hard stare but didn't respond.

"In another tribe, the boy had to hang from a rope tied to thick sticks stuck through the skin of his chest," Walter continued.

"Jeez," Koot said. "That sounds painful." He drank again.

"But the Indians around here, they had their own way." Walter said.

"What was that?"

"Trial by fire."

"By fire? How did they do it?"

Walter smiled. "A boy would walk through a bed of hot coals in his bare feet. If he made it all the way across, he'd be called a brave and every-one would respect him"

Koot looked suspiciously at the fire, which looked like it had died out. He took another long drink and jumped to his feet, pulling off his big brogans and tattered socks.

"I'll do it!" He announced.

"Now Koot," Walter said. "Nobody's asking you to walk through that fire. You could hurt yourself."

"I'm tougher than any Indian!" Koot said loudly. With that, he took a long drink off the jug and stepped into the coals.

Koot got about three steps before he screeched and jumped. He wasn't a nimble man, just big and heavy. He landed right back in the coals. He howled and danced for a few moments before he toppled over sideways and rolled out of the coals. He curled up into the fetal position and moaned.

"What the hell did you do that for?" Walter asked him after a bit. "It looks like you burned your feet pretty bad."

Koot rocked back and forth on the ground, trying to soothe his burned feet. "How did they do it, those Indians?" Koot said

Walter pointed out that Indians went barefoot most of the time and each one had a thick layer of callous built up on the bottoms of his feet.

"You never told me that, damn you Walter!" Koot said.

Walter got some ice that he'd brought along and helped him cool his feet. After a while Koot put his boots back on and began limping away.

"Don't worry," Walter said. "Nobody here will tell anyone about this. And if anyone calls you "Squaw Boy," they'll have to answer to me!"

They never saw Koot much after that, and he never picked on any of the gang again.

• • • • • • • • • • • • • • • •

As Walter talked Neil guided his Chevy down the interstate, the big engine purring. We were headed north to a place called Chadwick Bay. According to Walter, there was a big power plant there that expelled hot water into the bay. "The hot water attracts all sorts of fish," he said. "Schools of calico, walleye, and perch; they've taken trophy smallmouth bass there too," he added.

"The Erie Indians lived in this area," Walter explained as he puffed on his pipe. "Legend has it that they had found a way to domesticate the wild panthers that roamed these parts before the white man came in and destroyed their habitat. They used them for hunting and in warfare. The name Erie is the short form of Erieohogan – the people of the long tailed cat. They were the most feared of all the Iroquois," he added.

"What ever happened to them?" I asked.

"They were wiped out by the Senecas," Walter said. "They hated each other to begin with and then, during a Lacrosse game, a fight broke out. An Erie warrior killed one of the Senecas and, as the Senecas carried his body away, they vowed revenge. The Matriarchs of both tribes demanded a peace council be convened to avoid bloodshed, but at the council a fight broke out and there were several killed on both sides. Both tribes went on the warpath. By the time it was over, the Eries were wiped out."

"I thought the Eries were supposed to be so tough," I said. "How did they lose?"

"The Senecas had been trading with the Whites, who had firearms. They defeated the Erie warriors in a big, pitched battle and then went from village to village, slaughtering and burning 'till the Eries were no more, except for one man."

Uh oh, here we go, I thought, grinning to myself— another one of Walter's tall tales was about to be spun. He would take the shred of an idea and weave it into a complex story like my grandmother could take a ball of yarn and, with only two needles, weave it into a sweater that fit perfectly. It occurred to me that maybe that's why a tall tale is called a yarn.

"There was *one* man who survived the big battle," Walter said, packing a fresh pinch of tobacco into his browned pipe and lighting it. "He was a Chief and had fought bravely during the battle until a Seneca musket ball hit him in the head. He fell among the dead and dying. But he wasn't dead after all: the ball had only grazed his skull, knocking him unconscious. The Senecas, seeing all the blood, had left him for dead. When he woke, the Chief found himself among the dead and mutilated corpses of his fellow warriors. None was alive but him.

"He staggered off into the woods to clean his wounds. He stayed there for a time, waiting for his double vision to end. He fell back into unconsciousness. When he woke again, it was nearly dawn. A sense of profound dread came over him. He got to his feet and began trotting towards his village. When he got there, he found that his wife and children were all dead, along with the rest of the villagers. There had been no warriors left alive to defend them. They were defenseless old men, women and children. Unspeakable things had been done. The Chief sat among the corpses for hours, softly singing his death song. Suddenly, he felt a presence next to him. He turned and, opening his eyes, saw a panther, turned completely white. It was one of his own that had survived the battle and had come home, like him. The panther nuzzled him and purred, glad to encounter another living thing. Soon, another panther, also pure white, approached. Then another panther came and another, until the Chief counted twelve, a sacred number for the Eries.

"The white cats circled the dead, sniffing at their lifeless bodies and growling softly. The Chief noticed that his own hair had also turned white. Was it from the shock of the slaughter, or were they all ghosts still walking the Land? The Chief prayed and the gods revealed to him his mission: he was to go go on a campaign of revenge.

"The Chief and his band of cats tracked the warriors who had raided his village to a camp deep in the woods. The cats crept up on the guards and silently pounced, ripping the men's throats out before they could sound the alarm.

"At the camp, the Senecas were asleep, exhausted from their rampaging. Fresh scalps hung from their stacked lances. The Chief knew that they were the scalps of his family and friends. He silently took the lances, set them on the fire, and stood alone in front of them. When the fire flared up, the Chief held his lance and tomahawk high and let out a bloodcurdling scream.

The Senecas, startled awake, scrambled to their feet. They went for their lances, but their lances were gone. Who was this strange screaming apparition, they wondered. They pulled their tomahawks and their war clubs out of their belts and faced the Chief, who they greatly outnumbered. But, before they could attack, there came a chorus of unholy screams from the surrounding woods. Confused and terrified, the

Senecas backed into a defensive circle. An instant later, the cats were upon them.

"The battle was over quicker than it can be told," Walter said." The Chief left the mutilated bodies where they lay as a message to the other Senecas. He then led his cats from camp to camp, killing all that he found— warriors only."

Walter paused for a minute, relighting his pipe.

"Some say the Chief and his cats roam these hills to this day," he said softly— "Chief Nothing" they call him. No one who has seen them has lived to tell about it!"

Walter turned and faced me. "Alone, at night in the dark, a stranger might hear the soft pads of the panthers and the Chief's moccasins as they approach. He might hear a low throated growl and then…they *pounce!*"

At "pounce," Walter's hand snaked out, grabbed my thigh just above the knee and squeezed. I let out a scream and shot up from my seat, ramming my head into the roof of the car with a dull thud.

"Ahh!" I shouted as I sank back into my seat. Walter was laughing along with Neil, who almost went off the road watching me in the rear view mirror. My face went red as I realized that the whole family would hear about the incident that night – and for years to come.

After Walter's tall tale, he continued his discourse on the history of the region.

"This was the dividing line between the French Fur Empire and the English settlements," He said. "The English encouraged settlers to come into the region. If there were enough of them they could form a militia to fight the French. The settlers were pioneers; indentured servants who paid off their passage to the Colonies by working on plantations in the East. They didn't have much more than a musket, a knife and a lot of guts.

They built cabins out of logs, hunted deer and small game and gathered wild ginseng root to sell for its energizing properties. They called it "sang." Deerskins brought a dollar to traders; that's why a dollar's called a 'buck.'

"The French didn't like the pioneers coming into their territory and incited the Indians to attack them. The British didn't want the expense of sending troops to protect the settlers, so the settlers formed their own groups; Rangers, they were called. Colonel Benjamin Church formed some of the first companies. They used the Indian way of fighting: stealth and sudden attacks, usually at dawn. Colonial volunteers and friendly Indians fought the French and their Indian allies. Later Robert Rogers formed the most famous Ranger outfit: Rogers Rangers. He taught them to learn the 28 rules of rangering, which the Army still uses today. They had to memorize the Ranger Creed, twenty rules like: "don't use your musket if you can kill 'em with your hatchet."

"Militia companies were formed too; and provincial units, like the Virginia Blues, led by George Washington. They defeated the French in the French and Indian Wars. But, after the war, the British went back on their promise to pay the men in land west of the Appalachians. They forbid settlement in the region in order to promote peace with the Indians and to profit from the fur trade. Settlers went in anyway.

"The British encouraged the Indians to attack the settlers and paid them for scalps. It didn't matter if they were from men, women or children. The Indians would stretch each scalp on a hoop made from a willow branch and paint the circumstances of its taking on the skin side. One of the Indian leaders, over in the Ohio Valley, was a full-blooded Dutchman named Marmaduke Van Swearingen, he was known to the Shawnee as 'Blue Jacket.'

"How did the Indians let a white man be their leader?" I asked. "How did they trust him – and why did he do it?"

"They captured him as a child in a raid," Walter said. "Tribes did that. They'd decide to go on the warpath against a rival tribe for some insult or grievance. The war party would sneak up on a village in the night and attack at dawn. They'd kill or capture the warriors and carry away the women and children. The captured warriors were marked for torture, unless some squaw who had lost her husband wanted to claim one of the prisoners as a husband. Families claimed the children and raised them as their own. Young braves took the girls as wives.

"To the Indians the Pioneers were just another tribe and isolated settlements were raided and captives taken. Sometimes family members would try to get the captives back. A father might look for his daughter, a husband for his wife. But if the captives were with the Indians very long, a couple of years or more, they might not want to be rescued."

Walter paused to fill and light his pipe. He liked to build suspense. Neil broke first.

"Why wouldn't they?" he asked.

"The women would have children with their new husbands, friends among the other squaws. The children had brothers and sisters that they didn't want to leave. It's a known fact that many women who were recaptured snuck away at the first chance and went back to their tribe. That was the way of it, in those days."

• • • • • • • • • • • • • • • •

We drove for a while in silence, Walter puffing languidly on his pipe and Neil guiding the '57 along the smooth pavement, the engine purring and the tires singing. I drifted off, dreaming of Indians and panthers. When I awoke dawn had broken – we had left while it was still dark in order to get in a full day of fishing. The sky was blue, with a soft orange glow beneath it as the sun rose.

"A bluebird morning," Walter announced. "It's an omen, a sign of good fishing today."

Walter was always doing that: making predictions based on a circling hawk, or a cruising Heron or a bluebird morning.

We came to a hilltop and saw Chadwick Bay laid out before us on the Lake Erie Plain. A small craft harbor, it was bordered by a restaurants and shops, a marina and a hotel. Docks, jutting out into the harbor, contained lines of boats of every description. On its west side stood a large coal-fired electrical power plant which sent plumes of smoke into the morning sky from three large smokestacks. To the north was the great lake itself, deep blue beneath the bluebird morning sky.

Chapter Two

The Chadwick Bay Marina, so promising as seen from the hilltop, turned out to be an old rickety building, built over the water in the harbor. The upper part was a restaurant-bar that advertised "Lake Erie Blue Pike" and "Carling Black Label" in flickering neon lights. Below there was a series of docks built among the massive wooden pillars that served as the foundation for the building— whole tree trunks, I guessed. They reminded me of the giant masts on a square-rigged ship from the age of sailing, but, on closer inspection, I could see that they were soft, spongy and riddled with rotten holes. I looked up at the joists that supported the restaurant's floor— they were old and rotten too and covered with thick green moss. The walkways were covered with the same slippery moss that seemed to be everywhere. The smell of the rotting moss, stagnant water and gasoline from the boats made me gag. I looked at Neil, who was wrinkling his nose at the smell. I saw him look down at his new tassel loafers, covered with the stinking moss.

We made our way towards a faded hand-painted sign that read "Rentals."

A man whose greasy work shirt identified him as "Bob" came out of a dingy office. He was short, with a gray two-day stubble on his face. His skin was slightly yellow and as he walked, slightly hunched, he had a noticeable limp. Chewing a cigar stub, he regarded us with a glowering expression.

"Help you?" He said. It was more of a challenge than a question.

"Thought we'd give you a bit of rental business," My father said. "What do you charge?"

"Depends on what you want," the man said.

"Two boats with motors and some bait."

"Ten dollars apiece for the boats for the day, five dollars apiece for the motors," the man said. "Gas is extra, bait is extra."

"Fifteen dollars for a motor boat is too much," my father said. "And gas should come with it."

"Well, it don't," the man said. "And fifteen apiece is fair, and firm. You don't like it, go somewhere else."

"Where's another boat livery?" my father asked.

"Ain't one," Bob said. There was an insolent tone to his voice.

"We'll take the boats, but not the motors," my father said. "The oars aren't extra, are they?" He added sarcastically.

"Suit yourself," the man said. "But it's a long row out to the perch grounds."

"We aren't going to the perch grounds," my father said. "We're going out to the break-wall. I'll give you fifteen dollars for the two."

The man shook his head. "The price is twenty dollars, and it's a dollar extra for the life vests— apiece. Law says you gotta have 'em."

I saw the red creep up my father's neck and into his face. A little vein was standing out on the side of his forehead. It took a lot to get my father angry, he prided himself on his self-control. But sometimes someone would make the mistake of going too far and it was clear that Bob just had.

"That's bullshit," Pete said in a loud whisper that everyone, including Bob, could hear. My other uncles murmured angrily.

The trouble was that after my father was done with Bob, we would end up fishing off the pier for the day. I looked over at Walter, the only one who might be able to rescue the situation. He was puffing on his pipe, seemingly unconcerned with what was going on.

My father took a step forward. "I don't like your attitude buddy," he said. There was menace in his voice.

"I don't give a shit," Bob said. "You don't like the price, don't take the boats."

"You can stick the boats up your ass," my father said. "Along with the oars!"

Bob suddenly stood tall and stepped forward. He was much larger than he had first appeared. There was a glint in his eye and he appeared ready for a fight.

"I think you'd better clear out of here while you can," he said threateningly. "I'm sick of you damn tourists coming in here and acting like you own the place. I don't need your money and I don't need your snotty rich-folks-on-vacation attitude!"

Suddenly Walter stepped forward. He had an easy smile on his face.

"Where'd you get that hitch in your get along?" he asked.

"What's it to you?" Bob said. It looked as though he was ready to fight anybody and everybody on the dock.

"Well," Walter said. "Unless I miss my guess, you didn't get malaria in the States and you have the look of someone who spent time in the Pacific, during the War."

The man seemed to relax a little. My father relaxed a little too.

"Were you in it?" the man asked Walter softly.

Walter nodded. "CBI, then the Pacific." he said.

"With Chennault?" Bob asked.

Walter nodded again. "I was on C-47s."

"Ah, "Goony Birds!" They took a lot of our wounded out and brought us food and ammo when the ships couldn't get in close enough."

"Where were you?" Walter asked.

"Pacific, Marines," the man said.

My father stepped up to Bob. His demeanor had softened and so had his voice.

"Were you on Iwo?" He asked.

Bob nodded.

My father grabbed the man's right hand and put it in his own, shaking it firmly.

"You guys saved my life," he said. "I was with LeMay."

"Off Tinian?" the man said.

"Yep," my father said. "B-29s." He let go the man's hand and stepped back. His eyes took on a vacant look, the kind of look that comes over a man when something causes him to remember a thing that he'd spent a lifetime trying to forget.

"We were coming back from a mission, shot up pretty bad." My father said. "We'd lost one engine and a second one was beginning to malfunction; our hydraulic system was cut and we were losing fuel. We weren't going to make it back to Tinian. They'd briefed us on the new airfield on Iwo. We headed for it. I saw it first, from the bubble up front, I was the bombardier. That little black speck was one of the most welcome sights I can ever remember seeing."

"What was your plane?" Bob asked. "What were its markings?"

"Circle "R" on the tail, number 13. Jake's Jernt was the name," my father said.

"I remember that plane," Bob said. "We looked up and saw a number thirteen coming in." He shook his head. "Number thirteen! We all thought that that was a strange number to give a plane. Why would the Air Corps put that number on a plane? Lots of buildings don't even have a thirteenth floor, they skip up to fourteen! Guess it was lucky enough for you guys, though," he added.

"Not for all of us," my father said grimly. "The tail gunner and one of the waist gunners were already dead. We never got the belly gunner out – the hydraulic system was cut."

"Bad deal," Bob said. "But you made it, and here you are – one of the guys from a plane that I watched land on that Godforsaken piece of volcanic sand. I lost a lot of friends on that island, and more still on Okinawa; but if it hadn't been for you guys bombing those bastards into submission, we'd of lost a lot more taking the Home Islands."

The man paused for a moment; then he stuck out his hand. "My name's Bob Hiller, and I'm proud to meet you."

My father shook his hand, smiling, glad to be back in the present.

"Owen Edwards," he said. "These guys were in it too: Frank was with Patton, and Charlie was with Nimitz in the Navy. Pete here was in the Philippines," he added.

Bob shook hands around. He looked at Pete. "Bataan?" he said.

Pete nodded.

"Bastards!" Bob said. "You should've seen what they did to our guys that they captured."

Pete nodded again.

My father introduced the rest of us and then stopped for a moment, considering his words. "We're not rich, by the way – far from it."

"Sorry about that," Bob said. "We do get some real assholes in here sometimes. I shouldn't have prejudged you. He turned and gave a whistle towards the stairs. A few moments later, a tall boy about my age came clambering down. He had buck-teeth and a cowlick.

"Yeah, Dad," he said, glancing at us dubiously. Bob walked over to him and gave him a few terse instructions. The boy raised his eyebrows a little, glanced at us again and began readying two boats, complete with motors, gas cans and life preservers.

"This one is on me," Bob said as he handed us buckets of minnows, soft shell crabs and night crawlers. "It's not often that I get to see some of the guys who were in it, the rich types stayed home, or in the rear with the gear."

"You got that right," Pete said.

Bob explained how to fish each type of bait and then pointed out a spot near the end of the break wall where he thought we'd have the best luck. "These boats would just be sitting here all day anyway," he said as we began to climb on board. "Just leave 'em where you found 'em when you're done."

I saw my father open his wallet and take out a bill. It was a big one. As he stepped into the boat, he reached out and stuffed it into Bob's pocket. "Semper Fi," he said with a nod.

"How did you know he was a Marine" Neil asked Walter as we motored out into the bay.

"I saw a million of those Marines come out of the jungle," Walter said. "They all had the same weather-beaten, jaundiced look from the heat, the combat and the malaria. "Besides," he added, "He had a Marine tattoo on his forearm."

• • • • • • • • • • • • • •

The break-wall was a long concrete structure that protected the harbor from the waves of the open bay. It was several hundred yards long and maybe a dozen feet high. The side facing the open bay angled steeply into the lake and the side facing the harbor was vertical. There was a four-foot wide walkway on top, covered with squawking gulls and mottled with white bird shit. It was a perfect fishing platform. Walter, Neil, Calvin, Joe and I clambered up on some rocks piled at the eastern end of the wall and spread out along it. The two boats, with the rest of the bunch, prepared to go out into the open bay.

We immediately rigged up and began to fish. Everyone had a different idea about his goal that day. Walter was after perch.

"There's no better eating fish than a Perch," he said. "And you don't have to scale 'em, just gut 'em, head 'em and throw them in the pan."

My father favored Calico bass. "Perch are tasty, I'll give you that," he said as he headed out into the bay. "But a few measly perch aren't going to feed our bunch. Once you light into a school of calicos you can fill your boat."

Pete was after Yellow Pike, or better yet, Lake Erie Blue Pike. "Troll a worm rig deep," he advised. "When you catch one, drop a marker over the spot. You'll catch one or two on every pass. One Walleye will feed two people!"

Me, well, I was going for smallmouth bass. They weren't very good eating in the summer, but it was a fighting fish that was hard to land, and a trophy smallmouth would give me bragging rights. I was fishing a soft shell crab right on the bottom. I noticed that Neil was doing the same thing. Once again, we were in competition.

Walter got the first fish, a nice Perch. He unhooked it, put it in the big bucket that we had for the purpose, re-rigged and cast back out to the same spot. A few minutes later he had another. "Why aren't you boys fishing over here?" He asked Neil and me. "The Perch are biting."

Neil and I looked sheepishly at each other and shrugged.

"Lookin' for trophy bass, eh?" Walter said with a smile. "Well, good luck. I got five bucks each for biggest and most bass."

Neil and I smiled, looked at each other with that squinty-eyed look competitors give each other and concentrated on our lines.

Calvin, who still hadn't got his rig together, was trying to keep his pipe lit – a hard job in the stiff breeze on the break wall.

"What's this about a prize?" he said, strolling over towards us.

"Five dollars for biggest bass, another five for most," Walter said.

"How come just bass?" Calvin asked. "Why don't the other fish count?"

Walter laughed. "Alright," he said." Biggest bass, most bass, biggest overall fish and most fish overall. Five bucks each."

"Don't worry about it, Calvin," Neil said over his shoulder. "You don't even have your line in yet. The only prize you could win would be most matches used to try and light a pipe."

Walter and I started laughing. Calvin turned away mad. "Shut up Neil," he said as he started to walk away. But he wasn't paying attention and accidentally kicked Walter's new plastic tackle box that was guaranteed not to sink. It clattered down the steep slope of the break wall and hit the water with a splash. It floated for a moment and then began to sink slowly.

"Jesus," Neil exclaimed. "What have you got in that thing?"

"Sinkers," Walter said.

"I'll get it," Calvin said, clambering down the break wall after it. He plunged his arm into the water, but he slipped on some moss and slid partway into the water. He looked silly there in the water: he had the box in one hand, the other braced against the break wall and his smoldering pipe clenched in his teeth.

"Toss it up," Walter said, extending his hand. Calvin threw the box, but his position was bad and so was the throw. The box sailed over Walter's head and went into the lake on the other side of the break wall. Walter stared at it balefully as it sank from sight.

"Jesus, Calvin," Neil said. "You are lame!"

"Shut up Neil," Calvin said, his teeth chattering against the plastic mouthpiece of his pipe. "This water sure is cold – help me up out of here."

"Just clamber up the side," Neil said, reluctant to put down his rod. "I think I've got a nibble!" He added.

Walter was still staring over the other side of the break wall in the hopes that his box would somehow pop back up to the surface. I was fishing near to where Calvin was and watched him, amused, as he struggled to climb up the steep break wall, his pipe still clenched in his teeth. He would make it part way up but then slide back down as his feet struggled to gain purchase on the slippery moss. On his last try, he flailed madly and then slipped all the way down and into the lake.

"I can't swim!" He announced, suddenly tiring. There was a note of panic in his voice. His boots and clothes, now thoroughly soaked, were weighing him down. He went under briefly and came up spitting water and thrashing. I threw down my rod and skittered down the steep concrete.

"Grab my hand," I said.

Calvin lunged forward and grabbed my outstretched hand. I began pulling him up, but a panic had gripped him and he tried to scurry up over me. The action caused both of us to fall into the lake; I went in head-first with Calvin on top of me. Calvin managed a weak "help" before he went under, clinging desperately to me. I had taken a lifeguarding course at the Community Pool and worked there as a guard during the summer, but none of my training, all done in a pool, had prepared me for this situation. I began to feel the presence of the great killer: Panic. She crept up on me like a monster in the dark.

Summoning every bit of self-control I could muster, I did the only thing that I knew could save us both: I swam straight down towards the bottom, breaking away from Calvin's flailing legs. My aching lungs screamed for air as I turned and swam upwards. After what seemed an eternity, I broke the surface and grabbed a lungful of air. I looked towards the break wall, but didn't see Calvin. Meanwhile Walter and Neil had noticed that something was wrong. Neil was signaling my father's boat to come in and Walter was pointing desperately at a mass of bubbles – the spot where Calvin had gone under. I did a surface dive and swam down towards the spot at an angle. A moment later, I spotted Calvin's limp form, drifting down towards the bottom.

I grabbed him from behind, under the armpits, and thrust forcefully towards the surface. Weighed down by my wet clothes and shoes, and Calvin's dead weight, it was a desperate struggle. Again, I felt my lungs screaming for air. Panic re-appeared, urging me to let go of Calvin and save myself. I ignored her and swam for the light.

We broke the surface with a crash. I grabbed a lungful of air and maneuvered Calvin into a cross-chest carry. The action forced the lake water out of his lungs in a fountain that rained down upon me. As I scissored my legs, Calvin came to and began struggling. I gripped him tightly and headed towards the jumble of rocks at the end of the break wall. When we got there, I pushed him up onto a rock, and fell back into the lake, rolling into back float, exhausted. The whole event had only taken a few moments.

Calvin scrambled up the rocks, puking lake water the whole way. Neil and Walter grabbed him and pulled him up onto the walkway. Walter looked down at me.

"Are you alright?" he asked.

I nodded and climbed up the rocks.

My father's boat, with Frank and Donnie in it, pulled up moments later.

"What the hell happened here?" Frank demanded angrily.

Calvin came up to his knees, covered with white bird shit and seaweed.

"I fell in," he said weakly. Joe was cackling and pointing at Calvin, unable to form words.

"Did someone push you?" Frank asked, looking from Walter to Neil to me. We pulled a prank now and then, and Calvin was often the brunt. He noticed my soaked clothes and gave me a hard look.

"Nobody pushed me," Calvin said angrily. He was brushing himself off and trying to restore his shredded dignity. "I was trying to get Walter's stupid tackle box. Someone knocked it into the water."

"Well," Frank said. "Did you get it?"

"It sank," Calvin said.

"I thought it was supposed to float," my father said.

"It was full of sinkers," Neil said. "It sank like a rock!" The crisis over, everyone burst out laughing, except Walter, who lit his pipe with angry puffs, his face growing redder and redder in the process. Walter could give a ribbing, but he didn't like taking one.

I sat down and emptied the water out of my shoes. Calvin was checking his pockets; he fished a sodden package out and looked into it.

"My tobacco's soaked," he announced to no one in particular. Then he looked accusingly at me. "You knocked my pipe out of my mouth when you fell on me," he said. "Now it's lost!"

"Maybe you better buy a bubble pipe next time if you're going to go swimming with it." Neil said over his shoulder. He was back to fishing, intent on winning the contest.

Walter laughed; glad to have the attention drawn away from himself. "The next time you go in, take a bar of soap with you. A fella can never be too clean."

Walter looked around with a smile. We all knew what was coming: "Myself, I like to bathe once a week," he said. "Whether I need to or not!"

• • • • • • • • • • • • • • • •

We fished the rest of the morning, but it wasn't until about ten O'clock that Neil and I began catching bass. I'd done a lot of snorkeling in the big lake near our house and knew that, during the summer, bass tended to travel in loose groups, feeding on crabs, minnows, grubs, and worms. I was fishing a soft shell crab right on the bottom on a weighted rig— I don't like bobbers, so I kept the line on my finger so I could feel the crab moving around.

When the first fish struck my bait, it came as a surprise to me: I hadn't had any action yet and had been daydreaming a little. Bass hit hard when they're hungry or angry, and they're usually both. When the fish snatched the crab he felt the tug of the line and made a run for deeper water. I set the hook and realized immediately that I had a big fish. I was using six pound line so I flipped open the bail on my spinning reel and let him have his run. I could see the bare spool through the last few layers of line when the big fish finally slowed. I flipped the bail shut, raised my rod tip and began playing him.

Walter stood next to me holding a long handled net, gently coaching me. His voice came in a monotone, like a fisherman's mantra: "Keep your rod tip up, don't horse him, let him run if he wants to, let him tire himself."

Fishing's a funny thing: it requires a particular skill set that includes concentration and focus in rigging up, presenting the bait, detecting a hit, setting the hook and playing the fish. But the most important attribute of an angler is patience. You might sit for hours waiting for a nibble, the urge to reel in your line and check your rig is almost irresistible. You think about relocating, changing rigs or bait, or even giving up and trying it on another day. But a good angler will banish those thoughts and focus on the job at hand. Like the solitary heron who stands on one leg for hours at a time, waiting for an unwary fish to swim by, the angler persists.

Patience is especially important in playing and landing a big fish— a lesson I learned the hard way that day on the break wall. I'd played the big bass for a good twenty minutes, letting him have his runs, teasing him in ever closer until he was on the surface next to the break wall, exhausted. It was the biggest bass I'd ever seen.

"The net!" I yelled to Walter, who was standing right next to me, holding it at the ready.

"Wait," Walter said. "Don't try to bring him in yet. He's apt to have one more run left in him. When he sees you…"

But I cut Walter off by letting go of my reel handle and grabbing the net. I held the rod tip up with one hand, lifting the big fish slightly, while I bent down with the long handled net, trying to get it under him. The fish was lying on his side, his red eye staring vacantly at the sky. But, as I bent down, I could see the eye suddenly focus on me. In an instant, the fish came back alive, struggling to dive. The rod bent double and I was unable to release the bail to let the fish have his run. I almost lost my balance as the fish wriggled desperately into the murky depths.

"Drop the net and open your bail!" Walter shouted. "He'll break your line, if he doesn't break your rod!"

I dropped the net and grabbed the bail on my reel, but before I could open it the fish changed direction and shot up and out of the water. He danced on his tail for a moment, shaking his head from side to side on the slack line. I swear I saw him look once more at me as he threw the hook and plunged back into the lake.

"Lost him!" Neil said, his voice tinged with triumph. "He spit the hook on you!"

"No shit," I said, slumping into a sitting position on the concrete, ignoring the thick layer of bird shit that I was sitting on.

"That was a big fish," Calvin said, sucking on a toothpick in lieu of his lost pipe. "Too bad you lost him."

"Shut up, Calvin," I said weakly.

"It wasn't that big," Neil said over his shoulder. "There's plenty of fish bigger than him in this lake, and I intend to catch one!" He turned his attention to his line as if he was getting a nibble. I knew he wasn't. I stood up, brushed myself off and began re-rigging.

By noon, I'd caught four decent keepers, but none the size of the first one. Neil had five. Walter measured each one of our fish and Neil's beat my biggest by a quarter inch. Since Calvin had quit fishing and nobody else on the break wall had caught much, all four prizes went to Neil, twenty dollars in all.

"Not a bad morning's work," he said triumphantly as he slid the bills into his wallet. "I might have to go pro!"

"Who'd pay someone to catch fish?" Calvin said derisively.

"Walter just did, you mullet head!" Neil shot back.

Calvin just stood there, his toothpick poised in his hand as if he was about to make an important point. He stuck it back into his mouth, chewed on it thoughtfully for a second and then said: "I wish I hadn't lost my pipe!" He glanced accusingly at me, turned and walked away.

Shortly after that, the boats came in. Pete and Charlie had caught a half dozen yellow pike and a huge carp, which they had kept just to show everyone. As soon as we had all gawked at it, Pete released it. My father, Frank and Donnie had caught over thirty pan fish, mostly calico bass but also bluegill, rock bass and a couple of smallmouths. It looked like we were going to have fish for dinner.

On the way back, we stopped at a railroad car diner, painted deep green with white trim. It was the type of diner you'd see in every little town in the country. When automobiles replaced trains, railroad companies liquidated their stock; people bought the surplus dining cars cheap and turned them into diners. A large sign above it read "Eat."

"Order whatever you want everybody," Walter said. "I'm buying."

The waitress, a woman named Mary, stood by with her pad and pencil, ready to take our orders. She was thin and short, with a friendly smile.

"Cheeseburger, fries and a milkshake for me," I said when it was my turn. "Vanilla, malted." Neil ordered the same, but with a chocolate shake. Walter ordered a steak.

"Steak?" my father said when Mary left with the order. "In a place like this? It'll be tougher than shoe leather!"

"Well, what did you order?" Walter asked, sounding a little miffed.

"Wieners and beans," my father said. "They specialize in that type of thing in these little diners. Nobody ever orders the steak; it's just on the menu for show. They'll probably have to go over to the supermarket to get one."

Walter's face began to redden, but you could see that he wasn't going to take my father's bait, not this time at least.

A little while later the waitress began bringing out the meals— a man in a white apron assisted her. He introduced himself as Mel, the owner. Mary was his wife, he told us. He was tall, wore steel-rimmed glasses and had a thin mustache. The burgers were big, thick and juicy and were served on homemade rolls. The plates had piles of French fries – the kind fried in lard with gravy on top. There was a large homemade pickle on the side. Walter's steak was huge and, with a large pile of onion rings and steak cut fries, barely fit on its large platter.

"We're famous for this steak," Mel said. "It's Black Angus. I have it shipped in from Kansas twice a week. I lose money on it, but that's offset by the other dinners I sell. The steak brings in a lot of families."

Mel looked over at my father. "I'm real sorry," he said. "But there'll be a short wait on the wieners and beans; we don't get many orders for them and we ran out. But don't worry, I sent my son over to the supermarket. Your order will be right out."

Walter nearly choked on his steak, suppressing the urge to laugh.

After lunch, Walter decided to ride with my father, so I jumped into the front seat of Neil's Chevy. He gunned the engine and we sped off towards the interstate. He was unusually quiet, working his jaw, staring straight ahead at the road. Funny, I thought, I expected a forty-five minute brag session on the fishing contest that he'd just won. Finally, after he had turned onto the interstate and come up to speed, he looked over at me.

"Remember the book?" Neil asked.

"How could I forget it?" I responded.

"I think Walter's got it with him," Neil said. "I've seen the men at night, looking at something and arguing."

I looked over at him. "I know," I said. "I saw it this morning. It slipped out of his satchel, along with something else."

"What's that?" Neil asked.

"A pistol. A Japanese Nambu, from the looks of it," I said.

"Jesus!" Neil exclaimed. "What's Walter doing with a pistol?"

"Damned if I know," I said, trying to suppress the shiver that was traveling up my spine.

"I've never seen Walter shoot a gun of any kind," Neil said, clearly surprised at my news.

"Even for plinking," I added.

"You've got to read it," Neil said abruptly and forcefully.

"Why me?" I said, cringing at the thought of even touching the book.

"You sleep in your Father's car, don't you?" Neil said.

I swallowed hard and stared out at the road. I knew where Neil was going with this. I knew that he was right, but couldn't bear the thought of touching the book, let alone opening it.

I shook my head. "I don't think I can do it. The thought of it gives me nightmares," I added weakly.

Neil gave me a piercing look. "Those guys are up to something," he said firmly. "They're poring over it every night after everybody else is asleep. I've seen them. But, whenever I come close, they clam up. I want to find out what they're up to."

"Then why don't you look at the book," I countered, a little hotly.

Neil shook his head. "Somebody would see me," he said. "You're sleeping in the car. You can crawl up to the front and look at it with your flashlight."

"I don't know," I said. "I'd hate to have Walter catch me going through his stuff."

"He won't, not if you're careful," Neil said. Then his face softened. "Don't you remember that night?" he asked.

I nodded. I had tried, but I couldn't forget it. I dreamt about it almost every night.

"Those guys went to a lot of trouble to get that book," Neil said. "It must be pretty important. I'd just like to know what it's all about. Besides," he added. "It might help stop my nightmares."

"I'll think about it," I said. "But I'm not making any promises. I'm not sure that I can bring myself to even touch it."

Neil smiled. "Just try, OK?" He paused for a moment. "I think we're owed."

Chapter Three

After we returned to the campground, I found myself on fish-cleaning duty along with Pete. Neil, Joe, Donnie and Calvin had managed to disappear somehow. Pete might have been grouchy, but he was an excellent cook, and he took great pride in cleaning and cooking fish and wild game.

"Most people butcher wild game and fish," he said. "They waste too much of the meat and then over-cook it. Cleaning and cooking wild game and fish is an art and is as important as taking the game or fish."

I felt a little bit honored at being chosen to help Pete clean the fish. He didn't let just anybody assist him.

"The key to cleaning fish is a good sharp knife," he said. He drew the blade of a wooden-handled filet knife across a whetstone methodically, spitting on the stone occasionally to keep it lubricated.

"Most knives used for general purpose should be sharpened to about a twenty degree angle," he said. "But for filleting a fish, you want ten. Ten will get you a blade as sharp as a straight razor."

As he finished sharpening his knife, he spit on his forearm and shaved some hair off of it.

"That's just about right," he said with satisfaction. "Here, try it," he said, handing me the knife. "But be careful."

I took the knife and gingerly shaved a small bit of hair off of my forearm.

"See," Pete said. "You could shave with that blade, if you had any hair to shave."

I ignored the comment and handed the knife back to him.

Pete took a small Calico Bass out of a bucket and clipped it to a ridged cleaning board. He held the fish down with his left hand and deftly worked the blade with his right.

"Make a slit just behind the gill," he said, drawing the blade lightly across the fish. The flesh opened up easily.

"Don't push it or saw. Let the blade do its work."

Pete then inserted the tip of the blade into the meat at the top of the cut.

"Work the blade along the ribs, right down the spine," he said. "Lift lightly on the filet as you do."

Moments later Pete had freed a thick filet from the fish's body, leaving behind only the shimmering ribs. He flipped the fillet over and pinned it to the lower part of the board with his thumb. He placed the knife just above his thumb and drew the blade forward against the skin in one smooth motion. The resultant fillet was a pure translucent white. He rinsed it and tossed it into a bucket of ice.

"Try one," he said.

I picked another small Calico out of the bucket and clipped it to the board. Carefully, I made a slit behind the fish's gill and began working the blade down its spine. The filet I produced was choppy and I noticed that I had left a considerable amount of flesh on the body. I prepared for a stinging rebuke from Pete. But he surprised me,

"Not bad, for a first try," he said. "Start with the smaller fish first. They're a little more tricky to clean, but you won't lose as much meat."

He produced a second cleaning board and sharpened another filet knife. "Re-sharpen your blade every two or three fish," he said. "You'll be able to tell when you need to."

We worked together for the better part of an hour and, I must say, I got pretty good at it; but nowhere as good as Pete. When we were done we had two large white buckets full of fish filets on ice. Then Pete surprised me again.

"Good job, Tom," he said, clapping me on the shoulder. We carried the buckets over to the shade by the dining fly.

After an hour of cleaning fish, I was ready for a swim.

The campground had a nice pool with a lifeguard and changing rooms, but it was packed with people. The only thing you could do was stand in one spot and maybe play a little catch with a beach ball. I wanted to escape the noise, the glaring sun and the heady smell of suntan lotion. I put on my suit and walked down a trail to the river that ran through the campground.

The water was crystal clear and cold. Only three or four feet deep on average, it ran over a bed of sparkling gravel through a thickly wooded valley. I waded out into the current, wincing at the cold, and plunged into the water. I swam against the current with strong strokes intended to generate some warmth in my shivering body. The current was brisk but not insurmountable and I made good progress. As I swam I noticed fish scattering along the bottom, surprised by my presence. They were trout, big browns and smaller, speckled brookies. Occasionally I saw the flash of large rainbow trout in the deeper pools. Walter had told us that the campsite brochure had bragged of the clear stream "teeming with trout, a haven for fly fishermen." For a change, it seemed that a brochure's claims were true.

I noticed that the trail along the section of river that I was swimming was scant; the main trail from the campsite ran downstream only. I began to hatch a plan.

That evening we had a fish feast. Pete fried the fish fillets, coated with egg and cornmeal, in a large cast iron skillet. The perch, headed and gutted, were brushed with oil and cooked on a camp grill over a wood fire. The Yellow and Blue Pike were wrapped in foil with wild leeks and baked in the coals. There was store-bought potato salad and baked beans cooked in a Dutch oven that had been buried in coals all day. There was plenty of fresh lemonade and, for the men, Carling Black Label beer.

"These are tasty fish," Walter announced. "Especially the perch."

"I didn't see you shy away from the calicos," my father commented.

"Or the Walleye," Pete added. "These are Blue Pike, by the way."

"I know how good perch taste," Walter said. "That's why I took the other kinds too. I like to share my catch so that everyone can judge for himself that perch are the best. He looked over at Calvin, who was meticulously picking away at his plate.

"Right Calvin?" He said.

Calvin looked up in surprise, he hadn't been paying attention.

"Right," he said. You could count on Calvin to agree with just about anything when you caught him not paying attention, and he usually wasn't. We often set him up to agree with something absurd, just to get a laugh. He didn't get jokes either. Often, someone would make up a nonsense joke and tell it to the group. We'd all laugh and ask Calvin if he got it. "Yeah," he'd say, laughing. "That's a funny one." Then we'd get him to go tell it to someone else and watch him fail.

Calvin sat, poking at his plate, wondering what he had just agreed to.

"See," Walter said. "Calvin agrees – there's few who know fish better than Calvin: he tried to become one himself today."

Everyone laughed and Joe cackled. "Fish boy!" he said, pointing at Calvin. He made a fish face by pursing his lips and fanning his hands alongside of his head, to imitate gills.

"Shut *up*, Joe," Calvin said. He returned his attention to his plate.

After dinner, I went down to the creek to do a little extra fishing. The water was gin clear and I could see deep holes loaded with brown trout. I tied a red devil spinner on my line and drifted it past the fish several times. There was no response. I tried a deep diving Rappala and worked it in front of them, but again the fish were not interested. Finally, I tied on the biggest, heaviest lure I had, hoping to hook one of the big trout in the lip. I knew that it was a bit shady, but I couldn't help myself. But the big hooks just slipped over the trout's slippery skin and all it seemed to do was annoy the fish.

I looked around at the surrounding woods; the pool I was fishing was remote, hard to get to and sheltered by trees and bushes. I waded part way in and, looking over my shoulder, extended my net towards the bottom of the pool. I quickly realized that the fish were far too deep for the net and that, if I really wanted to get at them, I'd have to swim down. I took another glance around, trying to decide if I should chance it, netting fish was illegal. I wasn't worried about breaking the law— my family had grown up during the Depression and any game was fair game for them; they ate whatever they could get: rabbits, squirrels and even woodchucks. "Woodchuck can be very tasty," my father used to say. "If you get a young one." It wasn't breaking a few minor laws that was frowned upon by our family, it was getting caught. Getting caught meant that you had done something stupid, and stupidity was viewed as a Cardinal sin in our family.

My father's distant whistle saved me from doing something stupid. I took one long last look at the trout and headed up the trail.

"Catch anything?" Walter asked as I trudged into the campsite. I shrugged.

"Weren't biting," I said.

"Too bad," Walter said. "Trout and eggs make a nice breakfast."

"The Indians didn't wait for fish to bite," he commented. "They'd scoop them out from under a bank with their bare hands."

"That's an old wives tale," my father said. "Bears can catch them that way, but no human, Indian or other, is quick enough to catch a trout by hand."

"They'd rub their bellies first, to calm them," Walter said. "Then slide their hands forward and grip them by the gills."

"Right," my father said. "Before or after they kissed them?"

"Mullet head!" Walter exclaimed. He didn't like to be doubted, especially by my father, the youngest of the brothers.

"I knew a couple of guys used to catch snapping turtles by hand," Pete said. "They'd pull a rowboat up next to a muddy creek bank and find a turtle hole. When they found one, they'd stick their arms into the mud under the hole – turtles go in head first and then turn around. They'd grab them by the tail and pull the whole bank out. Then they'd throw the turtle into a burlap sack."

"What if the turtle hadn't turned around yet?" Frank asked.

"Both men had missing fingers," Pete said. "Have you ever had turtle? It's tasty. They let me have some once. Different parts taste like different meats: one part tastes like steak, another part tastes like chicken and another still tastes like pork. Used to hang 'em from tree branches to let the blood drain. Cut their heads off and hang 'em by the tail. The head would keep snapping for hours."

I remembered those guys, they were old by the time I knew them, but they still hunted turtles and hung them from the tree branches of a large oak in their back yard. They were the DiFlippo brothers and lived down the street from the house that Charlie, Doc and Joe shared. Joe and I got ahold of some turtle heads once and Pete was right, they were still snapping. We wrapped them in some burlap and took them down the tracks to where the bums slept. The bums would make little shelters out of scraps of corrugated steel that they scrounged from the junkyard, all rusty and full of holes. The bums were gone during the day, probably panhandling downtown for enough money to buy a bottle of cheap wine. We tossed the burlap-wrapped turtle heads into one of the shacks and took off running. We laughed at the surprise they would get when they opened the burlap.

After a bit, my father began working on the nightly campfire. He prided himself on his fires and on starting them with one match.

"If you build your fire right," he said. "It should only take one match to light it."

"One match and a can of kerosene," Walter proclaimed.

"Start with the smallest kindling you can find," my father said, ignoring Walter's remark. He crushed up some pine twigs and made a pile. "Pine is best, but it burns fast, so you've got to gradually work in some other woods too."

I had heard him describe how to build a fire dozens of times, but I never grew tired of it. It was a ritual with him and I enjoyed it.

"If it's been wet out get your kindling from up in the trees," he continued as he selected pieces from the jumble of wood that he had gathered. "Dead branches are best, as long as they aren't rotten. Dry and dead: they should feel light and break easily."

To demonstrate, he snapped a few branches with his hands and carefully placed them on his growing pile. He preferred the teepee method, where bigger and bigger pieces of wood are braced against each other over the kindling. "Some like the log cabin technique, where the wood is stacked up in a square with the kindling in the middle," he said. "But the teepee method concentrates the heat in the center. It starts faster and is more dependable."

When he was done, my father stood up and took out a single Ohio Blue Tip match. "Stand back everybody," he said in his commander's voice, although nobody was standing nearby.

He flicked the match with his thumbnail and tossed it into the center of his teepee. The kindling flared up beautifully and soon he was placing some of the bigger pieces of wood that I had helped him gather earlier that day.

Walter, Neil, Calvin and Joe were standing around watching.

"It's easy to start a fire at a dry campsite in the middle of summer," Walter commented. "But to start a fire in the north woods during winter, with your life on the line... well, that's a different story."

"What's that got to do with anything?" my father asked, clearly annoyed. He hated having attention drawn away from his fire, just when it was reaching its peak.

"Well, nothin' really," Walter said. "I'm just saying that that would be the real test of fire making."

"That's a Jack London story," my father said, softening a little. 'To Build a Fire.' A lone lumber prospector is stranded in the Yukon with only his wolf-dog as a companion. The temperature is more than fifty below zero. He falls into a creek through the ice — his feet and legs are soaked. On the bank he builds a fire carefully, laying a base of sticks on the snow and then piling dry driftwood sticks on some kindling. At first it sputters and smokes. He gently blows on it and it finally catches. He builds it up and begins drying his clothes. But, just as he's getting warm, a big clump of snow falls on it, putting it out completely. He made the mistake of making his fire under a big pine tree and the heat from the fire loosened the snow caught up in the branches. He tries to start another fire in the open, but his hands are frozen and he drops his matches. Somehow he manages to find a dry match and strike it with his teeth. But, as he blows on the fire to get it going, he chokes on the smoke and blows it out. He collapses in despair. The last thing he sees is his wolf-dog, watching him slowly freeze to death."

"That's what I mean." Walter said. "That's the kind of thing people write about; they don't write about somebody making a big smoky fire at a campground."

"Who's writing about it?" My father asked. "And who says it's smoky?" He stood back and dusted his hands off, pleased with his efforts.

"The Plains Indians made their fires out of buffalo chips," Pete said. "There wasn't much available wood on the plains."

No one commented on Pete's information— everyone had heard it before.

"Buffalo chips," he said, a little more emphatically. "I bet that was fragrant!"

"About as fragrant as Calvin after he rolled around in that bird shit today," Neil said.

Joe cackled loudly and pointed at his friend.

"Did you think to take a shower and change your clothes?" Neil asked his brother. "Or are you just letting that bird shit mellow?"

Joe cackled louder. "He's letting it mellow," he said. "He figures it ain't Saturday yet!"

"Shut up Joe," Calvin said, a threatening tone in his voice. "I haven't seen you head off to the shower in a while either."

"Joe likes to maintain his protective film," Walter pointed out. "It keeps you waterproof and insect-proof. The Indians and frontiersmen added bear grease to their film, they wouldn't think of stripping it away."

"Those Indians must have smelled pretty fragrant," Pete said. "With bear grease and buffalo chip fires."

No one commented on Pete's opinion. Everyone stared at the fire as it grew. Every so often my father would poke at it a little and add some more wood. Pretty soon it was roaring and everyone had to move back a little.

"Tell us the story about the Japanese prisoners, Walter," Donnie said. "The one about the prisoners on your plane." He was Neil's youngest brother and it was the first time that he'd be allowed to go along with the men. He'd heard most of the stories second-hand, but had never heard them directly. He was just barely a teen and had a high voice that cracked and squeaked when he spoke.

Walter laughed, puffing his pipe and warming to the story. He had volunteered for General Claire Chenault's AVG: the American Volunteer Group, in the early part of the War, before Pearl Harbor. He was a radioman on C-47 transport planes that supplied the Chinese who were fighting the Japanese on the mainland. Fighter pilots with the group painted shark's teeth on their Curtiss P-40 Warhawks. The airmen called themselves the Flying Tigers.

"We were flying supplies into China from India," Walter said. "Food, fuel, ammunition, medical supplies and Chinese soldiers. On our way back we carried Chinese recruits to be trained and equipped for Chiang Kai Shek's army. They were a bunch of poor wretches, those Chinese. Half starved, dressed in rags, filthy and lice-ridden. I guess Mr. Chiang didn't want to waste his precious resources on raw recruits.

"Once they got to India, they'd be washed, deloused and fed. Someone told me that it took a couple of months to bring them up to enough strength where they could be trained. I heard that some of them were too far gone and died.

"One time we were flying back a load of Japanese prisoners, guarded by some Chinese soldiers. We had to fly over the Himalayas to get in and out of China. 'The Hump' it was called. We were at maximum altitude when the plane began to shake. There was a loud commotion from the back of the plane at the same time.

"Go back and see what's going on," the pilot told me. I opened the cockpit door and saw that the Chinese had opened the side door of the plane. One by one, they were shoving the Japanese prisoners out of the plane. One of the Chinese turned and glared at me. I went back and told the pilot. "Shut the cockpit door and lock it," he told me.

"When we landed, an officer wanted to know what had happened to the prisoners.

"They escaped," a Chinese soldier told him.

"How come you didn't stop them," Calvin asked. There was a challenging tone to his voice. Calvin had developed a rudimentary grasp of sarcasm that only extended to rude questions, snide remarks and a scoffing "pah!"

Neil, standing behind him, cuffed him lightly on the side of the head.

"Hey!" Calvin said. "I was just askin'!"

"If I'd have tried I'd have been the next one out the door," Walter said, ignoring the interruption.

"Besides, if you ever heard what the Japs did to the Chinese, you'd understand. The Chinese sure hated the Japanese," he added, relighting his pipe.

"Those Japs were mean, that's for sure," Pete said.

"Amen," the men murmured in unison. As much as they found Pete annoying, they respected his experience during the war. Captured in the Philippines, marched to a prisoner of war camp on the Bataan peninsula, he had been tortured, beaten and starved. He was one of the few survivors left when the camp was liberated towards the end of the war. He was still skinny as a rail and was racked by bouts of Malaria from time to time. Pete tended to annoy everyone a little, and he could be a little short with us kids, but it was never doubted that he was one of them – a member of the Sleeper Street Gang.

Pete stared into the fire for a while and we all did the same. I tried to imagine being beaten and starved in a jungle prison camp and didn't like the thought.

"Hey," I said to Walter, trying to wipe the prison camp image from my mind. "Tell Donnie about the time you pushed old man Phelps into the canal."

Everyone laughed. The story was a classic and we had all heard it dozens of times.

"Yeah," my father said, needling Walter. "Poor old man Phelps! He might have drownt!"

"He had it *comin*," Walter said defensively. "He shot me in the ass with rock salt!"

"Somebody shot Uncle Walter?" Donnie squeaked.

"That's right Donnie," my father said. "Gram had to pick the rock salt out of his butt with a pair of tweezers. It took the better part of two hours."

"Why would the old man shoot a kid?" Donnie asked. "It seems a little ex*cessive* to me." Donnie liked to use big words whenever he could. He often emphasized one of the syllables.

"We had been stealing apples from old man Phelp's orchard at night," my father said. "Walter organized lookouts and pickers. We even wore bandanas over our faces, like outlaws in a Western. But someone always broke a branch or made a noise that alerted the old man. He'd come out of his house with a hurricane lantern and run us off. But we kept sneaking back. One night he decided that enough was enough. He had loaded his shotgun shells with rock salt and when he came out that night he started shooting."

"He scared the hell out of us," Pete said. "He shot up into the trees. Apples, branches and leaves came raining down on us. I thought the sky was falling."

"But why was Walter the only one that he shot?" Donnie asked.

"We all ran off when the old man shot," Frank said. "He shot into the air to scare us and he did. We ran like hell. Except for Walter, Walter wouldn't run."

"Why didn't you run Uncle Walt?" Donnie asked.

"I was sick of the old man running us off over a few lousy apples," Walter said. "He was a mean old cuss anyway."

"He always yelled at us if we came anywhere near his property," my father explained. "If somebody hit a ball into his yard, he'd throw it into the canal. Gram wanted to buy some apples for a pie once, but when Frank and I went there he wouldn't sell us any. He ran us off."

"He just used the apples to make hard cider and apple jack," Frank said. "He was drunk most of the time."

"Walter decided that we'd get some apples anyway," my father said. "That's why we started sneaking up there at night, and that's why he started shooting."

"I'd never been shot at before," Frank said. "It was pretty scary."

"I wasn't going to let that old bastard get his satisfaction," Walter said. "I stood my ground and looked right at him. 'Here's your damn apples back,' I said and threw the two apples I had in my hands at him."

"Walter missed him with the first apple," Pete said. "But he hit the old man square in the forehead with the other. As Walter turned to walk away, the old man took aim and shot!"

"Hit me right in the ass!" Walter exclaimed. "It felt like I'd been stung by a dozen hornets!"

"You should have seen Walter run after that," my father said. "He cleared the fence like a steeplechase runner!"

"Walter got him back, though," Frank said. "Walter had a plan: The old man had an outhouse that jutted out over the canal on a platform he had built out of planks. It was his pride and joy. 'I never have to shovel it out,' he bragged to anyone who would listen. "The canal flushes it out for me."

"Fine for him," Walter said. "But he was upstream of the town. Everyone got to see his brown trout float by."

"Walter snuck out in the middle of the night," Frank continued. "He used a crowbar to loosen the nails that held the outhouse to the platform. Then, shortly after dawn, the old man went into the outhouse to do his business. When he was inside, Walter ran out and pushed the outhouse into the canal, with the old man still in it!"

"I didn't know he was in it!" Walter said defensively. "I took the crowbar into the woods so I wouldn't have to run with it and then I went back and pushed the outhouse in. The old man must have slipped by me when I was gone!"

No one believed him.

"The best part of Walter's plan was that he ran into town and then calmly walked up to the bridge as if he was out for a stroll," Pete said. "He stood there, smoking his pipe and talking with passersby. When the outhouse came into sight, the old man was clinging to it, shouting for help. Walter dove in and dragged the old man to shore."

"Yeah," Frank said. "Everyone thought that Walter was a hero, including the old man! He was so grateful that he gave Walter the right to be on his land anytime. He even hired Walter to do odd jobs around his farm."

"Walter even helped the old man rebuild his outhouse – and old man Phelps paid him for it!" My father added.

"He also let me pick all the apples I wanted," Walter said with a laugh.

"They were good pie apples too, Northern Spies, as I remember. Gram always claimed that they were the best pie apples there were."

His comment led to a lively discussion about apples, each man arguing which ones were the best for cooking and which ones were the best for eating. I thought that Cortlands were the best for eating, but I didn't tell anyone.

The talk continued for a while, devolving into individual conversations, then back into stories told to the whole group. My eyes burned from the smoke from the fire and I was having trouble keeping them open. I started to drift off a couple of times, but forced myself to stay awake. Neil had given me a task, and I wasn't very excited about it.

"Time for you boys to head to bed," my father announced abruptly. I looked over and saw that Donnie was sound asleep in his chair. Calvin was dozing off and Joe was on his knees, trying to tie Calvin's shoelaces together. My father's announcement woke Calvin and he kicked viciously at Joe, who scrabbled away, laughing.

"Idiot!" Calvin said as he retied his shoes.

Neil was nowhere to be seen.

When I crawled into the back of the station wagon and into my sleeping bag, the tiredness left me. I was nervous about what I planned to do and I could feel my heart throbbing in my chest. I lay there, staring at the darkened ceiling, thinking about the journal and the circumstances that had brought it here. I could hear the men, still sitting around the fire, talking in hushed tones. I was convinced that the talk concerned the journal. I found myself wishing that they would get done so that I could get on with my task, a task that made me shudder.

After what seemed a like a very long time, I heard Walter quietly open the front door of the car and put his satchel on the floor. I kept my eyes closed until I heard the door click shut. Waiting a few minutes to be sure that he was away, I sat up and looked out the window. I saw Walter lay down on the old canvas army cot that he set up next to the tent, under the dining fly. I waited until I could hear him snoring. Walter had a loud and distinctive snore that my father described as "somewhere between the bellowing of an old cow and the mating call of a bull hippo." It was the reason Walter slept outside the tent. I crept forward, my flashlight gripped tightly in my fist. It was army surplus, OD green, with the lens at a ninety-degree angle from the handle. There was a red filter on the lens for reading maps at night.

Squirming over the front seat, I turned on the flashlight and located Walter's satchel. It looked strange, bathed in the red light. I felt guilty at the thought of going through someone else's stuff, especially Walter's. Screwing up my courage and swallowing my pride, I reached down, picked up the satchel and shined the light inside.

There, amid the personal items that I had seen in the morning, was the Nambu. Next to it was the journal. I took the book out and stared at the cover. "Journal" it read in embossed letters. Below that was a small embossed white flower with an inscription in what I guessed was Welsh: *"Na ad I'th dafod dorri'th wddf."* I had no idea what it meant. The flower surprised me, though: I had seen it before, but couldn't remember where. My heart began to race as I eased the cover open. This was it: this was the book I remembered from that rainy night in December, the night that haunted my dreams still. With shaking hands, I shined the red light down on the inscription. The roar of a car engine and two blinding headlights suddenly stopped me.

Surprised, I sat bolt upright, bumping my head on the dashboard and dropping the book and flashlight as I did. Brakes squealed and the head-lights went out. I heard car doors slam and the peals of a woman's laughter. My uncle Doc had arrived with his new girlfriend. There were shouts of greeting as someone opened the tent flap and turned on the lantern.

I put the book back into the satchel, remembering at the last second to fasten the clips. Peeking over the dash, I could see everyone clasping hands and hugging. Walter was on his feet, shaking Doc's hand and laughing. Although anyone could have seen me, bathed in the light, no one was looking. Fast as a rabbit heading for his hole, I scurried over the seat and into my sleeping bag. I lay there a while, wondering if I should crawl out and say 'hi'; but then I heard my father say that it was late and that they would talk more in the morning. He invited Doc and his girlfriend to sleep in the tent.

"No thanks, we'll sleep in the car," Doc said. I guess they didn't realize that I was in the station wagon, they kept me awake most of the night.

CHAPTER FOUR

My portable alarm clock woke me before dawn. I slithered out of the car and slipped silently up to the rear of the equipment trailer, using my red-lensed flashlight to guide me. There was a large compartment built into the back that held various tools.

I opened the compartment door and began pulling out a pair of swim fins, a diver's mask, a snorkel, a weight belt and a barbed trident affixed to a broom handle. The mask caught on something heavy and there was a loud "clunk". I stopped and looked around, but there was nothing but silence in the dark campsite. I stuck my head part way into the compartment and trained my flashlight on the obstruction. There were several long, heavy looking pieces of iron with holes for handles to fit. I realized that they were picks. Strange, I thought. Farther back, there were several wooden handles for the picks, also some sturdy looking shovels. At the far rear was a large canvas duffle bag, bulging with some additional equipment, and – most surprisingly – a welding torch and tank. What was all that stuff for, I wondered. Before I could investigate further I heard someone stir in the tent. I quickly freed the mask, closed the compartment door and slipped off down the darkened trail.

The path to the creek was steep and rocky and the red light made the rocks, trees, and bushes look two-dimensional. The ground was slick and muddy from the heavy morning dew and I had skinned a knee, bumped an elbow, bruised my tailbone and gotten covered with mud by the time I got to the creek.

I looked around furtively, nervous about what I was going to do. The eerie light of false dawn gave every bush and rock life. I felt like I was surrounded by ominous creatures, intent on doing me harm. I shined my flashlight at them, trying to get them to stay back. A crow's call startled me, its lonely cry echoing up and down the creek gorge.

The spring-fed creek was freezing. My teeth chattered as I waded across and began picking my way to the opposite bank and towards the big trout hole. Climbing up onto a big boulder overlooking the hole, I shivered, waiting for the sun to warm me.

The sun took a while coming up over the steep ridge above me. I lost feeling in my fingers and toes, and I knew that my lips were turning blue. But I felt that I had to see my mission through; I had grown up with the notion that we in our family weren't quitters. "See it through" was a mantra of my father's, one of many that he often repeated along with "any job worth doing is worth doing right," and "success comes to those who are ready when their opportunity knocks." I laughed to myself at Walter's favorite saying: "do unto others and then cut out."

When the sun finally cleared the trees, it did so with a flourish. Dew on the leaves and grass along the creek sparkled brilliantly. A light, swirling mist obscured the creek itself, but the sun quickly burned it off. When it did it lit the pebbly creek bottom through crystal-clear water. I looked and there they were: dozens of big trout, facing upstream and sparkling in the refracted sunlight. People say that fish don't sleep, but these seemed to be an exception— they were suspended just off the bottom, hardly moving. I climbed down off the rock and circled the big pool at a careful distance, trout are wary of predators on creek banks.

I readied my trident, mask, snorkel, weight belt and flippers and slipped into the icy water at the edge of the pool. Taking a big lung full of air, I drifted out into the pool towards the trout. To my surprise, I hadn't spooked them, the trout were still there, lined up like so many giant sardines in a can. I approached them from behind, downstream, figuring that any blood and thrashing would be less likely to spook the rest of the fish.

I targeted a big brown trout, hanging back at the rear of the formation. I thrust my trident at it, but my aim was off and the trident glanced off the silvery skin of the fish. Surprisingly, the big fish only rolled slightly and settled back into its former position. I tried again, thrusting lower and more firmly. This time the tines of the trident pierced the fish's body just behind the gills; it thrashed madly and I had all I could do to keep a grip on the slippery wooden handle. Crablike, I pushed off from the bottom, swimming backwards toward the shallows. As I surfaced I gulped some air and looked at my prize. It was a large brown trout, maybe sixteen inches long and weighing a couple of pounds. It was still wriggling weakly, its speckles glinting beautifully in the morning sun.

I looked around nervously. A blue jay shrieked, announcing my crime. I swiftly removed the fish from the trident and put it into a mesh bag weighted with a rock. I tied the drawstring to a low hanging tree branch and dropped the bag into the shallows. Glancing around once more and seeing nothing moving, I returned to the deep pool.

Amazingly, the other fish hardly seemed to have noticed the loss of their comrade, they were still where they had been, suspended just above the bottom of the pool. I approached another fish at the rear of the formation and speared it perfectly on my first try – another large brown for the bag.

After a half an hour I had a dozen big trout in the bag. I knew that I had more than enough fish and should get going, but I couldn't help going down again for one more fish. Call it greed, call it immaturity, call it stupid; call it anything you want. What it turned out to be was a big mistake.

When I surfaced, a big fish on my trident, I heard a noise on the trail. At first I thought it might be a deer or maybe someone's dog, but then I saw a flash of clothing and knew that it was a person, and that person was just about to come into my sight, which, I suddenly realized, meant that I would be coming into his sight. I slipped under water and swam across the pool to where there were some overhanging branches. Not wanting the loud noise of clearing my snorkel, I surfaced.

As I stood, freezing in the chest-deep water, I listened for a footfall on the trail. Strange, I thought: I heard nothing. Soon the squirrels began chattering again and the birds began chirping. Most likely, whoever it was had taken the trail that led downstream. I peeked through the foliage at the trail. No one was there. Relieved at escaping a close-call, I ducked under the foliage and waded out into the pool, prepared to swim across, grab my bag of fish, and get out of there. But before I could do anything a flurry of swift movement behind a bush stopped me— someone was there after all. I was transfixed, unable to think of anything to do but just stand there. Suddenly a young woman in a one-piece swimmers racing suit stepped out from behind the bushes and, in one fluid motion, dove into the frigid water.

The girl surfaced and began swimming upstream, directly towards me. Her stroke had the grace and power of a collegiate athlete. Halfway across the pool, at the deepest part, the mysterious girl did a surface dive and disappeared beneath the glassy surface. I was beginning to think that I had only dreamed her when she suddenly surfaced directly in front of me, not three feet away. She stood up and swept her hair back, a playful look on her face.

"So, what are you," the girl asked. "King Neptune?" She reached back and twisted some water out of her hair. It glistened in the morning sunlight.

My face reddened as I realized that I had my mask and snorkel on my forehead and a fish on my trident.

"Oh, um," I said, my voice quavering from the cold and embarrassment. "Just fishing for breakfast."

"Spearing's illegal," she said, a serious look on her face. Then she smiled. "Don't worry, I won't tell anyone."

I stood there, feeling stupid and unable to speak. The girl held out her hand.

"I'm Karen," she said. "Doc's latest girlfriend. You must be Tommy."

I shook her hand and nodded.

She looked at me appraisingly. "You're a lot older looking than the picture Doc showed me," she said. "Must have been an old one."

I nodded again.

"I didn't see you last night when we came in," she said.

"Oh, I guess I was already asleep in the back of the station wagon," I said.

"You were in the station wagon?" she asked, her face reddening slightly.

"Sound asleep," I lied.

"Right," she said with a doubting smile. She turned.

"Well," she said over her shoulder, "See you later, Neptune."

She slipped below the surface and disappeared. She didn't surface again until she was almost to the trail. Stepping out of the water, she turned, waved once, and then disappeared into the woods. I was left standing there, holding my trident with a dead fish on it.

"I hear you brought us a mess of trout for breakfast," Walter announced as I walked into the camp.

I raised the mesh bag for him to see. I had dropped my trident and snorkeling equipment off the side of the trail to be retrieved later.

He nodded approvingly. "You've redeemed yourself… Neptune." He said with a laugh.

My Uncle Doc got up from his lawn chair and shook my hand, a big grin on his face. He was a large man, head and shoulders taller than I was, and broad, his shoulders, chest and back stretched the fibers of the oversize polo shirt he wore. He played Tight End for the Lockton Essos – our semi-pro football team. He also played basketball in the winter and baseball in the spring. During the summer he played tennis and golf.

Doc made ends meet by working part time for a tree surgeon company, tending bar at Wagner's Tavern, his favorite hangout and playing pool. In pool, Doc had no equal and that was a problem. Very few locals were foolish enough to bet him on a game, or an individual shot. That meant that if Doc wanted to gamble on a game, he'd have to travel to a city where he wasn't known— a hard thing to do when you're six foot six.

Doc got his nickname from his time as a combat medic in Korea. My mother said that that was why Doc had such a devil-may-care attitude. "Doc saw too much in Korea for someone so young," she said. "He joined up when he was seventeen, in order to get the GI Bill for college and was sent to Japan. He loved it in Japan and had it pretty easy until the North Koreans invaded the South. The next thing he knew, he was in the middle of a nasty conflict. He got medals for dragging wounded guys away from the line of fire."

Doc had a thick shock of wavy brown hair, a strong jaw and dimples when he smiled, and he was always smiling. But it was his eyes that were his undoing with the ladies; big, brown and vulnerable, "bedroom eyes" my mother called them. Girls found Doc irresistible and he couldn't resist them. He had a succession of pretty girlfriends but never dated one for more than a month or two. "Because of the War," my mother would say. "It made him shy away from commitment."

Doc clapped me on the shoulder as he shook my hand.

"Hey Tommy," he said. "I heard you were fishing this morning."

"Yeah," I said, holding up the bag a little bit and shrugging. "I got a few."

My father came up from behind and took the bag from me. "Let's get these things cooked before the game warden comes around," he said. "Looks like they were speared."

My father and I cleaned the fish and Pete fried them in butter in a large cast iron skillet. He also made home fries in bacon grease and fried slices of my Grandmother's homemade bread in butter.

As we sat down at the big picnic table, I noticed that Karen was looking dubiously at the whole fish on her plate.

"You don't have to eat that if you don't want to," Uncle Charlie said helpfully. "I'm not going to either. I don't want my food staring at me."

Uncle Charlie was an unapologetic admirer of pretty women, and he openly admired all of Doc's girlfriends. Karen was no exception. As soon as she sat down, Charlie sidled up to her, a friendly smile on his face.

"No, I want to try it," Karen said, swallowing nervously. "It's just that I don't know how to go about it."

"Show her, Doc," my father said over his shoulder. "Have some manners!"

"Sorry," Doc said, flashing his signature grin. He turned his attention to Karen. "Here, let me help you honey,"

He showed Karen how to peel back the skin and rake the flesh off the bones. She looked at the pure white flesh, shrugged and put a forkful in her mouth. She chewed slightly, swallowed and smiled. "Better than lobster," she said, going for another forkful.

"What'd I tell you," Doc said. "Nothing like fried wild trout. Nice job Pete." Pete might have annoyed everyone a little, but he was an excellent cook.

"I think we should all thank King Neptune for this feast," Karen said. "Can we do this every morning?"

"As long as King Neptune here can pay the fine if he gets caught spearing," my father said sarcastically.

"Hey, leave the kid alone," Doc said. "Besides, you're putting Karen off her breakfast!"

"No, I'm fine," Karen said, pulling off another forkful. She looked over at Donnie. "I used to be a vegetarian," she said. "I quit eating meat after I visited a veal farm. Talk about cruel: those poor calves lived in their own filth in a narrow little box. The farmers didn't want them to get any exercise."

"Why not?" Donnie squeaked, intrigued.

"They didn't want the meat to get tough," Karen said. "And you don't even want to know how they kill them."

"Hold on," Doc said. "Now you're putting me off my breakfast!" Doc's favorite dish was Wiener Schnitzel, like his mother used to make.

After breakfast we loaded the cars and prepared to head north again. This time our destination was Lake Chautauqua, the fabled home of the Chautauqua Muskellunge. "Muskies," most people called them. They were the largest variant of the pike family, the record being sixty five pounds and fifty eight inches long. They were predators, long and sleek with a mouthful of teeth. They liked to lurk in the shallows where their greenish brown coloration and mottled stripes and spots camouflaged them in the weeds.

"Small pan fish and large creek chubs are their favorite food," Pete explained. "But occasionally, they'll take baby ducks." Pete had taken the lead on this trip, having fished Chautauqua before. He relished the role and never missed a chance to explain the finer points of musky fishing to anyone who happened to be within earshot.

"Muskies are territorial," he said. "They patrol certain areas in a predictable pattern, setting up ambushes along the way. Musky fishermen scout muskies during the off season, marking their movements in a note-book. I've heard it said that you can set your watch at the appearance of a big musky at a point or bay.

"You have to use a big lure that mimics a baitfish and slowly troll along the weed beds. It takes time and patience, but if you hook one – watch out!"

"Do people ever get attacked?" Donnie squeaked, his eyes wide.

"People get pulled under all the time," Walter said, a twinkle in his eye. "Sometimes they'll come out of the water and take someone standing on the shore. They've even been known to ram a boat to knock unwary fishermen into the water. A man, knocked out of his boat in the middle of a huge lake, watches hopelessly as the muskies circle, moving closer and closer for the KILL!"

At that, Walter grabbed Donnie's leg and squeezed. Donnie let out a high pitched scream and thrashed madly, trying to get loose of Walter's hand. Joe and Calvin giggled; glad to not be the brunt of the joke for a change.

Neil gave me a heads up as we prepared to leave. I was standing next to Doc's car, hoping to be invited to ride with him and Karen. But I was quickly disappointed.

"We're not going fishing, Tom," Doc informed me. "We're going to hang around the camp today, maybe play a little tennis and lounge by the pool. Karen wants to go into town to do a little shopping," he added.

"Oh, yeah," I stammered, feeling a little foolish for being so obvious. "I'm riding with Neil anyway." I turned and walked off towards Neil's car.

"Good luck, Neptune," Karen said.

I waved over my shoulder, feeling my face redden.

"She's out of your league buddy," Neil said as I climbed into the passenger seat, evidently Walter was riding with someone else this morning. My face reddened even more at the realization that my not-so-subtle move had been noticed by everyone.

"What are you talking about," I said weakly.

"Come on," Neil said. "You were following her around all morning like a little puppy! Everybody saw it, you couldn't take your eyes off of her."

I didn't reply, I just sat there, feeling stupid. It's funny how people see themselves differently than other people see them. Someone once told me that if you saw yourself walk into a room, you wouldn't recognize yourself, and you might not like the person that you saw at all. I guess it's like hearing your voice recorded for the first time, you don't recognize it as your own and you don't like it much.

"You've got to be subtle," Neil said. "Let them notice you. Girls like Karen like a guy who dresses well and drives a nice car," he continued. "Guys are always tripping over themselves around a girl like that, but it never works for them."

I had no comment. I was getting a little annoyed at Neil's lecture. He always held it over me a little, he being a couple of years older than me. When he turned thirteen he told me: "I'm a teenager now and you're not." I wondered if he would crow about turning seventy before me when the time came.

"I took a look at the book last night," I said after a long silence. Neil looked over at me.

"Did you read it?" he asked eagerly. "What did it say? What's it about?"

I shook my head. "Only saw the cover," I replied. After Neil's criticism of me I felt no need give him much of an explanation. He gave me a hard look. "All right, I'm sorry," he said. "I was just trying to get your goat a little. Looks like it worked," he added wryly.

I smiled and nodded. "Just a little," I said. We shared a laugh for a moment.

"Doc and his girlfriend pulled in just as I was opening the cover," I explained. "I thought I'd get caught with all the lights on," I added.

"Everyone went back to bed," Neil said accusingly.

"Doc was parked right next to me," I said. "I couldn't risk it. They were up for a while — I was afraid that they'd notice the light."

Neil gritted his teeth and stared at the road ahead. Somehow I felt like I had let him down. I've always been susceptible to feelings of guilt. Some people are like that: they'll do just about anything if you put enough guilt on them. I was one of those people.

"It's a journal," I said. "Pop's."

"Pop's journal," Neil said thoughtfully. He liked to chew on a toothpick and he moved it around in his mouth when he was thinking.

"What's in that journal that's so important to those guys?" He said.

"I don't know," I replied. "But I plan to find out – if I can."

Neil nodded and stepped on the gas a little. We drove the rest of the way in silence, absorbed by our own thoughts.

• • • • • • • • • • • • • • • • •

Chautauqua Lake is nestled in the hills of Western New York, just a few miles south of Lake Erie. But it doesn't drain into the bigger lake; instead it empties south into the Mississippi drainage basin. During colonial times, the French portaged the eight miles between modern-day Barcelona on Lake Erie and Mayville on Chautauqua Lake. It was an important part of their fur trading empire— or so Walter told it.

The lake is long, seventeen miles or so, but only a couple of miles wide at its widest. A narrow strait at Bemus Point separates the lake into two sections: north and south. Pete informed us that the northern section was deep and held walleye, smallmouth bass and bluegills, The southern section was much shallower and held calicos, perch and our quarry for the day, the mighty muskellunge. "Lunge," as Walter dubbed them.

"Chautauqua is a Seneca word that means "sack tied in the middle," Pete told us. "The water was crystal clear in Indian times but some Englishman had the bright idea of importing water plants for fish cover. The plants took over and now the shallower parts of the southern lake are choked with them by the end of summer."

We traveled to a boat livery halfway down the southern lake, located on a series of small canals. Snug Harbor, it was called. To his credit, Pete stepped up for this part of our trip. He rented two boats and motors and brought out a large tackle box filled with metal leaders, sinkers and huge musky lures. And he had a plan.

"We'll start here," he said, pointing to the dock. "One boat will head north and circle to the other side at Bemus, the other will head south and circle north, hugging the shore the whole way. We'll meet up somewhere near that big white pine on the opposite shore." He pointed at a big white pine tree, directly across the lake. "Then we'll head back here," he added. "That should take most of the day."

We rigged up and split into two groups. Neil and I ended up sitting side by side in the back of the boat heading south. Joe and Calvin would fish out to the side and my father would man the tiller. Pete was driving the other boat, with Walter, Frank, Charlie and Donnie fishing.

"Twenty bucks to the biggest fish," Walter announced as we eased out of the harbor.

"Guy could make a living," Neil said to me with a wink and a grin.

Trolling sounds easy, you rig up your rod, let your line out and run your boat slowly around the waterway. Instead of casting and retrieving, where your lure is in prime position for only a few seconds, trolling puts your lure in ideal position for very long stretches. But the problem with trolling is that, if you keep your lure where it needs to be, just off the bottom, you often get snagged. And the more lines you have out, the more snags you get, especially when Calvin is in your boat.

On paper, Calvin was in the best position in the boat, he was on the shore side, right on the edge of the weed beds. But it quickly became apparent that the only thing he was in position for was lots of snags. When trolling along a weed bed an angler has to be extremely watchful of his line. The first instant he feels a snag he has to pull his line in. It's especially tricky when the boat is rounding a point or when there is a submerged branch or clump of weeds. Calvin was not an attentive angler; he spent most of his time trying to keep his pipe lit and making comments on interesting things that he saw on the shore: a bird, some turtles on a log or a squirrel in a tree.

Almost as soon as we got started Calvin sang out.

"Fish on!" He shouted. We all reeled our lines in and my father reversed the propeller to stop the boat and allow Calvin to play his fish.

"He's a big one!" Calvin exclaimed as he heaved at his rod, bending it almost double. Calvin liked to use fifty pound test braided line on his rigs in order to prevent breaks and he used a heavy-duty saltwater rod he had found at a yard sale.

Normally with a fish on, a rod quivers and jumps as the fish struggles against the line. The drag sings as the fish makes a run and then the angler reels frantically when the fish slows. Calvin's rig did none of those things.

"You've got a snag, ya maroon," Neil announced. Neil liked to use

Bugs Bunny's corruption of 'moron' when somebody did something he judged as stupid. "Cut the line so we can move on."

"I'm not cutting the line, and I don't have a snag, I have a fish," Calvin said through clenched teeth, he still had his smoldering pipe in his mouth.

But, as he pulled and pulled, it became apparent that he did have a snag. A few minutes later he pulled up a sodden log, covered with stinking mud and some crawly looking things.

"Logfish!" Joe crowed from the other side of the boat. "Calvin's got him a big ole logfish!"

"Shut up Joe," Calvin said hotly. "I had a fish on, a big one! But it spit the hook and the hook caught on this log!"

My father reached over and freed Calvin's lure without comment and put the boat back into trolling position.

"What a maroon," Neil said as we let our lines out.

Calvin caught a series of snags on our way down the lake. He caught branches, clumps of weeds, logs, and in one case, an old tire. It seemed that once we had finally freed Calvin from a snag and got going again he caught another. Even my father, who was a patient man, was becoming irritated at Calvin's inability to pay attention.

"Tree ahead," he announced at one point. "Reel in!"

"What tree?" Calvin said looking around at the shore.

"Right there!" My father said, pointing. "That tree right there in the water ahead of us!"

He had shifted the boat into reverse and turned it sharply away from the tree, but it was too late.

"Fish on!" Calvin announced as his lure tangled in the submerged branches. We all reeled in, subjecting Calvin to an assortment of verbal abuse.

When we finally made it to the end of the lake and prepared to turn northward, my father had us reel in and change places. He tried to make it seem like he was just being fair to everyone, but Calvin felt slighted nonetheless. After we all switched sides, Calvin began casting his big lure out towards the middle of the lake and retrieving it in fast, jerky motions.

"You'll never catch anything out there," Neil said. "Muskies lurk in the shallows. Everybody knows that," He added.

Calvin refused to respond and kept casting and retrieving as we made our way north.

Joe kept his line much closer to the boat than Calvin had and was much more attentive. As a result we made good progress. Neil, now on the shore side of the boat since we had switched, worked his lure as close to the edge of the weeds as he could. I was a little annoyed that he was able to fish more effectively than I had been with all of Calvin's snags constantly interrupting us. But soon my annoyance turned to simmering envy as Neil's rod suddenly bent with a quiver.

"Fish on!" He announced. The drag on his reel sang as the fish made a run for deep water. My father stopped the engine and maneuvered the boat with a paddle in order to keep the line from going under the keel. The rest of us reeled in, except for Calvin who kept stubbornly casting and retrieving, but judiciously away from Neil's fish.

The fish was obviously a big one and it fought furiously. But Neil played him expertly, letting the fish have a run if it wanted and reeling slack line when the fish slowed or turned. As he brought the fish in closer we all held on as Neil stood and held his rod out to keep the fish from going under the boat, stepping over seats and anglers as he did so. My father tried to guide the boat out into the lake and away from the weed beds. The action caused the boat to sway and rock, coming dangerously close to swamping on several occasions.

"Get out of the way Calvin!" Neil shouted every time he had to step over his younger brother. "And reel your line in!"

Calvin would duck and maneuver his rod out of the way, but every chance he got he'd cast out into the lake again.

Finally the big fish was exhausted and Neil was able to bring him close to the boat. You could see, just beneath the surface, the pre-historic looking fish with alligator jaws. I was manning the net and I swiftly scooped the fish into it head first. But the net wasn't big enough and when I hefted the fish out of the water it thrashed violently, throwing its tail side to side. I managed to get the fish over the gunwale before it shook itself free. By this time the big musky had thrown Neil's lure and it hit the deck free, snapping its jaws viciously. Joe and Calvin jumped in alarm, threatening to flip the boat as I tried to get the net around its head.

Each boat was equipped with a club the size of a small baseball bat, to be used to dispatch a caught musky. My father, with cool aplomb, put the musky out of its misery with one swift, carefully aimed strike to the head.

"Look at the size of that fish!" Neil announced triumphantly as the fish lay dead on the floor of the boat. He stole a glance at me but I just smiled. I knew that he wanted me to be envious, but I wouldn't give him the satisfaction. He was like that about everything: his car, his new loafers, a new jacket or pair of pants, his job in the clothing store and now, his big fish.

"That's a beauty all right," I said, keeping any hint of sarcasm out of my voice. "Biggest fish so far, except for Calvin's tire."

Everyone laughed at my joke except for Calvin who was furiously working his rig. "I think I just got a hit," Calvin said.

"Yeah," Neil said, hefting the big musky onto a metal stringer and easing it over the side. "I guess I'll be twenty dollars richer in a little while." He gave me another look as he washed his hands in the lake and sat back down. "A guy could make a living," he added.

I nodded, concentrating on getting my line back out. We had drifted out into the deeper part of the lake during Neil's fight with the big musky, and my father powered the motor up to get back into trolling position.

"Snag!" Calvin suddenly announced. We all looked to see his rod bent with Calvin pulling at it. Another big log, I thought, but my father thought differently.

"That's a fish, Calvin," he said. "Don't horse it!"

"Doesn't feel like a fish," he said, his teeth clenched on his pipe. "Feels like a snag."

But he stopped heaving at his rod and raised the tip. Sure enough, it quivered as the fish resisted.

"Looks like you might have a walleye on," my father announced. "They don't fight much, but they're good eating."

"Is a walleye anything like the blue pike Pete caught yesterday?" Joe asked. For once it was a serious question.

"Same fish, different name," my father said. "In Canada they call them pickerel."

My father turned out to be right. Calvin's fish was indeed a walleye and a big one, a fact not lost on Calvin.

"This is bigger than your musky," Calvin informed Neil as we boated the big fish. It was the biggest walleye I'd ever seen. We put it on a separate stringer, then put the two fish side by side for comparison. Calvin's fish was bigger by a good deal.

"That means I win the twenty bucks," Calvin said, lighting his pipe.

"No," Neil said. "Walter meant twenty bucks for the biggest musky."

"He said biggest fish," Calvin said. "That's what he said."

"But he meant the biggest musky, right Uncle Owen?" Neil said, appealing to my father. "That's what we're fishing for today."

"You'll have to ask Walter what he meant," my father said. He looked thoughtful for a moment. "Although he's not always certain of what he meant himself," he added, more to himself than to anyone else.

We finally got settled back into a trolling pattern, but I was the only one who was really fishing. Joe and Calvin, bored, had reeled in their lines and busied themselves with a series of silly pranks on each other. Neil had his line in the water, but I noticed that he was keeping his lure high and close to the boat, he was in a hurry to meet up with the other boat and be done, his reward the quicker to collect.

I was in the best spot possible and worked my lure assiduously along the edge of the weed bed, but by the time the big white pine came into sight I hadn't gotten so much as a nibble.

"Well," Neil announced reeling in his line. "Here we are. Looks like you guys got skunked!"

Neil couldn't help gloating; it was part of his nature. Neil just had to rub it in.

"What do you mean skunked?" Calvin said. He had been busy trying to put a worm down Joe's back while Joe fiddled with something in his tackle box. "My fish is bigger than yours!"

"That's right," Neil said. "Your fish— not your musky. The reward is for biggest musky, not fish."

"I thought we were going to let Walter decide that," Calvin said. "It's his contest!"

Neil had clearly gotten under Calvin's skin, something he liked to do. Like a knife fighter, Neil twisted his blade.

"You foul-hooked your fish anyway," he said. "Walter would never accept a foul-hooked fish."

"He wasn't foul hooked!" Calvin exclaimed angrily. He was still holding the worm and it was dangling from his fingers. Joe turned sharply to see what the argument was about and turned his face right into it.

"Hey!" He said, slapping at the worm. He dislodged it and it flew through the air, landing with a plop on one of Neil's new tassel loafers.

"Idiots!" Neil said. He picked up the worm and threw it at Calvin, who ducked. It looked as though the two brothers were about to get into a fight right there in the boat when my father suddenly spoke up.

"Look," he said, pointing. "Look at that!"

There, rounding the point on which the white pine sat, was Pete's boat. In the front was Donnie, struggling to hold up the biggest musky any of us had ever seen. He had it cradled in his arms and he wore a huge grin on his face.

"Now that's a big fish!" My father exclaimed.

"Wow," I muttered. Reluctantly, I reeled in my line. Game over, I thought. But at least I hadn't been beaten by Neil. Involuntarily I started clapping. The rest of us in the boat did the same, including Neil, he might have been a bit of a braggart, but he wasn't a sore loser, especially to his little brother.

When we got back to the harbor, Donnie was walking on air. He recounted his fight with the big fish a half a dozen times, his voice squeaking with excitement. I saw Pete talking with the owner of the harbor, a grizzled old man with a grey beard and deep, gruff voice. His name was Aubry and he'd run the harbor since before the war. Pete pulled out his wallet, counted out some bills and shook Aubry's hand.

"What's Pete doing?" I asked my father.

"He's having Donnie's fish mounted," he informed me. "We'll pick it up on the way back through."

That night we feasted on Calvin's big walleye. Pete stuffed it with cans of mandarin oranges and buried it in some coals, wrapped in tin foil. Karen, back from the mall and sitting in Doc's lap, proclaimed the fish excellent.

"This camp is turning out to be a first class seafood restaurant," she said, sipping a glass of white wine. I idly wondered where she had gotten such a nice glass.

Keep those fish comin', boys," Doc said with a big grin. "They are mighty tasty!"

Charlie made a comment about doing all the work, but Doc just laughed. Nothing fazed Doc. He was a person comfortable in his own skin and happy with life.

Later, around the fire, stories were told and beers were drunk. Frank regaled us with a tale about Walter.

"There's a bridge in Middleport that opens like a double door, except straight up," he said. "You know the one, the one on Second Street." We all nodded, we knew the one.

"Well, one time, Walter was driving his old Model-T, and he was late for something. As he got to the bridge lights were flashing and the operator was starting to raise the bridge. Walter, well, Walter being Walter, decided that he didn't have time to wait or go to the next bridge, so he gunned the motor and made a run at it, hoping to leap the car over the gap. Problem was, Model-Ts have a gravity fed gas line – sometimes people would have to back them up a steep hill in order to keep the gas flowing. Just as he got to the top, the engine stalled. The front tires caught on the lip and the bridge kept going up. Finally, when the angle was really steep, the tires slipped off and the car shot down the bridge backwards – really fast! Walter tried to slow it with his brakes, but the bridge surface is un-surfaced steel grid. The tires just slipped." Frank took a long swallow of beer and continued.

"The car shot down the street with Walter madly trying to steer it. It finally came to rest in a big cluster of metal garbage cans. The cans burst and Walter and his car were covered with garbage!"

Everyone laughed at the image, including Walter.

"Did that really happen?" Donnie squeaked. Frank was known to exaggerate a story from time to time.

"Sure," Walter said. "Happened just that way!"

CHAPTER FIVE

That night I decided to try looking at the journal again. I went to bed in the car, as usual, while the adults sat up playing cards in the common squad tent. It was a place where the food boxes and coolers were kept, along with lawn chairs and camp tools. There was a big camp table to one side of the center post and a sputtering Coleman lantern hanging above it. The men sat and played cards, smoked, drank beer and talked. I knew that Neil was trying to eavesdrop on them and I felt that I needed to do my part.

Doc and Karen had driven off somewhere. I knew they wouldn't be back until later. Walter didn't play cards, but he always sat around watching the game and talking. He usually went to bed long before the rest of the men. All I had to do was stay awake and wait, which wasn't hard to do considering that my heart was beating like a rabbit's.

After a while Walter walked out to the car and put his satchel on the floor. I waited until he had closed the door and walked over to his cot before I sneaked a peak. Sure enough, Walter was in his cot, wrapped in his army blanket. I gave him a few minutes to get to sleep and then crawled into the front seat of the car. I turned on the red lens of my flashlight and extracted the journal from the satchel. Gingerly I opened the cover. An overwhelming musty smell hit me in the face. I realized what it was and began to gag. I sat up, sweating and cranked down the window. Drinking in the cool, fresh air, I tried to settle myself.

I looked around the campsite, bathed in the flickering glow of the lantern inside the tent. I could hear the spirited sounds of the card game: my father's deep voice, chatter and laughter from the men, and the sputtering sound of the lantern. It was a familiar sound, a sound from my youth. It calmed me. I saw that no one was stirring outside so I kept my face by the window and opened the book again. Bathed in the dim red glow of the flashlight I could see text written in neat copperplate.

"*This is the journal of a simple Welsh coal miner named John Edwards,*" it began. "*My brothers, Sam and Don, and I left Swansea, hoping to find fame and fortune, or at least jobs in America. This is our story. In it you may find salvation, if you're bold enough and brave enough. You may also find some small measure of forgiveness or at least understanding for a man who hurt many people, but never by plan.*"

I set the book down for a moment in order to clear my head again of the musty odor. Taking another deep breath of fresh air, I reopened the book.

"*My brothers and I were born in Swansea, South Wales. Coal mining is in our blood – it's all we know, but we know a lot. Most of what we learned we learned as lads working in the mines as hauliers, carters and air door boys. Carter is the hardest, but pays the most for young lads. The carter takes the coal from the miners in a small cart pulled by hand up to the bigger cart that the haulier drives. It's pulled by mules; most of them are blind from being in the dark mines for most of their lives. I was the haulier on our shift. My brother Sam, being older, bigger and stronger, was the carter. Don, the youngest, was the Air-door boy— he opened the door at the mouth of the mine for the haulier. Our father, Tom, worked down in the mine with a crew of six others. He had worked in the mines since he was twelve. His father had done the same.*

We learned how to detect the gasses; the drifts that could choke a man to death or catch fire and burn everyone. Sulfur is easy: it smells like rotten eggs. Firedamp is the worst, it has no smell and the least spark can touch off a deadly explosion. In America, I heard that they call it methane gas.

Cave-ins are a constant threat, the company doesn't use enough bracing and a shudder from a dynamite blast can take a whole shaft out. Miners are buried alive or trapped in small air pockets. The company always makes a big show of trying to rescue trapped miners, but time and cost usually prevail over persistence. The company has called off many rescues too soon, in the view of most miners.

To me, flooding is the most frightening accident in the mines – I've always feared drowning. The thought of being submerged with no way to get a breath and having a minute or two to think about imminent death terrifies me. I still have nightmares about it. Flooding took my father's life.

It happened one day, right at the end of our shift. I was driving my cart when I heard shouting behind me. An alarm bell sounded. I turned around and saw Sam and three miners running up the shaft. "Go!" they shouted. "The mine's flooding!"

I whipped my mules as the men ran past me, clambering over my cart in a mad rush to get out. I jumped off the cart, abandoning the mules to their fate, and ran with the fleeing miners. I could hear the mules braying in panic as I ran up the steep slope. When I got out, I looked around for my father, but I didn't see him. At first I thought that maybe he had gone to get help, but then one of the older miners, a man named Robert, came up to me. Tears had streaked his blackened face. "Your Pa didn't make it out," he said, *clasping both of my shoulders in his big hands. "He went back in to get his brother – your uncle Cal. There were two others."*

My head swam as it dawned on me that I'd never see my Pa again – or my uncle Cal. Usually a flooded mine would be simply closed off – it was too costly to drain the mine in order to recover bodies. "Buried is buried," was the expression.

I often dream that I'm with him, down in that mine. We're all working our picks, extracting the coal and filling the cart. I hit a seam and suddenly pressurized water shoots out, knocking me down. I try to rise, but it's no use: the water is holding me down, like the hand of a great invisible giant. "Run!" I hear, but I just lay there, unable to breathe. The water closes over me like a shroud, shutting out all light and air. I panic and struggle, fighting the cloying water, but it's no use. I try to scream, but the scream is muffled.

As a lad, my mother would wake me at this point and comfort me. I've come to realize that I was comforting her too, that she had the same nightmares.

My father's death devastated my mother. Her name was Ida and she's the one that taught me my letters, how to read and how to write in copperplate during nights by candlelight. She tried to teach my brothers, but they saw no point in it. "Knowing how to read and write won't help your coal tonnage, Lad," Sam used to say.

She was German— her family had immigrated when she was a little girl. Her father was a coal miner too. He left Germany for Wales because of the violence between Germans and Poles, and Catholics and Protestants in the coal fields. When I was a lad, he would talk German to my mother. One day when I was very little they talked about going for a walk in the park that had a duck pond. "Duck pond, duck pond," I shouted with glee. I loved the duck pond. I remember it still, so peaceful and clean, with people tossing bits of bread to them and them quacking and splashing and fighting for the bits.

I didn't realize it at the time, but I was speaking German. I must have picked it up by being around them. After that, my mother spoke German to me as often as she could, thinking that it might come in useful to me one day. She did the same with Sam and Don. After my grandmother died and my grandfather was injured in an accident, he moved in with us. He tutored us assiduously. I remember that he would grab my face with his big strong hands and squeeze, trying to make me get the umlaut right.

Times were hard after my father died and soon Sam was working as a full time grown up miner down in the pits, even though he was still too young for it. He lied about his age and no one seemed eager to check. After a year, I did the same.

One day, after our shift, we were having a tipple at the bar. A man named Gerald came over and offered to buy Sam and me a drink. I knew he was in the union. His father had died in the same accident that our father had.

We tapped glasses and drank. "I'd like to bring you into the union," he said quietly. "You have cause."

"I don't have cause to lose my job," Sam told him.

Gerald nodded. "I felt the same way when I was approached," he said. He ordered another round.

"But I figured that somebody had to do something about the company before it killed more miners," he continued. "It has to be forced to change its policies."

"I agree that we have cause," I said. "But I have a family to feed. How can I feed them if I'm discovered and blackballed or killed?"

"You're right," Gerald said. "You can't feed your family if you're dead. But if you continue to work in Number Five, you'll surely die. The mine is a death trap, and the Company won't close it."

"I know," Sam said. "But what can the union do about it?"

Gerald stepped a little closer and looked around to make certain no one was listening. "We can close it. We need a couple of good hands that know how to handle explosives. Ones we can trust."

Sam looked at me. I nodded. Gerald bought another round and we toasted Number Five.

Two days later, in between shifts, an explosion closed Number Five. The miners blamed it on a firedamp explosion and there was no evidence otherwise. The company investigated, but no one was talking – everyone knew that lives had been saved. "Firedamp," the miners would say when a company official asked. "Lucky no one was down there when it went." That was the suspicious part: no one was down there when the explosion happened, not that the company wanted deaths, deaths in the mines brought bad press. But still, they thought it strange that the explosion happened when it did. There was one other mysterious thing: a white flower had been left near the entrance to the mine, the sign of the Blodwyns; the most radical and violent section of the miner's union. The name means "white flower" in Welsh.

The union itself was outlawed and miners belonging to it or even associating with known union men could be blackballed and never work in the mines again. But the bad conditions in the mines, the constant threat of death, the poor pay, and the cheating engaged in by the company over pay-per-ton were the things that caused unions. The members used secret signs, spies and noms de guerre to

keep their identity from the company detectives. Sam's was "Gavin."
Mine was "Dylan." We swore the Blodwyn oath: "Na ad I'th dafod
dorri'th wddf." It means: "let not your tongue cut your throat."

"Once in the Blodwyns, you're never out," Gerald said. "But
there are perks," he added with a wink.

We soon found out what the perks were: lighter work schedules,
better shifts and cash – operating capital, Gerald called it— to be
used for bribes or materials. There was no accounting of any money
left over. "The widows will need something when they finally catch
us," Gerald often said.

I found that I had a talent for slipping into buildings unnoticed
and listening in on the conversations of the detectives, who seemed
to be everywhere. I could pose convincingly as a foreman turning in
tonnage reports or reporting on a suspected company spy. I learned
the art of disinformation, throwing detectives off someone's trail or
planting information that was false and then following its trail.

In this way I was able to alter tonnage reports so that miners
got their fair pay – and maybe a little more. I was also able to
identify company spies and informants, some of whom met with
unfortunate accidents. The accidents were Gerald's specialty, which
he seemed to enjoy more and more as time went on.

Sam and I suspected that we were not the only team that Ger-
ald worked with, nor did we know who he got his orders from. If
either of us were discovered, torture could only give the detectives
Gerald. He told us that if he was caught, he would kill himself rath-
er than give up any of the Blodwyns. Sam and I pledged the same.
We both thought that death was preferable to torture anyway.

Gerald came to enjoy the notoriety that came with being a
Blodwyn. He began to flaunt it dangerously, dressing better than

the average miner, carrying himself with a self-important air and buying round after round of drinks at the bar. Sam and I knew that it was only a matter of time before some informant tipped off the detectives and Gerald would be picked up. Whether he would be able to kill himself or keep quiet under torture was an open question. In the Blodwyns, if a man was picked up, we had to assume that he would break and give up his contacts. There seemed to be no way out for us except capture or death. Then two big things happened to change everything: our mother, sick with sorrow after losing our father, passed away from a bout of pneumonia, and war was declared. Sam and I volunteered.

I sat up, rubbing my tired eyes from the strain of reading to a dim red light. I looked around and saw that the campsite was still dark and quiet. My head was swimming: my grandfather – old Pop with the bad cough – had been a member of a violent miners' group. He had had a price on his head and deaths on his conscience. I wanted to read on, but it was getting near dawn and Walter was an early riser. Plus, I could hardly keep my eyes open. It wouldn't do to fall asleep with the journal in my lap. I put it away and crawled back to my sleeping bag.

It seemed like only moments later that the dome light came on. Somebody shook me, it was Walter.

"Thomas," he said in a loud whisper. "Let's go get some more of them trout of yours."

I sat up and looked around. Except for the light thrown by the dome, the campsite was completely dark. I crawled out.

"Have you got your flashlight?" Walter asked. I reached back in the car and grabbed it. When I turned it on to check the batteries Walter looked at me funny.

"Why the red lens?" he asked.

"Oh," I said, quickly changing it to clear. "For the trail, yesterday. I didn't want to be seen." I knew that my answer sounded weak and that I stammered a little. Was he suspicious I wondered? But he said nothing further.

I started to pick up my spinning outfit.

"Leave it," Walter said. He didn't explain.

The flashlight beams danced crazily on the roots and rocks of the trail, slippery with dew. With the clear lens on my flashlight, I could see much better than I had the day before, but the advantage was offset by our pace. Walter, sure-footed as a goat, was moving down the trail with incredible speed. It was all I could do just to keep up with him and I fell several times before reaching the bottom of the trail.

We headed upstream on the edge of the creek-bed, pausing only briefly at the big pool where I had speared the trout the day before.

"You left a few after all," Walter said as he shined his flashlight into the deep water. We could see a couple dozen big shadows at the bottom, suspended.

Continuing upstream, Walter stopped at a riffle just above the pool. He waded out into the stream and pulled a couple of ears of corn out of his pocket from the previous night's meal, and began shaving kernels off the cobs with his jackknife.

"Chum," He explained. "The trout will soon smell these and move up to feed."

He waded back to shore, lit his pipe and began leisurely assembling his fly rod. Walter seemed unaffected by the cold water, but that was no surprise. I had often seen him standing, facing a stiff cold wind, in nothing more than the short sleeve cotton shirt that he wore in every kind of weather. His only concession to winter was a light blue spring jacket, unzipped.

Every year, on his birthday and at Christmas, Walter received jackets, coats, shirts, hats and pants from almost everyone in the family. But he never wore them. "Saving them for good," he would say if someone asked about their gifts. He stuck to his cotton shirt, threadbare slacks and worn Florsheim shoes, just as I wore my low cut Converse All Star sneakers, pocket T-shirt and Levi jeans. "I don't like to spend time breaking in new duds," he used to say. "Not when the familiar ones work well."

When he was through rigging his fly rod, Walter took out a second one, rigged it up and handed it to me. I looked with curiosity at the long rod with its heavy green line, monofilament leader and strange reel. As a kid, I had fished with a push button Zebco reel, then, saving money from my paper route, I graduated to a spinning reel – a Martin 350. It worked well for me and I felt that I had developed a certain skill set with it. Like most of my friends, I viewed fly-fishing as a strange hobby, with its bewildering assortment of buggy looking wet and dry flies and streamers.

Fly fishermen seemed to hold themselves above ordinary anglers. They had special waders and vests and hats with flies stuck to them. Standing in the middle of a wide river with their long fly rods poised, they worked their flies back and forth in huge loops, touching the flies to the water in series, like flat rocks skimmed across the still surface of a pond.

They went to places like Montana, Alaska, New Zealand and Iceland, tying their own flies for each specific river. I read about "matching the hatch," where fly fishermen would find out what the trout were feeding on and then tie a fly that imitated it. Sometimes they'd suction the food from a trout's belly with a special tube. It was all beyond me.

But Walter didn't have any of that special equipment, he kept his tackle in a box that fit into his back pocket, and waded out into the creek in his pants and shoes. He worked his old fly rod in short rolling loops, changing flies only occasionally. He used it for bass and pan fish mostly

– in between times when he was helping one of the kids with a snag or a bird's nest of tangled line. Once, when we were younger, Calvin caught a large crayfish, which terrified him.

"Just grab him by the shell and pull him off your hook," Walter said. But Calvin was too afraid. Walter walked over and snatched the crayfish from his line, and then, to show us that the claws were harmless, stuck his thumb in between the pincers of one of the claws. The crayfish bore down with its sharp pincers and punctured Walter's thumb. Walter yelped and shook his hand, trying to dislodge the creature, but it was no use: the crayfish's grip couldn't be loosened. My father had to pull it off with a pair of needle-nosed pliers.

The crayfish left a large white scar on Walter's thumb, which Walter would show when anyone mentioned the story. "That son-of-a-gun just wouldn't let go," he said.

As the sun began to illuminate the creek gorge, Walter explained the rudiments of fly-fishing to me.

"Just remember, the line is your weight, the fly has hardly any weight to it at all. You use the rod to throw your line and the line throws your fly. The leader and tippet put the fly on the water just like an insect landing; no splash or noise. The right fly, presented the right way, will look to the fish like their favorite food."

He showed me the flies that he had tied on the tippets. They looked like little brown bugs on a tiny hook. "Nymphs," Walter explained. "The larvae of mayflies. The trout eat them like candy. They lay in the riffles and hoover them up as the current washes them downstream. "

I watched, still unconvinced that a big fish would go for such a small lure. After all, Musky lures were huge, with several sets of sharp treble hooks. And bass liked big crayfish or creek chubs. A tiny little hook with a little bit of brown thread wound around it seemed a reach to me.

Yet Walter had a reputation for catching fish when no one else could. While the men drank beer and watched their bobbers, and we kids fought over position, casting and re-casting, Walter would slip off on his own with his fly rod. He usually returned with a stringer of perch, bluegills or calicos.

Walter showed me how to make a roll cast, the most basic cast of flyfishing.

"I'll teach you the other casts another time," he said. "But, for today, with all of the overhanging brush, the roll cast is what we'll use."

He stripped off some line and twitched his rod tip so that the line lay on the water the way he wanted. Then, with one smooth motion, he described a counter-clockwise semi-circle with his rod tip, drawing the line back at first, then sending it forward in a large loop. The heavy fly line lay down in a perfect straight line, with the leader, tippet and fly following. The fly landed softly upstream, just inches from the far shore.

"Now you let the fly bounce along the bottom," Walter said, his teeth clenched on his corncob. A pleasant plume of tobacco smoke drifted up into the morning air.

Walter deftly gathered his line with his left hand, letting it fall in coils at his feet. He didn't use the reel at all.

"Let the fly drift on its own," he said. "Don't pull at it – it won't look natural and the fish will avoid it. You don't want to let too much line belly down-stream either," he added. "It'll pull the fly downstream faster than it would travel naturally. Flip the belly upstream every so often and then gather the extra line."

When the fly had completed its journey, drifting across the water on a lazy diagonal and ending up downstream from us on our side of the creek, Walter repeated the process. I was amazed to see that the fly landed in almost exactly the same spot as before.

I tried my hand at it and, after a few embarrassing failures, began to get the hang of it, coached by Walter.

"Now," he said when he was satisfied that I had a decent grasp of the process. "We'll wait for the trout to come upstream after the chum. He re-lit his pipe and sat on a rock, looking up into the sky and enjoying the beautiful morning.

After a time, I noticed a shadowy shape moving upstream. I alerted Walter in a whisper.

"Wait a few minutes 'till they get their feed on," he said, readying his rig. "We don't want to spook them too early."

When the trout were fully in the riffle, Walter began working his fly. I moved a ways upstream and did the same, watching Walter out of the corner of my eye and trying to imitate his motions. His actions were so seamless and smooth that he seemed to be doing an imperceptible dance to some melody in his head. He handled his fly rod like a conductor handled his baton, setting the tempo, dynamics and intensity of an orchestra. But Walter's orchestra didn't consist of musicians, it consisted of trout, and they seemed to be moving in the stream as if to his direction.

Walter's rod tip suddenly bent. He responded quickly, raising the rod high and setting the hook. He then lowered the rod tip, the drag on his reel turned completely off. He let the fish take all the line he wanted on his first run. The trout ran upstream and towards the far bank, seeking to spit out whatever it was that had caught in his mouth and was tugging at him. Walter let him go. The fish jumped, shaking his head as he danced on his tail. The sun caught brilliant flashes of color on the trout's body, sparkling and vivid.

As the fish danced, Walter deftly took up the slack line, everybody knows that if a fish gets slack he can spit the hook, or break the line. I'd even heard of rod tips snapping, although I'd never seen it happen myself.

As the fish plunged back into the water, Walter let the line go again. This time, the trout circled left and Walter began to gently fight the fish, with his rod tip high and a bit of pressure on the line. The fish fought against it, but was tiring. He made a couple of more short runs and, each time he slowed, Walter took in a little more line.

Soon the fish, a big brown, was in the shallows, thrashing desperately one moment, laying still the next, gathering himself. Walter waited longer than I would have, holding the rod high and ready to let the fish have another run if he wanted. But he didn't, and Walter slipped his net gently under the fish, flipping the mouth of the net to close it. He walked over to the big bucket that he'd brought along for the purpose, unhooked the fish and slipped it in.

Walter never looked upstream towards me at all. He didn't need a thumbs-up or grin from me. He quickly re-rigged and got back to fishing.

Walter got two more trout before I finally hooked my first fish. It was a big relief for me; I didn't want to get skunked. I set the hook and, struggling against my impatience, let him have the line. He ran upstream for a while and then into a long pool just above the riffles. Once in the safety of the pool's deeper water, the trout decided to keep going. The line sang off my reel until I could see the white backing. Holding my rod high, I ran upstream as fast as I could, stumbling and slipping and trying to keep up with the fish.

He finally turned and I was able to put some line back on my reel, but, as he began to come back my way I found that I couldn't keep up with the slack with the slow and clumsy fly reel.

"Strip the line," I heard Walter say behind me. I hadn't realized that he'd seen me with a fish on and had come up to watch. "Don't use the reel at all; let the line slip through your fingers."

I did as he said and was able to regain control of the fish. But a new problem had come up. The big fish was heading back to the riffle and the safety of the big pool below it and, standing in the middle of the riffle, I was in his way. He came right at me and swam between my legs. I kicked my right leg up and rolled to my left, keeping the rod high and the line taut. I ended up sitting in the creek, facing downstream with the wriggling trout still somehow on my line.

"Jesus," I heard Walter exclaim. "I've never seen one do that before."

I jumped up and began playing the fish again, wondering if he would ever tire. But he did and, after a few more short runs, I was able to bring him close enough for Walter to net. Walter was laughing the whole time and shaking his head. "Never saw one do that before," he repeated several times.

After a while we both had our limit of trout for the day. Although the trout were still in the riffle, Walter began securing his gear. I suggested that we stay and catch a few more but Walter shook his head. "I saw the Game Warden skulking around yesterday," he said. "It wouldn't do to be caught out of compliance with the game laws. I hear they fine out-of-staters pretty stiff."

I thought that a strange comment from Walter. Everyone always talked about outfoxing the government, with its *rules*. It was an attitude born of the Depression – snatching apples from a farmer's orchard, stealing day-old donuts from a bakery and shooting, cooking and eating any wild animal they could find. So why would Walter hesitate to take a few extra trout, I wondered. Moments later, the answer came walking up the trail.

His name was Weeb Toliver, the Game Warden informed us. He was short and pudgy and wore a handlebar mustache and a state-issue campaign hat – the kind of hat they used to wear in the army before the First World War. It had an impressive state shield on it.

"Whatcha got there in the bucket?" He asked. There was an insolent tone to his voice.

"A few Creek Chubs," Walter said sarcastically. He made no effort to show them to Weeb.

"All right," Weeb said, his short patience already gone. "Set it down and show me your licenses." Mine was in my wallet, in a plastic bag in my pants pocket. I dug it out and showed it to him. Weeb seemed a little near sighted and squinted to read it. As he did he looked up at me two or three times, as if unconvinced that it was really me.

"Thomas Edwards?" He said.

I nodded. He asked my address and age. I told him. He seemed disappointed as he handed me the license and turned his attention to Walter, who was casually lighting his pipe.

"License," Weeb said, holding out his hand.

"You checked it yesterday," Walter said, not moving.

"Got to check everybody's license," Weeb said. "My job."

Walter laughed and showed him his license. "One day older," he said when Walter asked him his age. Weeb was unamused. He looked at the bucket and made a mental count. "Both caught your limit," he said, relaxing a little, satisfied that we were in compliance. Then he smiled. "Nice Creek Chubs," he said.

Walter didn't respond, he just puffed languidly on his pipe.

"I heard talk that someone was down here yesterday, spearing fish," Weeb said. "Know anything about that?'

"We're fly fishermen," Walter said. "We don't need to spear them."

"No, I guess you don't," Weeb said, looking at the bucket again. "Well, have a nice day," he said. He turned and walked up the trail, whistling a toneless tune.

"I guess you're lucky old *Weeb* didn't come down here early yesterday," Walter said after we had walked down the trail a ways. He emphasized

"Weeb" and drew it out a little. The effect was comical, but I didn't laugh.

On the way up the trail to the camp, I was tempted to ask Walter about Pop. He was the oldest of the brothers and sisters and might know the most. Plus, he lived with Gram – maybe she had told him things. But I rejected the notion. I was afraid that he would wonder what had sparked my imagination and might guess that I had found the journal; after all, he kept the journal in the car – the car that I slept in. My fear was that, even if he only suspected, he might keep the journal close and not put it in the car. I was anxious to read on.

As we approached the campsite, Walter suddenly handed me the bucket. "Carry this on in, Thomas," he said. "I have to go to the toilet." Without another word he set the bucket down and walked off towards the restrooms.

I walked into the camp with the bucket in one hand and my fly rod in the other. Everyone looked up as I arrived and I suddenly realized what Walter had done and felt the fool for it.

"Hey!" My uncle Charlie exclaimed. "Here comes Neptune with another bucket of trout! Someone get the fry pan ready!"

Everyone looked at me expectantly. I held the bucket up with a half-hearted grin. Inside I was feeling sheepish: Walter had caught most of the fish, and taught and coached me in catching the few that I had. But here I was; the hero of the moment and no way to get out of it.

"Let's see what you got," my father said as he walked up to me and took the bucket. "Jeez, a few more days here and there won't be any trout left in the county," He added. He looked at my fly rod. "I see you took these legally," he whispered with a wink.

"Yeah, Walter and I…" I started to say, but the commotion and noise of everyone crowding around to see the bucket full of fish cut me off. Walter had gotten me again, I thought wryly. He liked to do that kind of thing: do something special and then watch as someone else got the attention. He didn't like attention himself, and avoided it when he could. But he couldn't help himself from setting up an event and then watching from off to the side – just another spectator.

But everyone always knew that Walter was usually at the bottom of any event. His personal stamp would be on it, and no one would be fooled when he walked up to the crowd and asked what was going on.

Of course, sometimes the event took on a negative aspect. Once, when we were little kids, Walter took a bunch of us on a walk down a steep trail at Outwater Park while the rest of the extended family was setting up a big picnic. On the trail he convinced us that a cave in the shale wall was the famous "Dead Man's Cave."

"A pioneer was being chased by Indians," he told us. "He ran down this trial and ducked into this cave. But as he wriggled far into its depths, he found he wasn't alone, there was a bear sleeping in there."

We all stared into the darkness of the cave, trying to imagine the terrified man, caught between a group of rampaging Indians and a vicious bear.

"The bear was asleep, so the pioneer, a man named Miles Hafner, curled up next to it, hoping the Indians wouldn't investigate. They stopped by the entrance and looked in, but didn't see him. Soon, they moved on. When Miles thought they were gone, he carefully crawled out. The Indians were gone, but as he turned to head back up the trail, the bear woke up and charged. The last thing Miles Hafner heard was the bear's *roar!*"

At that, Walter grabbed Calvin by the side at the small part of his ribs and roared. Calvin screamed, we all did. But Calvin bolted and ran straight off the trail and down the steep hill. He must have hit every tree, rock and thorn bush on the way down, because, when he reached the bottom, he was cut, bruised and crying.

"I'll buy everyone here ice cream at the snack bar this afternoon," Walter announced as he cleaned up the crying Calvin. We all knew that we were being bribed, but we didn't care. Calvin kept saying "you pushed me," over and over and examining his injuries, none of which were serious.

"Shut up Calvin," Neil finally said. "You're not hurt and nobody pushed you. You got scared and ran off on your own." Neil was a little out of sorts anyway: he hadn't expected the trail to be muddy and he thought his new loafers were ruined.

"Did too," Calvin said. He started crying again.

"Did *not*," Neil said. He was starting to lose patience with his little brother. "Everybody here will say you're lying if you tell, so you better *not*."

Calvin looked around at the bunch of us and we all nodded with serious expressions on our faces. We didn't want to miss out on the ice cream. He sniffled a few more times and began walking back up the trail.

"What happened to you, Calvin?" My Aunt Yvonne demanded when we got to the picnic area. She was a small woman, but firm and wasn't above snatching one of her sons – or nephews – by the ear when confronting an issue that displeased her. She stepped forward and snatched Calvin by the chin, turning his face towards hers.

"Nothin," Calvin stammered. "I... I...fell down."

She ignored his remark and twisted his face this way and that, examining his cuts and bruises. She looked him up and down for a minute. "Looks like you fell down a hill," she said. "Did someone push you?"

"No," Calvin said, his voice shaking.

She let go of Calvin and glared at Donnie. If anyone would break under questioning, it would be him, being the youngest.

"Did someone push him, Donnie?" Aunt Yvonne said. Her voice was clipped and incisive. Donnie began visibly shaking.

"No," he squeaked, his lip trembling. "Nobody pushed him. He...he *fell!*"

"Neil!" Aunt Yvonne said, turning her attention to Calvin's older brother. He had been slowly easing away from the scene – as had I. He stopped dead in his tracks.

"What happened to Calvin?" Aunt Yvonne asked. She had a disconcerting habit of turning her head slightly sideways at times. Later, I would find out that she had an astigmatism; a slight imbalance of one eye which makes a person's vision level only if the head is tilted. The effect is that the person looks slightly quizzical – or doubtful. Neil, normally strong and independent-minded, wavered under his mother's astigmatic stare. The moment of hesitation was all she needed.

"I thought as much," she exclaimed. "He *was* pushed." She looked around at the rest of us accusingly.

"Who pushed you Calvin?" she demanded again.

Calvin burst into tears, rubbing a scrape on his arm. "Walter scared me and I ran," he blubbered. "Then I fell."

"Walter!" Yvonne said. "I might have known." She looked around but Walter was nowhere to be seen.

Chapter Six

We ate the trout that Walter and I had caught with eggs and home fries for breakfast, but I was disappointed: Doc's car was missing, and so were Doc and Karen. My Uncle Charlie noticed me looking around.

"I miss her too," he announced loudly. "She's a cute one; sure brightened up this campsite. Smells a lot better than this bunch does too," he added.

"Doc said he'd meet us at the next campsite," Charlie explained. "Seems Karen felt uncomfortable sleeping in the car; they'll be staying at a motel nearby."

I nodded, pretending to be interested in my plate of trout and eggs.

"They'll be over for dinner, though," Charlie added. He gave me a wink and I felt my face go red again.

After breakfast, we broke camp and prepared to move on. The Allegheny Valley was our next goal: tributary rivers and streams of the Allegheny River, meandering through the foothills of the Appalachian Mountains north of Pittsburgh. Pete had heard that they were loaded with trout.

"They'll bite on a bare hook," Pete exclaimed as we gathered around the loaded cars. "Anything shiny; they've never been fished before and have no fear of man."

"They have a fear of bears though," Walter said. "Those hills are swarming with huge black bears; Coyotes and Cougars too. I wouldn't be surprised to find a few rogue Indians there; the mean ones who never gave up."

Calvin was standing next to Walter, working on his pipe. When he heard the word "bears," his eyes widened. He overdrew on his pipe and began coughing. Walter struck. He sank his fingers into Calvin's side and roared. Calvin yelped and spit his pipe out; he slipped on some wet grass and fell, writhing and coughing.

"Goddamn it Walter," Frank exclaimed. "Leave the kid alone for a change!"

But his words fell on deaf ears: everyone was laughing. Joe let out a cackle that sounded like a rooster caught in a fence. After a while, Calvin was able to compose himself and scramble to his feet, clutching his muddy pipe.

"Jesus," Joe said. "You looked like a piece of bacon frying."

"Shut up Joe," Calvin said, brushing himself off. "This ground is slippery."

"Looks like you shit your pants Calvin," Neil said, wrinkling his nose. "Smells like it too."

"Did not," Calvin said, looking over his shoulder at the seat of his pants. "That's just mud."

"Right," Neil said. "But you're not riding with me."

"All right people," my father broke in, barking in his commander's voice. "Let's saddle up!"

"Jawohl, Herr Oberst!" Charlie said snapping to attention and clacking his heels together.

Walter made a snorting sound into his hand.

CHAPTER SEVEN

We traveled south-east into the Allegheny Mountains. Walter had found a campground that advertised trail riding by horseback, hiking trails with spectacular views of the mountains and, most importantly, trout fishing.

The caravan arrived at the campground late in the afternoon and it was more than anyone had expected: the road wound up a long, well-tended field, bordered by white fences behind which a small herd of horses neighed and whinnied at our approach. They ran alongside the cars as we drove into the campground.

A large brightly lit brick recreation center sat in the middle of a fenced-in area that contained a playground, tennis courts, a basketball court and a large in-ground pool.

"Looks more like a country club than a campground," Donnie commented, a grin on his face.

"It ought to," my father said. "It cost an arm and a leg." He shot a glance at Walter, who was enjoying his pipe.

The choice of the campground with horseback riding had been Walter's and the other men had vigorously argued against it.

"We can't just only fish," Walter had said. "The boys need a little entertainment. Besides, every man should know how to ride. They advertise excellent horseback riding instruction," he continued. "Equestrian instruction, the brochure calls it."

"They probably have a fancy name for horse shit too," Pete said. "But that don't make it anything else but horse shit."

The men grumbled, but they finally gave in to Walter's idea. They always did.

"It's worth every penny if it's got a laundry and hot showers," Neil said. "Next trip, I think we should use motels." Neil liked his comforts.

"Next time I think we might," my father said. I thought that a strange response. Whenever somebody mentioned eating out or staying in a motel he would shake his head. "Too expensive and not worth it," he would say. "You save a lot when you cook your own food, and camping beats a motel any day. It wasn't that he was cheap; it was just that he'd grown up poor.

My father started our family camping experience when I was little and my sisters were just Toddlers. He bought sleeping bags, army surplus cots, a canvas wall tent, a Coleman lantern, a camp stove and off we went.

My father liked State Park campgrounds. They were cheaper, more rustic, and there were always open sites. I still remember the smell of canvas mixed with pine and the sputtering sound of the lantern. My mother hated it, every bit of it. My sisters were constantly tripping over roots and skinning their knees, there was dirt everywhere and she was deathly afraid of snakes, which she thought would slither under the tent flap and lay there, coiled and ready to spring at her in the morning.

After two years of tent camping, my father relented and bought a trailer. It was a Yellowstone, made by Amish workers in Indiana. We drove out there to get a better deal and avoid shipping costs. "It pays to go right to the source," he said several times, unasked. "Eliminate the middle man, that's the trick." No one mentioned the cost of gas for the trip.

My mother liked the trailer. It had a built in stove, a sink and most importantly a bathroom. The bathroom was small and cramped and stank of the blue fluid used in the tank. But it was a lot better than running through the rain to the State-built outhouses with their cold toilet seats and open cesspools. I rarely used the trailer's bathroom, somebody always seemed to be in it, so I used the outhouse or the nearest tree.

The other victory that my mother managed was that we began using private campgrounds. They were more expensive, but they had showers, laundry facilities, playgrounds, pools and recreation centers. My sisters, getting a little older, loved having other kids their age to play with. I missed the tent and was glad when my father decided to use it for our fishing trip instead of the trailer.

We parked our cars at the administration building and the men went in to register. I tagged along. Neil went off the check the facilities.

Two college-aged kids in matching green polo shirts were behind a polished wood counter. Their shirts were embroidered with the campground logo, the letters ATC in front of a mountain, and their names, Betsy and Thad. Betsy, a girl of medium height and bright smile, introduced herself and said "Welcome to Allegany Trails Campground."

Thad, taller than Betsy but clearly her brother, pulled out a thick registration book and said "Party?" with a smile.

"Edwards," my father said. "We should have reservations."

"Right here," Thad said. "Three nights for the group."

My father nodded, signed the book and pulled out his wallet.

"Already paid for," Thad said. "Check signed by a Mister Walter Edwards."

Everyone looked at each other in surprise. Walter just smiled.

We settled in to a loop of semi-private campsites located on a bluff that overlooked the Allegheny River. A pair of eagles soared high above, lazily riding the air currents up into the blue summer sky. No fishing was planned for the afternoon so Neil, Calvin and the rest of us grabbed our swim suits and headed down to the swimming pool.

Looking around, I saw groups of kids of varying ages heading here and there, carrying bridles, ropes and other horse riding tack. I realized that the real money in this particular campground was in youth riding camps. Parents would send their kids for a week or more to learn horsemanship, along with tennis and basketball. It was obvious that quite a few parents chose to stay at the camp themselves. There was a restaurant and bar in a large western-style building, tennis courts and swimming pool. I also noticed that the cars in the parking lot were mostly Mercedes, Lincolns, BMWs and Cadillacs.

Most campground pools are there just so the owners can advertise "heated pool." They're not much bigger than a large hot tub and are usually so over-chlorinated that your eyes start watering when you open the gate. Your skin itches for hours afterwards. Not this one.

This pool had three separate sections. There was a deep diving pool with two competition boards: one meter and three meters; there was a four lane section for swimming laps and a large recreation pool with slides, tubes and a waterfall. At each section a lifeguard was on duty. There were men's and women's locker rooms, a large hot tub and steam rooms. Fresh towels were stacked neatly at various locations. At the end of the pool area, between the recreation and diving areas, there was a cabana bar from which kids could be comfortably watched. A few adults, their kids most likely off to riding or tennis lessons, sat at the bar and at tables, leisurely sipping drinks and talking. Soft rock music played through speakers discretely positioned behind some large ferns.

The section of the pool for swimming laps was empty. Joe, Calvin and Donnie headed towards the recreation area, grab-assing and laughing. I saw the lifeguard at that station sit up a little and put his whistle between his teeth.

Neil had been a diver for the Niagara Falls High School swim team, our arch-rivals. He was very good, I remembered. I think he read my mind.

"C'mon," he said with a grin. "Let's hit the boards. I'll show you a few tricks."

I shook my head "no." I could do the basic required dives but lacked the grace and coordination required for competitive diving. Plus, I like swimming. After all, it was called a swim team, not a diving team. I also didn't relish spending the afternoon being one-upped by my cousin.

"Nah," I said. "I'm going to swim a few laps. Shake the rust off."

"Suit yourself," Neil said. He stopped for a moment and gave me a hard look.

"Did you read it?" He asked. "The journal?"

I nodded. "Not all of it," I said. "Just the beginning." I gave him a brief summary of what I had read.

Neil whistled softly. "I never heard about any of that stuff," he said. "Have you?"

"No," I said. "No one ever told me anything about Pop. I just knew that he had been a coal miner at one time."

Neil nodded and walked off towards the diving area without saying anything else. But I had an idea what he was thinking: that somewhere in that journal we would discover the mystery that the men were keeping from us.

I walked over to the laps area, knelt and splashed some water on myself and stood, stretching and shaking out my stiff muscles. I crouched and sprang into a flat racing dive and hit the water smoothly. It felt good. I kicked with my arms stretched in front of me until I surfaced; when I did I went into my distance pace, hoping that the swim would somehow wash away the troubling thoughts that I couldn't seem to shake.

Swimming to me has always been a meditative exercise. The rhythmical and repetitive mechanics of the stroke and kick, the isolation and support of the water and the mental repetition of the lap count repeating over and over, like a swimmer's mantra. The only interruption was the brief slap and glide of the flip turn at the end of the lane.

But, despite my efforts, I couldn't shake the journal. I lost count of my laps. I began daydreaming. I found myself in a flooded mine with no escape. I swam along a darkened mineshaft, holding my breath and hoping to find a pocket of air. After one of my turns, I stayed in my glide and swam the length completely underwater. I could feel the drag of a miner's clothes and heavy work boots. I imagined the hopeless realization that must have consumed drowning miners in their last moments.

At the wall, I decided to keep going. I had always been pretty good at swimming lengths underwater and found that I still had that skill. Plus, I wanted to purge myself of the haunting daydream of a drowning miner. At the far wall, I went for a third length. I began to feel the panic that comes when you finally run out of air. A coach told me once that it's not lack of oxygen that forces you to breathe, it's the carbon dioxide build up in your lungs that triggers the breathing response. I let out some air and kept going. The danger of purging CO_2 is that you can pass out from lack of oxygen, it's called shallow water blackout. The other problem is that, if you let out all of your air, you sink. Fortunately, as I started to feel my consciousness fade, I reached the wall.

I stood with a rush of splashes and bubbles, inhaling with a loud, indescribable sound. I looked up to see the lifeguard giving me an enthusiastic thumbs-up. I heard a smattering of applause from the bar area, which embarrassed me. I hadn't realized that anyone was watching. I pushed off and went back into my swim, cleansed for the moment of my dream of the flooded mineshaft.

After I had swum a few more lengths I became aware of another swimmer in the lane next to me, swimming in my blind spot. "Neil!" I thought. It would be just like him to wait until I was a little tired and then push me. I accepted the challenge and picked up my pace.

At the wall I did a flip turn and picked up the pace a little more. But, as I swam, I noticed that he was still with me, pushing me from my blind spot. I was getting tired and knew that Neil was a pretty good distance swimmer, but not a sprinter. I decided to go all out at the next turn and settle the race.

I went into my turn hard and came out sprinting for all I was worth. Determined to beat Neil by as much as I could, I put my head down and did the length without breathing. My lungs screamed for air and my muscles screamed for oxygen. I kicked and stroked even harder, bouncing in the water as I did. I touched the wall forcefully with both hands out-stretched and turned to see how far back Neil was. But there was no one there, the lane next to me was empty.

"Nice race, Neptune," I heard a woman's voice say. I turned and there, sitting on the edge of the deck and wringing her hair out, was Karen. I must have looked a little surprised because she laughed a little.

"I didn't expect you to kick into a sprint at the wall," she said. "I thought that you'd be a little tired after swimming all those lengths under-water. It was all I could do to beat you."

"Nice race Tommy," I heard from the deck. I looked over to see Doc sitting comfortably in a deck chair, a bottle of Carling Black Label in his big fist raised and pointed towards me in a toast. "I thought you were going to beat her at first," he added. "You got the jump on her."

"I am a little rusty," Karen said. "I haven't been in the pool for a while."

"Me either," I said. "You beat me pretty good, you don't even look winded," I added.

"Karen swims for Syracuse," Doc informed me. She made Nationals last season."

"Wow," was all I could manage. Neil was right, I thought. She was totally out of my league.

"Any chance at the Olympics next summer?" I asked after I recovered my voice.

"Trials are this coming fall," Karen said. "But I'm not sure how I'll do; I've missed a lot of training already."

She gave Doc an accusatory look. He grinned and held his hand up like a basketball player charged with a foul. "Guilty as charged," he said.

Karen splashed at him playfully. Swimmers are good at splashing and she soaked him.

"I don't know what I was thinking, coming on this trip," she said, half seriously.

"Hey!" Doc exclaimed, jumping up. "My shirt!" But he was laughing, as usual. Nothing much bothered Doc. He could change a flat tire in a rainstorm and still keep his happy go lucky demeanor. "How often do you get to change a tire in the rain?" He said once after doing just that.

As he took his shirt off to dry it I noticed again how big Doc really was. His shoulders, chest, arms, and back were massive, the result of lumberjacking in Montana right after high school. Charlie told me that he went west because he liked skiing and trout fishing. He financed his hobbies by lumberjacking and smoke jumping – parachuting into the mountains to put out forest fires.

"Doc was there, working on a section of a big fire," Charlie said. "A dozen of his friends were caught in a crown fire in a canyon on the Missouri River. He was on the recovery team. Only four guys lived, but one, one of Doc's closest friends, died a few hours later from his burns. He joined the army after that and became a medic. As far as I know, he's never fished or skied since," he added.

But the thing that was striking about Doc with his shirt off wasn't just his build, it was his scars.

"He was hit with shrapnel and small arms fire," Charlie explained. "Pulling wounded guys out from under fire. He's got a shitload of medals in a drawer, but he'll never talk about any of it. Combat veterans never do."

Doc also had a tattoo of a hula girl on his left upper arm, the result of a night of binge drinking in Honolulu while on R and R. He would occasionally pull up his shirt sleeve and make it dance with his arm muscles if he'd had a few beers.

Doc laid his shirt on the back of a deck chair and walked over to the cabana bar for another beer.

"Ever tell you how he got those scars?" Karen asked me when he'd gone.

"Nope," I said.

"Me neither," she said. "Charlie told me that he saw a lot in the war," she added sadly.

Neither of us said anything for a while. Then the unmistakable sound of a diving board bouncing on its fulcrum caught my attention. I looked over at the diving pool and saw Neil, using the three meter board, perform a flawless two-and–one-half somersault with a twist, layout position. I'd seen it before, when Neil was diving for The Falls and I was a skinny frosh swimmer, sitting on the bench.

"Seven," Karen said, judging the dive. "He was a little too far out on his entrance. What do you think?"

He'd gotten an eight at the meet. With the degree of difficulty so high, he got major points – enough to put The Falls ahead to stay. "Yeah, seven," I said. I wasn't about to give my cousin any acclaim if I could help it. "A little far out and not quite straight either," I added.

Karen laughed and I realized that she was on to me.

"Seven might even be pushing it," I said in a serious tone. "More like a six – or even a five."

"He's your older cousin, right?" Karen said.

"Yep," I said. "And he thinks that he's hot shit."

Doc whistled and waved from the cabana. He was holding up a martini glass and motioning to Karen to join him. She got up and waved back.

"Well, see ya later, Neptune," she said, shaking her head. "He's relentless," she added.

I watched Karen settle in with Doc, positioned to watch Neil's diving exhibition. Doc waved for me to join them, but I waved him off. I'd already done enough damage, I figured. I pushed off the pool wall and settled into a long swim.

When I returned to the campsite later I saw a large cast iron pot suspended over the campfire by an iron tripod. I could smell the bubbling stew right away – it was my father's famous Hunters Stew. He was busily stirring it and adding ingredients as the other men sat around, drinking beer and offering advice, opinion and comment, much to my father's annoyance.

"Hunter's Stew is a Polish dish," Pete said as I walked up to the circle. "It's called "Bigos," and it has pork, polish sausage and sauerkraut in it. I had it once when I was working in Dunkirk."

"Dunkirk?" Walter said. "Dunkirk's not in Poland. It's in France."

"Not Dunkirk in France, you mullet-head!" Pete shot back. "Dunkirk in Western New York. There's a lot of Polish people there."

Walter was sitting on a lawn chair, leaning back and smoking his corncob pipe. He seemed to be enjoying himself, getting under Pete's skin.

"Hunter's Stew is whatever a hunter gets that day, cooked over an open fire." Walter said. "It would be venison, rabbit, squirrel, wild leeks, tubers and greens. There wouldn't be pork and sausage. And there wouldn't be sauerkraut."

"Why not?" Pete demanded.

"Hunters don't carry around sauerkraut with them. And they don't hunt pigs."

"Hunters stew is beef," my father said as he sliced a carrot into the stew. "It's what the hunters came home to after a long day of hunting. Mine has carrots, celery, potatoes and onions," he added.

"That's just beef stew," Frank said. "I agree with Walter. Hunter's Stew is made with game and whatever vegetables can be gathered. It's how the Indians lived."

"Indians!" My father said. I could tell he was getting a little annoyed at the criticism of his stew recipe. "Indians couldn't cook a stew— they didn't have metal pots until the White Man came. They roasted every-thing."

"No," Charlie said, rattling the ice in his drink. "The Indians cooked in leather bags, held over the fire by a wooden tripod."

"The bag would catch on fire and burst," Frank said. The other men nodded and muttered their agreement.

"The water in the bag sweats through, keeping it wet," Charlie informed us. "It would only burn if it got too close to the flames."

"I don't know," Donnie squeaked a little too loudly. Ever since he had caught the big Musky, he had become more assertive. "That sounds a little dubious to me." He emphasized the first syllable, drawing out the 'doo,' then repeated: "A little doo-bious."

"What do you know about it, Donnie?" Calvin demanded. It was clear that Calvin's feathers were a little ruffled by Donnie's new-found confidence. There's a pecking order in families, and ours was no exception. Calvin wasn't about to be by-passed by his little brother. But Donnie wasn't going to back down.

"More than you do, bone-head!" He squeaked.

Calvin was sitting in a lawn chair, imitating Walter and trying to keep his pipe lit. Having no retort, his only option was to try and give his little brother a beating, which was often threatened but which never really happened; Donnie was too fast for Calvin. Calvin started to get up anyway.

"Sit down Calvin," Frank said sharply. He was kneeling in front of the fire, fiddling with a Dutch-oven that he had sitting on some coals at the edge of the fire. He was making cornbread to go with the stew and, once he poured the batter into the big cast iron bottom, he'd put on the lid and shovel coals onto it.

"Donnie's getting a big mouth on him," Calvin muttered. But he sat back in his chair, settling for a dirty look which he leveled at his younger brother.

"What is it that makes a regular stew a hunter's stew?" Walter pressed. He wasn't about to let my father off the hook. "You haven't enlightened us."

My father paused in his ministrations for a moment, considering whether or not to answer Walter.

"It's made in a cast iron kettle over a campfire," he finally said. "Gives it a unique flavor, the cast iron, and the campfire gives it a smoky taste."

"More like ash and chunks of burnt wood," Walter commented. "Now that's a special flavor."

"Won't slow your fork down," my father said. Walter was known for his voracious appetite and, despite being thin, his legendary capacity for food. He also claimed to have eaten every kind of meat and game at one time or another. "Owl is the only thing I didn't like," he said once. "It just has a sort of bitter taste to it."

"When did you ever eat owl?" I asked him at the time.

"I was aiming for a possum, but an owl swooped down on him just as I shot— got the owl instead of the possum."

"I thought owls and possums only came out at night," I commented.

"They do," Walter said. "You hunt possums with a flashlight taped to your gun barrel. Possum stew is a tasty dish," he added.

We sat on a long picnic table, the bunch of us, eating steaming bowls of hunter's stew and big chunks of cornbread, slathered in butter. I was a little morose, Doc and Karen not having yet returned from the cabana bar.

Charlie, sitting next to me, rattled the ice cubes in his glass and poked me a little with his elbow.

"I miss that little Karen," he announced to the table. "She sure brightened things up around here, right Tommy?" He poked me again, a little harder and a lot more noticeably.

I decided to stop being so embarrassed all the time and being made the fool.

"That's right," I said. "I couldn't help but notice that everybody's personal hygiene improved a lot after she arrived, except for Calvin's," I added.

"Wuddiya mean?" Calvin sputtered, choking on a mouthful of stew.

"Yeah, Calvin," Joe said. "I haven't seen you head to the showers since you rolled in the bird shit the other day!"

Everybody laughed and Joe cackled.

"You neither," Calvin managed, shooting a dirty look towards Joe.

"Yeah, maybe, Joe said. "But I ain't covered in bird shit."

"Shut up both of ya," Neil said. "Calvin, you need to hit the showers, and you too Joe. It's getting so a guy can't even stand to sit UP-wind of the two of you."

"They're just maintaining their protective film," Walter said over his third bowl of stew. "They're getting so even the mosquitos won't come near them!"

My father looked over at Walter, who was busy sopping up the last of the gravy in his bowl with his fourth piece of cornbread.

"I see you like my stew just fine," he said.

"Oh, it's passable, I'll admit," Walter said, pushing his bowl away. "But I'd have had more if it had been beefalo. Now that's a tasty meat."

Pete shot a dirty look at Walter. Beefalo was a sore spot with Pete. A few years back, he had heard about a guy out in Montana that had managed to cross a domestic cow with a bison bull, which produced a bull that was fertile. The new hybrid was called a beefalo and it promised to provide consumers with quality, nutritious beef that was higher in protein and lower in cholesterol and saturated fat than regular beef cattle. They were also hardier, more able to tolerate the cold and required less care than standard breeds. Pete was always a sucker for get rich quick schemes. He immediately emptied his savings account and ordered several breeding pair.

The problem was that the Beefalo Association wouldn't allow delivery of the animals unless the potential beefalo rancher met certain conditions. There had to be a farm with good water, a substantial barn and adequate fencing. Pete had none of those.

"Talk about taking the cart before the horse," Walter told us once. We were sitting on his back porch, taking turns shooting at squirrels with a Daisy BB gun. Walter had bought the gun specifically for the purpose of scaring away the squirrels that had infested his yard. It was a spring loaded lever-action rifle that shot a BB in a visible arc. It only had a range of about thirty feet or so.

Walter had a couple of English walnut trees in his backyard and he gathered the nuts that fell every year and dried them in his attic. Walter's walnuts were a source of pride for him. "I got these from my tree," he'd say as people helped themselves from a big bowl he put out around the holidays. My father could crack one open by squeezing it with his fist.

But, to Walter's great annoyance, squirrels ravaged the trees every season, picking the walnuts with their little claws and carrying them off to their nests. Walter only got a small fraction of the nuts. He tried wrapping sheet metal around the tree trunks to keep the squirrels from climbing, but they leapt off the top of a garage roof into the trees. He tried cutting the branches back, but the squirrels just leapt farther. Finally, he bought the Daisy. He lived within the city limits, so he couldn't use a 22 or a shotgun.

That's how Calvin, Donnie, Walter and I came to be sitting on Walter's back porch, shooting at squirrels. Calvin gave up after a few shots, accuracy eluded him. Donnie was more interested in whittling a stick than shooting and Walter preferred smoking his pipe and telling stories. That pretty much left the shooting to me. Squirrels are quick and hard to hit with a BB gun and, when I did manage to hit one, it would just chatter angrily and scamper farther up the tree. I did manage to kill a starling though; hit it right in the eye.

"Pete bought a farm up in the hills," Walter told us. "He spent a small fortune modernizing the barn and putting up a specially reinforced fence; cattle fencing wouldn't hold those big beefalo. When he was done he called in the association inspector to get approval. But he was rejected again: his water source wasn't up to code. It was a pond, not a well. Pete had to go into debt to put in a well which cost a lot more than usual because the water table was so deep, up there on that hill.

"Trouble was, people didn't really like beefalo and Pete went broke. He had to sell his house and his car and work double shifts on his regular job to pay everything off."

"Whatever happened to his herd?" I asked.

"We ate 'em," Walter said.

"If Pete lost everything, then why do you tease him about it," Donnie asked. "It seems a bit excessive, if you ask me. A bit ex-*cess*-ive."

Walter looked at Donnie for a moment, smoking his pipe.

"Because Pete has luck," he finally said. "And not just bad luck. He's always winning something; an electric knife at the fair, a football pool, a raffle or a drawing. And he gloats like hell when he does. He brags about everything he has: it's always the best, the latest, or the most expensive; his Oldsmobile, his house, even his Franklin stove. Pete always puts suggestions in the suggestion box at the factory. One day the foreman came down and told him management wanted to talk with him. Pete thought that he was in trouble, but when he walked into the office they handed him a check for ten thousand dollars. It seems that one of his suggestions saved the company big money, millions over time. He was able to pay off his debt, buy a new house and car and invest in a new scheme, aluminum siding."

That night I lay with my eyes wide open, waiting for Walter to put his satchel in the car. It was late, the men had had another of their hushed meetings by the fire after everyone else had gone to bed. I had the feeling that I would spend another sleepless night reading, but that was OK: no sleep was better than the torture of my re-occurring nightmare.

Finally, Walter put the satchel in the car and went to bed. I waited until he was on his cot and snoring before I slipped forward and dug out the journal. The red light from my flashlight cast macabre shadows in the car as I opened it. Immediately the powerful musty smell hit me. Fighting a gag reflex, I opened the window, breathed in some fresh air and turned to the page at which I had left off reading.

Sam and I had mixed feelings about fighting the Germans. We were half-German ourselves, our mother had come from Germany. But she was dead, and the Army seemed a good way to get out of the mines and out of the Blodwyns. Plus, like everyone else, we thought that the Allies would quickly defeat the Germans and the war would be over. We were wrong.

We were in the 38th Welsh Infantry: the Red Dragons. Because we were miners, they put Sam and me into a Pioneer Company. Our job would be setting up defensive positions: trenches, barbed wire and mines and dismantling the enemy's positions before an attack. "First In, Last Out" was the motto of the Pioneers.

We had a short period of training and then went to France with the BEF: the British Expeditionary Force. We were in the thick of it from the start.

The war quickly settled into a struggle between two extensive trench systems with massed artillery barrages, poison gas, night raids and massed frontal assaults. The death toll was staggering. So was the stench. No Man's Land, the area between the trenches, became a morass of dead bodies, twisted metal and shell-holes filled with filthy mud, fetid water and sometimes pockets of poison gas.

We soon lost any sympathy for our German cousins: German machine gunners and snipers shot wounded men trapped in No Man's Land and killed medics and burial parties indiscriminately. In retaliation, we did the same.

One of the nastiest things the Germans did was called a "Box Raid." Artillery would box in a section of our trenches by firing on the sides and rear of the trench, the front was left open for German "Storm Troopers"— specialized volunteers who would charge into the section of trench with pistols and knives.

We captured one of those devils once – we found him uncon-
scious after a raid. He wasn't a big man, but he was fearsome look-
ing, with scars on his face and teeth filed to points. He had a crazy
look in his eyes and kept saying "ershiesst mich"— "shoot me"—
over and over. Without thinking, I asked him why in German.
He told me that he expected to be tortured. A Sergeant heard me
speaking with him and sent me to see our Company Commander.

"You speak German?" he asked me.

I nodded.

"Fluently?"

I nodded again. He nodded back and dismissed me.

The next day they summoned me back to the Command Post.
At first, I thought I would be an interpreter and be pulled out of the
fighting, a tempting prospect. Instead, they ordered me to infiltrate
the German lines at night to get information. Told that I could pick
one man to accompany me, I chose Sam. They gave us captured
German uniforms and sent us out that very night.

No Man's Land is a spooky, horrific place during the daytime.
At night, it's worse. We crawled through gaps in our own barbed
wire and across a landscape that could have been on the moon.
There was not a living thing; no tree, bush or grass existed there.
Artillery, machine guns, hand grenades and rifle fire had churned
up every inch of earth. Pieces of rotting flesh mixed with shell frag-
ments and bits of shredded clothing were everywhere. I could never
get used to the stench nor could I ever forget it.

We posed as soldiers separated from a patrol and looking for
our unit, a common thing at night in the trenches. Afraid that my
accent, though pleasing to my Mother, would give me away, I spoke
only brusquely to the soldiers we encountered, appearing to be

*impatient to rejoin our unit before dawn. But I listened carefully as
we bumbled along and soon found out the name of the regiment we
were facing. We also made mental notes of the positions of German
machine guns, redoubts and command bunkers.*

*Getting back through our own lines was the trickiest part of the
mission: we were wearing German uniforms. As long as we came
back in at the same place, we'd be okay, but both sides had patrols
out at night, ranging throughout No Man's Land and everyone was
trigger happy. Fortunately for us, Sam and I had spent a great deal
of time in dark mines and could get about better than most.*

*Sam and I were good at what we did, and we got better. My
accent improved to the point where I could ask questions without
fear of causing suspicion. We began posing as Storm Troopers, regular troops were afraid of them and asked few questions. Sam knew
enough German to get by, but mostly he just snarled if someone
spoke to him.*

*We got bolder as time went on and several times stayed the day,
sometimes traveling miles behind the German lines using commu-
nication trenches. Their trenches were much better than ours: better
designed and better built. But they were just as muddy and miser-
able as ours and the soldiers just as tired and scared. It became my
fondest desire to put the politicians who had started the war in the
center of No Man's Land and rid the world of their kind.*

*Our missions were dangerous to the extreme, we could be
discovered and tortured at any time, or shot by our own troops.
We could fall into a shell hole filled with gas or get hit by a random
artillery shell. But, because we were out all night, and the information that we got was so important, we were held out of the massed
assaults that took so many of our friends. During the Battle of the*

*Somme, at Mametz Wood, our Regiment was so badly decimated
that it had to be pulled off the line and re-formed. They kept Sam
and me at the front though. Lucky us.*

*As the war was ending word spread around the regiment that
the mines around Swansea were not doing well: foreign competition, especially from America, was hurting them. The Welsh mining
companies hadn't modernized and their production was down.
Sam and I decided to emigrate to America. I knew that Lucy and
the two boys wouldn't be happy about the move, and neither would
Sam's wife; they had family in Swansea. Still, the boys were almost
of an age to work and it didn't look as if there would be much of a
future for them in Swansea.*

I put the book down, shocked by what I had just read. Pop, married
to a Welsh woman, and two sons besides! Two uncles I had never heard
about! I shook my head in disbelief. I was about to keep reading when
I saw Walter stir. I looked at my watch and realized it was almost dawn.
I put the journal away and crawled back into my sleeping bag. But I
couldn't sleep. Thoughts about what I had read, about Pop's experiences in
the war, and about Pop's other family, swirled in my head.

CHAPTER EIGHT

The wrangler's name was Bob, and he didn't look anything like a cowboy. He wore a dusty John Deere ball cap, steel-toed work boots, worn jeans and an Allegany Trails Campground work shirt that he had thoroughly sweated through. But it became apparent immediately that he knew horses very well and riders too. He welcomed us and then, walking easily around the corral, began pairing horses with riders. He started with Karen.

"Little lady," Bob said to Karen," I have just the horse for you. He turned to Thad, who was helping.

"Bring out Darcy will you Thad?" Bob said.

Darcy turned out to be a spirited little buckskin mare that pranced and whinnied as Thad led her out of the barn.

"She's a handful if you don't know what you're doing, but, unless I miss my guess, I think you've ridden before."

Karen smiled and adjusted the stirrups expertly. "A little," she said and vaulted up into the saddle. Darcy whinnied and started to rear, but Karen yanked the reins firmly, touched her heels to the horse's flanks and put her into a light trot. She turned sharply left, sharply right; then she backed Darcy up.

"Bravo," Doc shouted from the gallery, clapping his hands. He had chosen not to ride. "I'm too big for those little critters," he had announced. "Unless they have a plow horse for me."

Bob nodded appreciatively at Karen's riding.

"That's right," he said with a smile. "Put her through her paces, show her who's boss."

But Karen was done. She clearly didn't like to show off and shot Doc a look for applauding. The look didn't faze him.

I got a big Chesnut named King.

"I can tell you've ridden a little," Bob said. "But mostly on a track in a line. King will be the best horse you've ever ridden in your life. He's real responsive, but don't give him his head – he likes to run."

I smiled and nodded, hoping that I didn't appear too nervous. Bob was right, I had ridden a few times at a stable just outside of town. You held your own reins but otherwise you sat in a line with a dozen other riders as someone led the group around a big circular track. King was the biggest horse I'd ever been on and I could feel his power through my legs.

"Bring Calvin out for this strapping lad," Bob said, nodding towards Calvin. We all started laughing.

"What's funny?" Bob asked mildly.

"His name is Calvin," Neil explained, pointing at his brother.

"Huh," Bob said. "Calvin riding Calvin— never had that happen before."

"I bet the horse is the smarter of the two," Neil said.

After everyone else was mounted, Bob started the riding lesson, with Thad and Betsy assisting. They were patient and competent and soon I began to feel more comfortable. King seemed to sense it too and he began anticipating my directions.

"It's not rocket science," Bob said. "It's just horseback riding, people have been doing it for thousands of years."

Strangely, Walter had not gotten a horse and was leaning against a post, watching. When the lesson was done and all of our questions answered, Bob dismounted and walked into the barn. A few minutes later he came out, leading a big Gray Stallion.

"As you requested sir," he said, handing the reins to Walter. "Our best horse. His name's Patton"

Walter thanked him and patted the horse's muzzle. He adjusted the stirrups and mounted. As soon as he hit the saddle, Walter's back straightened, his shoulders went back and his chin went up. He had short legs but a long torso and appeared to have grown several inches in an instant. "Tall in the saddle," my father used to say about him. "Like General Lee."

Gone was the easy-going, affable Walter. Sitting on Patton, he looked like the General himself.

As we headed down the trail it quickly became apparent that, despite Karen and Bob's obvious skills, Walter was the best horseman among us. Patton held his head up high, as if on parade and he had a proud bounce to his gait. It appeared to me that the big horse was enjoying the ride as much as Water, although neither of them gave any outward sign of it.

The trail ran down the hill on a gentle slope and then along a ridge with a view of the wide valley below. Bob explained to us that this particular section of woods was "Old Growth". It had not been forested. The trees — hemlocks, beech and white pines — towered over us. "This is one of the last bastions of the bald eagle in the east," Bob said. "If you watch the sky carefully, you can sometimes see a pair of them, cruising the air currents above the hills."

"We did, earlier!" Donnie said. "We saw two yesterday when we first arrived!" His voice squeaked and popped enthusiastically and he bounced around in his saddle, looking up into the sky and hoping to get another glimpse of the big birds.

I'd seen eagles in the wild before, in Algonquin Park in Canada, but Donnie never had and he had been thrilled when Walter pointed them out to us. There were two bald eagles, riding a column of air, high up in the summer sky above our campsite. As we watched them, they drifted lower and lower until they were just above our hill. You could see every detail about them: deep brown bodies, white heads and tails, huge menacing talons and big beaks meant for ripping flesh. But the most striking feature was their piercing eyes, taking in everything, including the small group of humans staring up at them.

"Magnificent, aren't they?" Walter said. "Two hundred years ago this region was filled with eagles, along with wolves, cougars and wolverines."

"And Indians," Calvin said.

"And Indians," Walter replied patiently.

We watched them until they cruised out of sight.

The trail ride only lasted for a couple of hours but I knew that I'd be sore for a week— riding muscles are muscles that are used in no other way. Some people think that riding only requires the rider to sit on the horse and let him do the work, but that's not true. A rider has to become one with his horse, gripping with his knees, pushing lightly on the stirrups and sitting light in the saddle. The horses that I'd ridden at our local stable were plodders, and we did just sit. But out here, on King, I had to work. Bob rode alongside me for a while, coaching me.

"Watch his ears," he said. "When they go back, he's getting annoyed, you're doing something wrong. Sit easy, heels down, back straight, shoulders back. Don't slouch. Grip him with your knees, but not too tightly."

I began to feel more comfortable and King seemed to notice it too.

"He likes you," Bob said after a while. "I knew he would."

After a while we came out onto a wide plain, flat and grassy.

"This is the upper meadow," Bob announced. "Keep their heads up— they'll try to graze."

Sure enough, just as Bob said it, King tried to put his head down. I pulled up on the reins and suddenly saw his ears go all the way back. He shook his head back and forth twice and then forcefully tried to bring his head down to grazing level. I leaned back, my feet fully in the stirrups, and pulled back with everything I had. King didn't like that. He circled twice, straining at the reins the whole time. I knew I must have looked like a fool, losing control of the big horse. I yanked harder on the reins and managed to turn him. King seemed to be coming under control. But I was wrong, he was only gathering himself. He skittered sideways, shaking his head, trying to shake the bit. Then he bucked.

I'd never been bucked before and had no idea what to do. I was thrown forward and almost slid off over King's head – he lowered his neck to help the process. I managed to flop back into the saddle but my feet had come out of the stirrups. Before I could get them back in, King bucked again. This time I went straight up into the air. I felt my legs going up above me, like a diver's. I was stretched out completely, looking down at the bucking horse and the saddle, where I needed to be. Fortunately, I still had hold of the reins; they pulled me back towards the saddle, but head first. I threw my head and shoulders back and tucked my knees into my chest; then I extended my legs and spread them. The action miraculously put me right back in the saddle, but not without a jarring pain that shot up my spine. I gripped the horse as tightly as I could with my knees and forced my feet back into the stirrups, yanking left and right on the reins the whole time.

Suddenly the big horse gave up. Just like that. He snorted a few times and shook his head a little, but he calmed down, trotted lightly for a moment, and then he slowed to a walk. I pulled back on the reins and said "woah." He stopped.

"Yeeeh Ha!" Neil shouted. "Nice job!" But I could see in his face that he was disappointed that I hadn't been thrown.

A couple of people clapped.

Bob rode up to me, looking a little sheepish.

"I've never seen him do that to anyone," he said. He patted King on the muzzle and the big horse snorted.

"Usually everyone just lets him graze for a while – he's too big to stop."

"But you said to keep their heads up," I said.

"I always say that," Bob said, gesturing towards the group.

I looked around. Everyone's horse was grazing, except for Walter's and Karen's.

I shook my head with a laugh, loosened the reins, and let King graze a while.

After a little bit, Bob led us across the big field at a light canter. We were spread out in a wide, loose line. Bob came up next to me.

"He likes to gallop," he said. Go on and give him his head if you want. He clicked his tongue and put his own horse, a big roan named Chester, into a gallop.

King didn't even need a click to break into a gallop, as soon as I flicked the reins, he was off.

The fastest I had ever ridden the stable horse was a trot, heading back to the barn. Riding the powerful chestnut at a full gallop was an amazing experience for me. I tried to get a comfortable, balanced seat but couldn't manage it. I was getting bounced around and found myself grabbing the saddle's pommel for support. I still had the reins, but they were loose, flapping around like a ripped flag in a windstorm.

I began to worry about the saddle being too loose; if it slipped, I'd roll around under the horse's belly and probably get trampled.

"Sit up a little and relax," I heard someone shout. It was Walter, riding alongside me on Patton. "Put a little more pressure on the stirrups and press in with your knees. And let go of that pommel!"

I did as he said and suddenly felt comfortable. So did King; he surged forward with renewed vigor. But Walter's grey kept up easily. I could actually see Walter holding him back a little. For Walter's part, he rode so easily that he could have been sitting on a park bench.

The ride back would have been uneventful except that, while crossing a small stream at the edge of a big open field across from the campground, Joe's horse decided that he didn't like Calvin being ahead of him. He he bit Calvin's horse near the tail, just as it was ascending the bank. Calvin the horse bolted up the bank, almost throwing Calvin the rider in the process. The only thing that saved him from being thrown was that he had been holding on to his pommel, absently looking down into the water at some crayfish.

The horse's reins went free and he went speeding off across the field. Calvin yelped and screamed and held on to the saddle for dear life.

"That horse is heading straight for the campground," Donnie said, sounding alarmed. "He's going to trample someone!"

Bob was already on it, spurring his horse into a desperate gallop, trying to catch the two Calvins before they did any damage. He was gaining on them, but it soon became apparent that he would never catch them before they reached the Campground.

There were shouts of alarm from people as they saw the runaway horse speeding towards them. Mothers grabbed their children, fathers shouted orders and people ducked behind trees and cars. But there were still plenty of people milling about, confused as to where they should run. We all sat dumbfounded, powerless to do anything but watch.

Then, suddenly, out of the corner of my eye, I saw Walter on his big grey stallion, galloping as fast as I've ever seen a horse go. Walter had an angle on Calvin and caught up to him at the edge of the field. Leaning forward and out, Walter grabbed the halter of the runaway, yanking hard and turning Patton at the same time. Calvin stopped, but my poor cousin didn't; he lost his grip on the pommel and went sailing over the horse's head and into a muddy ditch at the edge of the road.

A moment later, Bob arrived and took Calvin the horse, now calm but still twitching from his run, and put him on a lead rope. He seemed relieved and thanked Walter several times. We all rode up to see if my cousin was all right.

It turned out that the only thing damaged on Calvin was his pride. He came up out the ditch covered in mud and algae, spitting and swearing.

"Goddamn horse!" he said. "He took off for no reason! I could've been kilt!"

Joe began cackling. "Rascal bit yours on the ass, that's why," he said. "Took off like a bat out of hell!"

Bob handed Calvin's rope to Thad and dismounted. Although most of us were laughing, he was taking the event very seriously.

"Are you all right, son?" he asked Calvin.

Calvin nodded, scraping the mud off his face the best as he could. "Yeah, I'm okay," he said. "I just lost my grip on the reins."

"You never *had* your grip on the reins," Neil said. "You were just sitting there, holding onto the pommel. Horses will nip at one that's stopped in a line. Everybody knows that."

"Well I didn't know it," Calvin said. He patted at his pockets, looking for his pipe and lighter, which were certainly lost in the muck and mire of the ditch.

"You'll get the hang of it," Karen said helpfully. "It just takes a little practice."

"The rest of you can ride all you want," Calvin said. "I'll never get on one of those smelly beasts again as long as I live!'

Joe agreed. "For me, if it doesn't have a motor and brakes, I don't want it," he said."

That night I fell asleep at the campfire during one of Walter's stories—an unforgiveable affront. Neil kicked my chair and I fell over as I came awake. I scrambled to my feet, but the damage was done: everyone was laughing, even Karen, I noticed.

"You were *snoring*," Neil said.

I noticed that Calvin seemed especially pleased at my gaffe – he was laughing and pointing and poking Joe in the ribs.

"I'm fine," I said weakly and walked off to bed. I was too tired to be embarrassed. But not too tired to set my alarm for two hours later. When I woke everyone was asleep. I began reading the journal again.

> *Sam and I only returned to Swansea long enough to collect our families, our meager belongings and our younger brother Don. We used our muster-out pay to book passage to America on a leaky old ship called "The Atlantic Queen" in steerage. There were hundreds of others doing the same thing.*
>
> *The trip was horrific for our families. Fleas, rats and bilge were part of the landscape in steerage. Compared with the trenches, steerage was a paradise, but for our families it was hell. A fever swept through the ship and Sam lost his wife and two daughters. My Lucy caught the fever too, she lingered for days but finally the fever proved too much for her. She slipped away one night, leaving me, and the two boys, alone.*
>
> *We landed in Philadelphia and were processed at the city's Washington Avenue facility. Because of the fever outbreak on the ship we were quarantined on Reedy Island. After a few weeks there, we were released. Most new immigrants were recruited by representatives of factories and mines and immediately shipped out on the next available train, but, since Sam and Don were still*

being processed, the boys and I slipped away to the nearest park to wait. We considered ourselves a package deal and didn't want to be separated.

While in the park, I noticed a young lady sitting on a bench, feeding popcorn to some pigeons. There was a little boy with her, about four years old. He started chasing the pigeons but couldn't catch them, no matter how hard he tried. As we watched, Neil and Thomas started laughing and I did too. After the long trip in steerage, the loss of Lucy and the time in quarantine, it felt good. Years seemed to fall away from the boys— they became kids again.

Suddenly the little boy fell and skinned his knee. He looked down, saw blood and started crying. His mother ran over to him and tried to calm him, patting at his scrape with a section of her white dress. Neil walked over and tried to help, joking with the little lad to take his mind off his wound.

"Did one of those pigeons get you?" he said. "Those little birds can get mighty angry if you try to keep them from their popcorn."

"I felled down!" the little boy said. It was clear that he was in no mood for joking.

Thomas walked over and picked up a couple of loose pieces of popcorn. He held out his hand until one of the pigeons approached, as it went for the popcorn, Thomas snatched it with his other hand. Holding the bird gently, he brought it over to the little boy.

"Is this the little bird that hurt you?" he said.

"I felled down," the little boy repeated. "The bird didn't hurt me."

But he had stopped crying and stared at the captured bird. Neil gave the boy some popcorn. "Give him some," he said.

The little boy took the popcorn and held it out to the pigeon with an open hand. The bird took the popcorn and cooed. The little lad squealed with delight and gave him some more.

I saw that the mother was still trying to clean the scrape with her dress. I walked over to her and pulled out a clean handkerchief.

"Here Mam," I said. "Let me do that, you don't want to be ruining that pretty dress."

The lady stepped back and let me do it. After wiping her hands, she stood and introduced herself. "Name's Ella," she said and held out a strong but pretty hand. I took it and looked into her sharp grey eyes. I was immediately smitten.

We spent the rest of the day together, the five of us. Neil, Thomas and the little boy, his name was Walter, ran off a ways, chasing pigeons and playing tag. Ella had a sharp wit and a lively sense of humor. We talked about everything in the world. To this day, I can't remember ever having laughed so much or having felt so free. By the end of the day, we had decided to stay together. Two days later we found a Justice of the Peace and were married.

Ella wanted us to stay in Philadelphia. She would wait tables and I could find some kind of work as a laborer. But I knew that my only skill was as a miner and I knew that Ella only made enough to barely get by, living in a one room apartment. I was certain that I could make enough in the coalfields to support us all. I promised her that I would save every penny and, when we had enough money, we would move up north, where she had kin.

When Sam and Don were released from Reedy Island, we lined up at the recruiting table from the Layton Coal Company. There were many immigrants in line: mostly Poles, Germans and Italians but I could hear in the babble of voices the occasional Welshman.

The recruiter behind the desk, a short man with a balding head *and sweaty forehead, didn't need to do much recruiting, there were scores of people in the lines. He was brusque to the point of rudeness and I was about to suggest that we try another company when it came my turn.*

"Nationality?" he asked.

"Welsh," I said. He suddenly looked up, the beginnings of a smile on his face.

"City?"

"Swansea," I said.

"Experience?"

"My whole life was spent in the mines," I said.

His smile changed to a grin. "Welcome aboard," he said. "Experienced English and Welsh miners are in high demand around here. He took my name and pointed to a knot of men standing around a man with a clipboard. "Over there."

I walked over to the group and introduced myself to the man with the clipboard. His name was Paul Blair, and his accent was English.

"They made me group leader for the trip," he said easily. "Do you have people?"

"My two brothers are behind me. I have a wife and three boys."

He handed me five tickets and mentioned the time that the train was leaving. "Don't be late," he said.

I looked around at the group and nodded. I knew I'd be seeing those lads again.

The train trip to Wilkes-Barre seemed to be a dream realized: out of the mines of Swansea, out of the trenches of Flanders, out of the fever ridden bowels of steerage and into the new promised-land of America; a new wife, three strapping boys and my two brothers with me. Could it be that I would finally be happy? I never had been, and the sensation was foreign to me. I thought that I'd better just get a pick or a shovel in my hands and start working on my tonnage; thoughts of happiness could wait.

The first day in the mines we were met by our foreman, a nasty little man named Jonas Smith. He had a high-pitched nasally voice, beady little eyes and an uncompromising attitude.

"These picks and shovels are the property of the Layton Mining Company," He announced. "Rent will be deducted from your pay. If you break them, the cost of replacement will be deducted from your pay. Helmets and lanterns are the same."

We were living in Company housing and had a line of credit with the Company store. So this was wage slavery! I'd heard about it back in Wales, but thought it was just a scare tactic by the Company to keep the miners from leaving. I looked at my brothers: they grimaced, but then shrugged as if to say 'here we are, let's just make the best of it.' Besides, since we worked by the ton and not the hour, we shouldn't have any trouble keeping out from under debt.

As we traveled down the tunnel, I noticed that American mines were more mechanized than Welsh mines, better organized and more efficient. I guess that's why they're more profitable. Still, for us, it was the same work: blast a seam with dynamite, break up the big pieces with the pick and shovel the coal into the carts, shore up the room with more timbers, then blast again.

Another thing that I noticed was that American mines were dustier than the Welsh mines; the Company didn't want to waste time and money hosing down the walls with water, some of the old hands told us. The shoring process was not as safe, either; there were fewer timbers and more space in between them than in our

Welsh mines. Timbers were costly and time-consuming to install. To
the company safety measures seemed an unnecessary expense.

Veteran miners told us of horrific accidents: fires caused by
coal dust or methane gas that swept through the shafts, burning
men alive or asphyxiating them; floods that drowned dozens while
stranding dozens of others, dooming them to slow deaths caused by
lack of oxygen, and the ever present cave-ins that rumbled through
the chambers, causing weak pillars in other rooms to collapse. We
constantly felt rumblings as we dug and blasted our way deeper into
a seam, occasionally pausing to look at each other nervously.

But we kept on, driven by the need for as much tonnage as we could get,
and by the little foreman who we called "Corgi" behind his back.

I looked up, laughing to myself: "Corgi" was the name that my father
and uncles gave to any annoying, inconsequential person they encountered. They told me that it meant "little dog" in Welsh.

I was about to turn the page when I heard the roar of a motor and
saw headlights dancing through the trees. It must be Doc returning, I
thought. He and Karen had gone off to town for dinner and some drinks.
I ducked down, intending to wait until he parked before I continued reading. Another sleepless night, I thought wryly.

But the car continued on past me, skidding crazily right up to the
tents, the horn blaring. I saw Walter sit up, surprised. Moments later, my
father and Charlie emerged from their tent.

I put the book away and scurried quickly into the back of the car,
hoping that I hadn't been seen. I opened up the back door and got out to
see what the commotion was.

As I approached the car I heard a woman's voice, trembling with emotion. It was Karen. Uncle Charlie had his arm around her protectively.

"There, there, Honey," he said. Charlie called every woman Honey, just like he called every man Doc and every kid Bub.

"Don't you worry, Doc can take care of himself," Charlie said. He gave Karen an extra little squeeze and winked at my father.

"You don't understand," she said, struggling to get her emotions under control and to get out from under Charlie's arm.

"I heard them. They plan to let him keep winning for a while and then, when he tries to leave, they'll jump him. I think they might kill him!" She buried her face in her hands, stifling a sob.

Keep winning, I thought. Doc must be hustling pool in some local bar. Pool was one of the few things that Doc took seriously, and he was good at it. He played a lot on the full slate pool table in the house they had grown up in. Often Joe and I would watch him, trying to pick up tips on the game. He would gladly explain everything: strategy, bank shots, how to get english on the ball. But even when he coached us, neither of us could come close to making the shots he did. It was almost as if he controlled the ball with his mind. He was that good.

Every once in a while, Doc would drive a good distance out of town and hustle pool in some local bar. He'd go in, act drunk and put a few dollars on the table. Losing a few games on purpose, he'd let the locals think they had a patsy. After a while, he'd put a big bill on the table, trying to win back what he'd lost. When the locals matched the bet, he'd run the table, pocket the money and leave, if they let him. Doc often came over to the house sporting a black eye and torn knuckles. "I'd hate to see what the other guys look like," my father often said.

"We'd best go get him," my father said. "Tom, you might as well come along," he added, looking at me.

He told me to get in the station wagon, and then nodded to Walter and Charlie. "Let's go boys, you know the drill."

Walter headed towards the car, but I noticed that Charlie still had his arm around Karen, "Maybe I better stay here," he said. "Karen's quite upset."

"Get in the car Charlie," my father said in a flat tone.

"Worth a try," Charlie said sheepishly as he climbed into the car. My father just laughed.

"Aren't we going to get Neil and the others," I asked as we pulled out onto the highway.

"No," he said. "That would be too many. We have to get in without causing any suspicion and be able to get out again… in a hurry."

Karen had told us where the bar was; it was in the local town, only a few miles away. The bar was a seedy little place called "Jim's" and it was on a dark side street. My father went past it and then parked a little way up the street.

"You go in first, Thomas," my father said. "Order a beer and then go play the pinball machine nearest the door." He handed me a five dollar bill. "Ask for dimes and don't leave a tip," he added. "You can look at the pool game, but don't watch it, and don't make eye contact with Doc. When everything starts, I want you to make sure no one blocks the door— we'll be coming out fast."

"What do I do after you leave?" I asked.

My father laughed. "You come out with us, and get to the car as fast as you can!"

I nodded, swallowing nervously.

As I entered the bar I was assailed by the stink of stale beer and cigarettes. A juke box in the corner was blaring Johnny Cash's "Folsom Prison Blues" and greasy looking sausages spun on a cloudy glass-covered rotisserie. I could hear the 'clack' of pool balls from farther back in the bar. I stole a glance and saw a group of surly looking men standing around a pool table lit by a green shaded light. Doc, a cigarette dangling from his mouth, was taking a shot.

"Ten bucks you don't make that shot," one of the men said. There was a threatening edge to his voice.

Doc stopped for a moment and looked at the man. "Why not make it twenty," he said. His voice was slurred, as if he were drunk. Odd, I thought, I'd seen Doc drink a lot of beer, but I'd never seen him drunk.

The man pulled some bills from his wallet and threw them down on the edge of the table. "How 'bout fifty," he said.

"Done," Doc said. He hit the cue ball on the side, causing it to spin around the blocking eight ball. It kissed the seven ball and sent it into the side pocket, the shot he had called.

"You're a goddamn hustler!" the man exclaimed as Doc picked up the bills and stuffed them into his bulging shirt pocket. There was an angry murmur from the other men.

"Naw," Doc said, tottering from side to side and grinning. "I'm just lucky."

"You could never make that shot again," another man said.

"Put your money where your mouth is and set 'em up," Doc said. He picked up a pint glass of beer and emptied it in one swallow.

"Can I do something for you kid?" a voice said. I turned to see the bartender standing in front of me. He was short and fat, with a scrabbly beard and thinning hair. He wore a threadbare white short-sleeve shirt with a crooked clip-on bow tie; over it, he had a filthy bar apron.

"Black Label," I said.

"You old enough?" the man said, squinting at me.

"Goddamn right," I said, slapping the five-dollar bill on the bar. "And gimme some dimes for the pinball machine while you're at it."

The man looked dubiously at me for a moment and then scooped up the bill.

"What's going on back there," I asked as he brought the beer and change.

"Some guy came in here and started hustling the locals," the bartender said. "He's drunk as hell but he's still making shots."

I heard the cue ball clack and turned to see Doc make the shot again.

"Son of a bitch!" the bettor exclaimed.

"Just lucky," Doc said again. "Double or nothing I can't make it a third time?"

"He'd better watch it," the bartender said. "He's messing with some rough customers. They don't take kindly to hustlers."

I shrugged, grabbed my beer and change and walked up to the pinball machine closest to the door.

I was on my second dime when I saw my father, Charlie and Walter come in through the door. They were laughing and joking and shoving at each other, drunk as skunks. They staggered up to the bar.

"Three boilermakers," Charlie announced. He slapped a bill on the bar. "And keep 'em coming."

The bartender drew three half glasses of beer and poured three shots of whiskey. He dropped the shots, shot glasses and all, into the beers.

"Bottoms up," Walter said. The three men chugged the boilermakers.

"Can a guy get a pool game around here?" my father asked as the bartender poured three more beers.

"You can try," the bartender said. "But I doubt it. Those guys have been at it for a while."

I noticed that he didn't mention the hustler.

My father and Charlie drank their boilermakers and staggered over to the pool table. Walter stayed behind at the bar, nursing his drink.

Charlie put a bill on the edge of the table. "Can I get a game?" he asked looking around.

"Table's all yours," Doc said. He walked over to the cue rack and put his cue in it.

"Nice doing business with you boys," he added with a wave. He began walking towards the door. I noticed that his speech was no longer slurred and the stagger had gone out of his walk.

What occurred next happened faster than it takes to tell. One of the men, the biggest of them, grabbed Doc by the elbow and spun him.

"You're not leaving here with our money," he hissed. Another man, now behind Doc, picked up a pool cue and cocked it back, intending to blind side Doc on the side of the head. My father grabbed the cue on the backswing, snatched it out of the man's hand and whacked him across the bridge of his nose. Doc punched the man holding his elbow on the jaw, breaking it with a loud crack. The man fell backwards onto the pool table, unconscious. Charlie pulled the pool cue rack over, temporarily blocking the surge of the rest of the men, who were out for blood.

"Let's go!" Charlie shouted, making for the front of the bar.

The bartender was reaching for something under the bar when Walter pulled out a pistol and pressed it to the man's forehead. "Put it on the bar, real slow," he said. The surprised bartender placed a sawed off double barrel shotgun on the bar.

Walter put his pistol away— the pistol from his satchel, I thought— the Nambu! He picked up the shotgun, broke it open and dumped the shells on the floor. He looked at the gun thoughtfully.

"You were going to shoot my friend with this?" Walter said. He looked at the gun with a bemused expression on his face. Then, swift as lightning, Walter brought the butt end of the shotgun around and knocked the man unconscious. He fell backwards into his liquor shelf and slumped to the floor.

It was only then that I noticed that a weasely little man with yellow protruding teeth had slipped up to the door and was blocking it.

"Keep the door open," my father had told me. Now I knew why. I lowered my shoulder and drove the man into the jukebox as hard as I could. Johnny Cash stopped in mid-phrase, a loud screech went through the speakers as the needle skittered across the grooves of the 45. The sudden silence was surreal.

"Come on!" I heard my father shout. He grabbed me by the scruff of the neck and pulled me out the door. Charlie followed, tipping the jukebox over to block the door. We ran down the street, jumped into the car and sped away.

"You boys came just in time," Doc said with a grin. "You saved the rest of those guys a trip to the hospital."

Charlie got serious for a moment: it wasn't the first time he'd had to pull his little brother out of a scrape. "If we hadn't got there in time, you'd be floating face down in the river by now!"

"Naw, I wouldn't," Doc said. "Those guys weren't nothing, besides, I knew you guys would come!"

Charlie shook his head in disbelief. He rummaged around in a sack he'd brought along. He fished out some beers and passed them around. To my surprise, he handed one to me.

"Good job at the door, Thomas," He said. "I'm glad we brought you along."

I thanked him, uncapped the beer and took a long draught. I wondered again where Walter had gotten that pistol.

CHAPTER NINE

The next morning, while Neil and I were fishing alone at a little hole downstream from the campsite, I told him what had happened.

"Why didn't you guys come and get me?" He asked; a little miffed.

I told him.

"Well," he said. "I'm older than you, and bigger. I wouldn't have let that guy anywhere near the door in the first place. You're lucky you didn't get your ass kicked!"

"I took care of that guy just fine," I shot back. "And, in case you haven't noticed, I'm bigger than you are now."

"Baby fat!" he muttered.

I laughed for a moment, enjoying his discomfiture. Then I turned serious. "Walter pulled his pistol on the bartender," I said.

Neil stopped fishing and turned towards me, wearing a look of disbelief.

"I'm serious," I said. "The guy had a sawed off shotgun under the bar and was about to take aim. Walter put the pistol to his head, and then whacked him with his own gun."

Neil fished silently for a while, ruminating over what I had just told him.

"Another thing," I said. "Pop had another brother besides Sam. His name was Don."

Neil turned and looked at me.

"And he was married before," I said. "He had two sons – Neil and Thomas."

"Jesus," Neil said.

A loud crashing noise in the brush above caused us to cut off our conversation. We listened as someone slipped and scrabbled down the steep trail to the river, swearing and muttering the whole way.

"Must be Calvin," Neil said.

Moments later, Calvin emerged from the trail, a new pipe clenched firmly in his teeth. He fell the last several feet onto the stones lining the creek, kicking several into the water in the process.

"You're spooking the fish," Neil scolded.

"You catch any?" Calvin demanded, standing, brushing himself off and fishing around in his pocket for his lighter.

"Not yet," Neil said.

"Well then," Calvin said. "There's probably no fish to spook anyway."

He laughed at his own joke as he puffed maniacally at his pipe, trying to get it started. It finally caught and a cloud of smoke enveloped his face, causing him to choke and cough. The action blew a fountain of burning tobacco and ash out of the end of his pipe.

"Jesus, Calvin!" Neil exclaimed. "What the hell are you doing?"

Calvin sputtered angrily, trying to catch his breath. "Shut up Neil," he finally managed.

Calvin told us that it was lunchtime, and that we were wanted back at camp. When we had a moment out of Calvin's hearing, Neil told me to keep reading the journal. "There's a lot more to this than we figured," he said.

A lot more, I thought.

After lunch, which consisted of burgers and bug juice, we headed down to the stables. Walter had gone there to ride some more. It was a beautiful afternoon up in the hills; the sky was clear and the sun promised to heat things up pretty good. I began to wish that I'd worn my shorts: my jeans were already starting to feel hot and cloying. Kids were running to and fro, carrying towels and beach balls towards the pool. Dogs on lines barked greetings and challenges as we walked by the trailers and tents lined up along the road. People waved and smiled. The smell of wood smoke and cooking food filled the air.

At the stables, Walter was putting the grey stallion named Patton through his paces. The big horse responded to Walter's every command smartly, his handsome head held high, ears straight up.

"He enjoys it, doesn't he?" Bob said as he walked up to the fence.

"Walter loves riding," I said. "He was in the cavalry once."

Bob laughed. "I meant the horse, Patton," he said. "He doesn't often get ridden by someone like your uncle. I ride him as often as I can, but there are so many horses, I can't give him the time he needs."

"He's a beautiful horse," I said. Neil agreed.

We watched Walter work with Patton for a long time. After a while Bob walked off towards the stables.

"He's an interesting guy, Uncle Walter," Neil said.

"They're all interesting," I said. Our fathers and uncles."

"Pop's pretty interesting too," I said.

"Yeah," Neil said. "And the missing uncles."

I saw Thad and Betsy walking across the lots, they waved when they saw me notice them.

"Ready for a ride?" Betsy said. She didn't wait for an answer. She turned and walked towards the barn, Thad following.

"I'm out," Neil said. "I'm still sore from yesterday, plus, I want to clean my car— it's covered with dust." I wasn't surprised, the only thing Neil was more particular about than his shoes was his car.

King neighed as I entered the barn. I could have sworn that he recognized me.

"He's happy to see you," Betsy said, as if in answer to my thoughts.

Betsy talked me through the process of fitting the bit and saddling the big chestnut and helped me adjust the stirrups. "You've got long legs," she said as she fitted the buckle's tines into two previously unused holes. I mounted and found that the stirrups fit perfectly. I realized that I had adjusted them too short the day before.

Thad rode up, leading Betsy's horse, and off we went. Bob, riding a paint, and Walter joined us. We took the trail at a much faster pace than we had the day before. As the trail widened, Walter fell in alongside me.

"Getting the hang of it?" he asked.

"A little," I said. I looked over at him. He seemed to read my mind.

"The pistol's a war souvenir," Walter said. He sounded a little apologetic. "The firing pin's broken, plus you can't get ammunition for it. It's a Japanese Nambu, eight millimeter. I thought it might come in handy, in the bar," he added.

"Where did you get it," I asked.

"Traded a carton of cigarettes to an Aussie soldier," he said. He clicked his tongue twice, touched his heels to Patton and rode up the trail at a light trot.

I was surprised. Usually, Walter would have made up some lengthy story about how he single handedly charged a Japanese pillbox, or how he took the pistol off a Japanese Officer who was about to commit Hari Kari, something like that. He rarely missed an opportunity to make up a story. But he just had, and I wondered why.

That night I crept up to the front seat again and resumed reading.

The union man came to me one day, on the elevator on my way down to my shift.

"James East," he said. His handshake was firm and his accent was English. He was tall and thin and unusually clean for a miner. A burley man stood silently behind him, keeping watch.

"We have an organization," he said. "If you join we can help you with grievances against the Company."

"How much?" I responded. He laughed.

"We have dues, if that's what you mean. It helps with the families of miners who are injured or killed. There's also a strike fund, if we have to go that way. It'll help us get through."

He gave me the usual talk about unity in numbers and the brotherhood of miners. I told him that I wasn't interested in joining that which could get me fired and blackballed. Besides, I wasn't born yesterday and knew that it was just as likely that he was a company man – or company informant. Even showing interest would likely get me fired.

Later that same day a different man came to me and identified himself as a company detective. He had cold steely eyes, the kind that belonged to men who had lost all remnants of humanity in combat; the kind of eyes that men who survived the trenches had. He had the look of a kind of man that could slit a throat without blinking. He asked if I'd been approached by the union.

"Of course," I said. "I turned him down. I came here to work, not to cause trouble."

"Can you identify the man," he asked me.

"Yes, but I won't," I said. "I'm not a stooge."

He must have seen in me what I saw in him, because he didn't say another thing. He just turned and walked away. But I did notice that a couple of miners had been watching us. They looked quickly away when I noticed them.

Things went on well for a few years; after all, we were coal miners and good at it. Despite the crushing costs of housing, food, fuel and equipment imposed on us by the company, which owned everything, I still was able to put a small but comfortable amount of real money aside, seed money for a move north, which Ella desperately wanted.

"I don't want to see my boys in the mines," she said often. "I like my boys above ground."

With each year there was a new baby. First there was Betty, then Marcy, Yvonne and, finally, little Owen. We lost Marcy to a fever when she was only two, a terrible loss. It was then that Ella began pushing hard to move out of the coalfields.

"The air's full of coal dust," she said. "We breathe it in all the time. Everybody's got a cough. Just look at the hills – they're black with soot. Nothing will grow on them. That's why Marcy died."

I had to agree about the soot, it was everywhere. And everyone did have a cough, "Black Lung," some called it. I saw miners go down with it and never recover. But, coal was money, and there was a lot of it down in those mines. I told Ella to be patient; that we'd move in a couple more years. She told me that she would try, but I knew that it would only be a question of time before she just up and left. But for the time being, I was determined to soldier on, making all the money I could make.

But, a few weeks later, something occurred that changed everything.

It happened one afternoon just when our shift was up. Don, Sam and I, along with the rest of our team, greeted our friends on the next shift as they arrived at the tunnel we had been working. The team leader was Paul Blair, the man that we'd met in Phila-

*delphia. He and his wife and three children lived in the apartment
next to us. Our kids played together and our wives were friends.
We knew the other men on the team as well: Johnny Jones from
Swansea, Tim Abernathy from Cardiff, Little Jimmy Franklin, a boy
no older than fourteen, from Swansea and Roger Entwistle from
London.*

*We had no sooner left the shaft and stepped into the sunlight
that we felt an ominous rumble in the ground. Seconds later dust
and smoke billowed out of the mine entrance. A few bewildered and
scared looking men staggered out, coughing. One of them was Tim
Abernathy.*

*"Pillar collapse," he said. "Little Jimmy was trying to pull it
and the room caved in. "I was pushing the cart out and escaped,
but the rest are trapped." He looked around, dusting himself off and
regaining his composure. "We've got to try and dig them out, some
of them may still be alive!"*

*Tim turned around and hurried back into the mine. We fol-
lowed.*

*We dug for hours, occasionally stopping to listen for the tapping that we
had heard earlier, indicating that someone was still alive in the tunnel. After
a while the tapping stopped, but we kept digging, hoping that we might still
reach them. Finally the foreman, Corgi, called the rescue off.*

*"No use digging any further," he stated flatly. "There's no one
still alive in there."*

*"We've got to keep trying," someone shouted. I realized that it
was me.*

*Corgi looked at me, his beady little eyes angry. "Edwards," he
said. "If you want to keep your job, you'll go back to your shift over
in Number Five. It's already started and you're late!"*

I started to pick up my shovel. I had every intention of bashing the little man's head in. But a hand stopped me. I turned to see the union man who had spoken to me.

"Not now," he whispered. "There'll come a time, but not now."

I dropped the shovel and walked off with the rest of the men. I saw that their dusty faces were streaked with tears. I assumed that I looked the same.

I set the book down; not believing that the coal company would abandon men trapped in a collapsed mine. I'd read about the struggles of the United Mine Workers Union to get safety measures instituted in the mines, and I'd heard about secret groups like the Molly Maguires that used violence to shut down mines. Now I knew why.

Looking around, I noticed that it was still dark. I checked my watch— it was 3:30. The woods around me seemed to close in on me, like the wings of some large black bird, enveloping me in darkness. I felt the fear I had felt as a child waking with a fever in the middle of the night. I could feel my breath coming in ragged gasps and my hands, holding the musty journal, went clammy. The red light of my flashlight on the hand-written words of my grandfather's journal cast a macabre spell on the scene.

Rubbing my eyes, I was tempted to put the book away and go back to my sleeping bag. But, somehow I knew that I wouldn't be able to sleep. I rubbed my eyes, banished my monsters and went back to the text.

There was a memorial for the lads left in the mine three days later. We were all docked a day's pay for attending. After the cere-mony someone approached me from behind.

"Don't turn around," the man said. The voice was familiar, but I couldn't place it. He reached his hand around me and stuck a white flower into my suit pocket. "Only turn around if you're will-ing to join— without reservation. Like before."

I took the flower and stared at it. The voice belonged to Gerald, my leader in the Blodwyns in Wales. How was it that he had turned up here in Pennsylvania? I turned around. We shook hands. I must admit that I wasn't happy to see him again, but I was filled with a desire for revenge for the deaths of my friends.

Gerald nodded to me, a grim smile on his face. "I hear you learned some skills in France," he said. He spoke in Welsh.

I nodded.

"We'll be in touch," he said. "Same signals and codes – at least for now. Bring Sam along, if he's willing."

I nodded again. We shook hands again and then he slipped away.

Several days later, a small boy came to our door. He handed me a white flower and ran off. Attached to the stem of the flower was a small bit of paper. I opened it. "Read this and eat it," it said. It contained the location of a meeting and a password. I brought Sam along.

We exchanged no names. There was Gerald and two men I'd never seen before. One, a swarthy man with thinning hair and a big mustache, sat back a little, his arms crossed. He had on a loose fitting jacket and I figured that the chances of him having a pistol in each hand were one hundred percent. The second man, tall with sandy hair and green eyes, did all the talking.

"You had experience behind the lines," he said. He had an American accent, a surprise: The Blodwyns were a Welsh group. I looked over at Gerald, but he sat impassively, not talking at all.

"We're looking for some payback for the mine accident," he continued. "And we want to make a statement to the company." I began to realize that he wasn't a Blodwyn after all, he was a union man.

He was looking for the Blodwyns to do some dirty work.

"We need a mine explosion in number Six, between shifts—just like we did back in Wales," Gerald said, breaking his silence. Again, he spoke in Welsh.

I looked over at Sam. He nodded.

"Okay," the Union man said. "I'll leave the details to Gerald and the rest of his men. The less I know, the better."

He stood and headed towards the back door. "This meeting never happened," he said as he slipped out the door. The second man rose and backed out the door, his arms still crossed.

Sam took up position as lookout as Gerald spoke. He used Welsh.

"It's different than in Wales," he said. "In Wales we were on our own— independent. Here, we're part of the union. We're the eyes and ears, and enforcers, if need be. We do nothing without the say so of the union; the man you just met. They negotiate, we... well, we help push the process forward."

We sat quietly for a while.

"Questions?" Gerald asked. We had none.

"Well then, lads, welcome to the brotherhood," Gerald said.

Sam and I took the Blodwyn oath once more: "Na ad I'th dafod dorri'th wddf"— let not your tongue cut your throat.

A few days after the memorial to the buried miners, an explosion rocked Number Six in between shifts. Company officials descended on the scene before the dust had even settled. They interrogated the men who had just finished their shift, but they had seen or heard nothing. Corgi, the foreman, was beside himself. He, like the company officials, knew that the explosion had been no accident. He seemed to take it personally. "Stabbed in the back by *my own men," someone heard him mutter.*

Of course I knew how it had happened. Sam and I had set the charges the day before, during our own shift. We ran a fuse up the tunnel, which one of our men lit at the end of his shift.

After that, Sam and I were assigned to an espionage group. There were five of us: Evan, Marwyn and Bowen, along with Sam and me— "Gavin" and "Dylan." We worked at night, slipping into the company headquarters buildings, making copies of guard schedules, delivery dates, tonnage reports, maintenance schedules and payment records. We soon knew the company's business as well as they did.

We also gathered information on the detectives, the company's private army. We learned their names, schedules and pay. But, most importantly, we found out where they lived and who their families were.

Part of our job was to arrange more accidents like the one in Number Six, accidents that would shut a mine down as retribution for a pay cut or for a grievance. We were very active, and very successful. We became a thorn in the company's side. They offered a reward for information on us, but the miners would never give us up: we were heroes to them.

But the company detectives were crafty in their own right; they were ruthless and vindictive, and they didn't like being shown up by us. One night, while Sam and I were at the bar after our regular shift, a group of miners entered the room. We immediately recognized them as the shift that was working Mine Number Seven.

"The company closed Number Eight," one of the men said as he stepped up to the bar. "The detectives had it cordoned off when we arrived for our shift."

Sam and I exchanged a glance: we had men in there, setting charges. I didn't see any of them in the bar.

A violent explosion suddenly rocked the room, shattering glasses and bottles and throwing many to the floor. We ran out into the street and found that the explosion had happened in Number Eight. Sam and I knew that it wasn't supposed to happen for several hours.

The detectives would let no one up to the site of the explosion. An official statement was issued on a flyer posted to a large community bulletin board. It read: union saboteurs planning to disrupt mining operations in Number Eight were killed when their home-made explosive device detonated prematurely. The mine will remain closed until further notice.

It was obvious to us all that the saboteurs had been killed by the detectives, otherwise the mine wouldn't have been closed in the first place. The question in my mind was whether our men had been captured before the explosion; if they had been, they would have been tortured. We would have to operate under the assumption that they had talked and named names.

The next day, we heard that the detectives had picked up three more of our men— men on our own team: Evan, Marwyn and Bowen. Gerald came to me and my brother and told us that we should leave immediately. "Go to the coalfields in the west," he told us. "They are on strike there. They'll need you. Lose yourselves in the camps. Blend in. Wait for a man named Lloyd to contact you. He'll use the codes, you do the same. Use different names. Lay low."

He pressed a thick wad of bills into my hand. "Send your families away," he said. "Somewhere safe, where they can't be found."

He looked at me with sad eyes. "We're all in grave danger right now," he said. "I don't know if I can get out myself, but if I can, I'll join you. Look for me in the coalfields of West Virginia."

At that he slipped away into the shadows.

The next day I gave most of the money I'd saved to Ella and sent her north with the kids. As happy as she was to be leaving the coalfields she was perplexed by the suddenness of the move. And the big wad of money.

"Good fortune in a card game," I lied. "The rest of us will work for a few more months and then head up to join you."

She wasn't fooled and said as much. She wanted the boys, Neil and Thomas to go with her. "Whatever you men are involved in; leave the boys out of it. They belong with me."

I knew that was impossible. Families left all the time, sent away as soon as a miner saved enough to send them. But miners would be noticed, even ones as young as Neil and Thomas. As it was, we would have to travel in secret, using back roads and traveling at night. It wasn't something that a woman and young children could chance.

Ella knew that I couldn't be swayed; I can be a stubborn man at times.

"You watch those boys and bring them to our new home soon," she said. "And you be careful yourself," she added, fighting back tears. I didn't know it then, but it would be a very long time before I saw her again.

"Sam went ahead with Don and my boys, headed for the coalfields in West Virginia, but I decided to stay behind for a short while, under cover. I needed to know what had happened to my friends.

That night, using all the skills I had learned during the war, I *slipped through the tight company security perimeter and worked my way up to the building that the detectives used as a headquarters; the place where interrogations were held. I immediately heard muffled screaming.*

Keeping to the shadows, I circled the building and went up to a small, broken window that was in a darkened recess. I climbed up on an old barrel and looked inside. What I saw I hadn't seen since the war, and it chilled me to the marrow.

Far across the darkened room were three chairs, each one contained a tightly bound man. Two of the men were covered in their own blood and each had a gaping red smile beneath his chin; their throats had been slit. The third man was unrecognizable to me: his face was a bloody pulp from a vicious beating. Several detectives were standing over him, questioning him closely. I strained to hear what was being said.

"You see what your friends got for not talking," a man with his back to me said. His voice was instantly familiar – it was Corgi! I was shocked: foremen were usually miners who had been promoted from among the ranks of average miners. They might be seen as company men and they might be bossy bastards, but they lived in company housing with the rest of us and shared the same conditions in the mines. But Corgi was obviously a detective of some rank. Working in the mines with us, he must have picked up all kinds of information through idle chatter among the men. He was the worst kind of traitor to us, and he had just murdered two of my friends!

As I watched, powerless to intervene, Corgi slapped the third man and demanded an answer to his question.

"Fuck you!" the man shouted. I recognized the voice as Bowen's.

He spit a glob of bloody spittle into Corgi's face.

Corgi staggered backwards, wiping the mess from his face.

"Do it!" he ordered one of the detectives who was standing behind Bowen..

The man grabbed Bowen by the hair, yanked his head back and drew a straight razor across his throat. Bowen's body convulsed for a moment as his life's blood drained from the wound. He then slumped backwards into the same position as the other two men, dead.

I screamed a silent scream, shut my eyes and held onto the window sill, trying to keep from falling off the barrel on which I was perched. It's funny, I'd been around death my whole life; in the mines and in the war. Yet the murder of Bowen hit me harder than any of the many I had seen. He had just saved my life by not giving me up to the detectives and had died because of it. I felt a murderous rage rising inside me, and it was directed at Corgi.

"Take them to the bridge and hang them by their heels," I heard him order the other detectives. He turned and walked out the door.

The next morning there was a murmur among the miners as the news spread: there were bodies hanging from the bridge – four of them. One of them was Corgi.

I sat bolt upright and read the last sentence again to see if I hadn't read it wrong. Then I read it again. My Grandpa, Pop, had murdered a man in cold blood and hung his body from a bridge! Unbelievable! I could feel my heart racing at the thought. I rubbed my eyes and read the passage one more time, but the words hadn't changed. Hands trembling, I closed the book and slipped it back into Walter's satchel.

I looked around at the quiet campsite and realized that dawn was beginning to break. I saw Walter stir and then sit up. Crap! I thought. I was still sitting in the front seat of the car with my red light on. I flipped the switch on the flashlight and slithered over the seat and into my sleeping bag. Moments later the car door opened and I was bathed in the bright white light of the car's dome.

"Are you awake Thomas?" Walter asked softly.

"Huh?" I mumbled.

"I thought I saw the car rocking around and thought you might be awake."

"Oh, I was having a bad dream," I lied.

"Well, if you're awake, why don't we go down to the fish pond they have here. The owner claims it's stocked with big bass."

I gathered my new fly rod and tackle box and followed Walter down the trail.

Walter moved well in the woods. He had a natural woodsman's gait from having spent years hunting, fishing and hiking and I found myself having to hustle to keep up. He had a little limp, though and his shoulders dipped and twisted slightly to compensate for it. The limp, I assumed, was caused by injuries he had sustained during the plane crashes he had been in during the war. He had been in seven.

My father once told me the story about the last crash, the one that broke Walter's legs in several places. He found out about it from an airman he encountered while stationed in Hawaii right after the war. His name was Alvin Barkley and had noticed my father's name on his uniform.

"Are you related to Walter Edwards?" Barkley asked casually.

"I've got a brother by that name," my father said. "He was with the 14th Air Force under Chenault."

"That's him," Barkley said. "Hell of a story."

"What story?" My father asked.

Barkley laughed. "He didn't tell you?"

"I haven't seen him since he joined up," my father said. "I found out from my brother that he was with Chenault in the Pacific, that's all I know."

Barkley, who was on the rescue mission, told my father the story.

It began with a milk-run. A milk run is an easy mission, one usually far away from any combat and designed to get some future politician his combat experience or to map a region that hadn't been explored. An anthropologist named Herman Kramer had convinced someone high up in MacArthur's Command that certain parts of New Guinea that had never been mapped needed to be. He had ulterior motives, of course: after the War, he intended to do Doctoral work on the primitive native tribes of the island. He would need maps.

A C-47 was fitted with special cameras, a team of Army cartographers was gathered and a flight plan was drawn up. Walter was assigned as the mission's radioman.

The mission itself was a flight that would take less than half a day. The pilot, a veteran named Curtis Leypold, flew the plane expertly across the narrow strait and high over the escarpment that separated the island's interior from its coastal region. They found the gorge, actuated the cameras and flew slowly up the hidden valley. Kramer and his team crowded at the windows to see the sights: high, wispy waterfalls cascading down from the highlands and into the glistening ribbon of river that ran through the valley; towering merbau and mahogany trees forming a lush canopy intertwined with dozens of climbing vines and creepers. The whole scene was shot through with thousands of brilliantly colored orchids.

Captain Leypold put the plane into a leisurely turn at the top of the canyon, preparing to fly back through the valley. It was then that, coming out of the sun, a pair of rogue Japanese fighters descended on the hapless plane. Leypold took evasive action but, flying so low and slow, the plane had no chance at all. The Zeros riddled the pane with machine gun fire, killing Leypold and his co-pilot. Walter climbed forward into the cockpit, trying to get to the controls. But it was too late; the plane wobbled crazily, its engines on fire. Moments later it crashed into the side of the mountain in a huge fireball. The Japanese fighters waggled their wings in victory and flew away.

The Army sent out search flights and found the smoldering remains of the flight. No signs of life could be seen. Radio operators intercepted a Japanese transmission describing the kill. It was decided that it would be too difficult and dangerous to send a ground team in to the crash site for body recovery; there could be no survivors from such a crash. The crew and passengers were declared KIA – Killed in Action.

But there was a survivor. Somehow, Walter had been thrown out of the cockpit just as the plane hit the mountainside. He landed in a jumble of ferns and vines battered, bruised and broken; alive but unconscious. When he awoke, he found that he had been unconscious for some time. The wreckage of the burned out plane was cold. Summoning all his strength, he crawled over to the wreckage, only to discover what he already suspected: there were no other survivors, the bodies of the passengers and his crewmates, burned beyond recognition, were scattered among the twisted and charred metal pieces of the plane.

Walter began crawling down the mountainside, his shattered legs useless. When he got to the valley floor, he found a faint trail used by native hunters. It took him two days, but he followed it to a small tribal village.

Walter was exhausted, starving and near death with a fever. He wasn't sure how the villagers would treat him. He'd heard stories, but he had no choice but to crawl on into the village and hope for the best.

A little girl, hoeing a garden on the side of the trail, saw him first and shrieked. A man, probably the girl's father, ran to her, brandishing a machete. He saw Walter and gasped.

"American, American," Walter said. "Friend."

Other villagers appeared, all carrying various farm implements as weapons and shaking them threateningly. They shouted at the pathetic creature on the trail who seemed to be begging them for mercy.

Finally an old man pushed his way through the crowd and approached Walter.

"American?" He asked in broken English.

"Yes, yes," Walter said. "American."

The old man turned to the crowd and said something that Walter didn't understand. The people relaxed. Some even smiled at him.

Once the villagers realized that he was an American, Walter was welcomed as a hero; the Japanese treated tribal people very badly, frequently sending patrols through the rural areas, committing every sort of atrocity imaginable.

Walter was cleaned up and fed. An old shaman smeared a paste on his shattered legs and bound his broken bones with the vines of some strange plant that took away the pain. He was given a vile liquid of unknown composition and made to drink it. Within a few days his fever broke and he began to regain his strength.

A runner was sent down to the coast and, after a few weeks, a rescue patrol arrived and took Walter out. Doctors at the military hospital were astounded at his recovery and asked him about what the old shaman had used to mend him. Walter didn't know.

Still, the Doctors told him that he'd probably never walk again. But Walter, stubborn as he was, began going to a nearby athletic field in his wheelchair and circling the track for hours at every day. When he was strong enough to use crutches, he spent even more time on the track.

Eventually he was able to walk on his own, although with a noticeable limp.

No one in the family knew about his injuries; he simply showed up at home one day in his uniform, kissed his mother, stayed for a few days and then left again. He never said where he went but, after a few years, he showed up again and got a job at the Henry Motors factory.

"That's the way Walter is," my father explained. "He plays his cards close to his chest."

CHAPTER TEN

At the pond, Walter peered into the water, stroked his chin thoughtfully and rummaged around in his tackle box. He tied a strange looking fly onto his line, it looked vaguely like a small caterpillar, and cast into the far end of the pool. As it sank, he began retrieving his fly along the bottom, jerking it sharply from time to time.

"Wooly buggers are the best flies for bass," Walter said. "They're all-purpose— they can be fished like a minnow, a crab, or a big fat grub. And they're easy to tie," he added.

Suddenly his rod bent almost double as a big bass hit the fly. Walter raised his rod tip to set the hook and released the drag on his reel. The bass circled to the left, then turned and broke the surface, shaking desperately to throw the hook. The greenish-brown scales of the fish sparkled in the morning light and specks of water cascaded around it. For a moment, the bass seemed to be dancing on its tail. It then plunged back into the pond, heading towards the bottom.

Walter played the fish expertly, giving it all the line it wanted on its runs and then taking up the slack when it slowed or turned. The only time he really fought the fish was when it headed towards a big patch of lily pads; Walter knew that the fish would twist and turn in the tangle of tough lily stems and break the line.

Finally, the fish tired and Walter scooped him up with his net. He pulled the smallmouth out by its lower lip and held it up, admiring it. He removed the fly and let the bass slip back into the pond, which surprised me.

Walter pointed to a sign by the dock. "Catch and Release Only," it read. I nodded and started working my own fly, trying to copy what Walter had done.

I got my first fish on my third cast. It hit hard, fought hard and broke my line when I couldn't keep it away from the lily pads. I re-rigged and went back at it, landing my second fish after a twenty-minute battle.

After a couple of hours Walter and I had each caught several fish— we both thought that we had caught one or two of them twice.

"These fish know how to play the game," Walter commented. "They've been caught a lot."

As Walter and I put away our gear and got ready to leave he suddenly launched into a well-worn joke. "Seems there was a new Game Warden in town," he began. "He had heard about a particular local called Nip who was notorious for violating game laws. Evidently, he sold illegal fish to a local restaurant for beer money, traded venison to a filling station owner for gas and even paid his rent in venison and fish.

"Deciding to take the bull by the horns, the Game Warden approached Nip one day on the street and introduced himself. "I hear you're a pretty good at fishing," he said.

"What's it to ya?" Nip said.

"Well, I love to fish on my days off and was just wondering if you could show me around, you know, maybe show me a few good spots."

Nip considered the request for a minute. "Sure, I'll take you fishing. I'll even take you to my favorite spot!"

"The next day the Game Warden picked Nip up early in the morning. They drove far out of town and up a dirt track through some woods. At the top of a hill, surrounded by pine trees, there was a small lake.

"They rowed out into the lake and anchored. As the Game Warden was gearing up, he saw Nip reach into a duffel bag and pull out a stick of dynamite. Het lit the fuse with the stub of his cigar and tossed the dynamite into the lake. Moments later, there was a loud thump! Fish began floating to the surface. Nip scooped them up with his net.

"What are you doing?" The Game Warden shouted. "Dynamiting fish is illegal! You know that! I'm the Game Warden for Christ's sakes! Are you crazy?"

"At that, Nip reached into his duffel bag and pulled out another stick of dynamite. He lit it and tossed it into the Game Warden's lap.

"What are you gonna do," Nip said. "Fish or sit there?"

I laughed. "First time I heard that joke…today!" I said.

• • • • • • • • • • • • • • • •

"Oh, I was hoping that there'd be trout for breakfast again!" A woman's voice announced as we approached the campsite. I immediately recognized it as Karen's. I thought that she would have made Doc take her home after the pool-hall incident.

"I told Doc that I didn't want to miss out on Neptune's breakfast trout," she said. "So I got him up early."

"Hey Tommy," Doc said through a big grin. "I told Karen you wouldn't let her down!" He was drinking a Carling Black Label, not a care in the world.

"You'll have to settle for bacon and eggs," my father said. He glanced at Doc. "Unless you want beer for breakfast."

Doc held up his beer bottle as if in a toast, and then drained it.

Karen ignored him. "No trout?" she said, sounding disappointed. "I was getting used to trout and eggs."

"I guess you'll have to settle for one of Owen's breakfasts," Walter said, his voice heavily laced with sarcasm. "He believes that eggshells are good for you."

"Shut up, Walter," my father said over his shoulder. He was stirring up a big mess of eggs in a large cast iron pan and the smoke from the fire was getting to him. He squinted his eyes against the stinging smoke, causing him to slop some of the eggs over the side of the fry pan. They sizzled loudly in the fire.

Walter snickered into his hand and poked at his pipe thoughtfully. "I don't mean eggshells in the eggs," he said. "That would spoil the chunks of firewood and ash that he's mixed in. No, he likes to crack a couple of eggs into the coffee – he claims they clear the grounds out."

Walter was referring to an incident a long time ago, when my father had first tried his new blue-speckled coffee pot. Everyone complained about the coffee grounds that got through the tin strainer during the percolation process. My father claimed that cowboys boiled their coffee straight, and then cleared the grounds with a couple of raw eggs. When he made the next pot he cracked a couple of eggs into the brew. But they didn't clear the coffee, they scrambled. Everyone ended up with chunks of brown egg in their cups, something that Walter never let my father forget.

"Put some bacon in it, and you'll have a complete breakfast," Walter had declared at the time.

My father was a lot of things: an engineer, a talented carpenter, an excellent painter and a fixer of just about anything. But a cook he wasn't.

"Your father could burn water," my mother often told me.

Everyone shuddered when it was his turn to cook and, whatever mélange he came up with, it was invariably over-salted.

"Ya gotta have salt," he would say in answer to a complaint. "The Romans paid their soldiers with it. The expression 'Worth his salt' came from that."

"Pillar of salt' is more like it," Walter responded. "If the Romans ate as much salt as you put in, they'd be petrified!"

Walter's comment always brought a laugh, but everyone knew that, as bad as my father's cooking was, Walter's was worse. By common agreement, Walter was left out of the cooking rotation.

Later that day I told Neil about what I had read in the journal.

"He killed a guy and hung him from a bridge?" Neil exclaimed. "Pop?"

"That's what he wrote in the journal," I said.

"Holy crap!" Neil said.

"Yeah, that's what I thought," I said. "Pop! Remember how shriveled up he was with Black Lung? How he coughed all the time? Hard to believe he killed a man, though it sounds like the guy deserved it."

"I remember the last time I saw him," Neil said.

"Me too," I said with a shudder.

That night Walter kept his satchel with him. He stayed up late, sitting by the fire and reading the journal by flashlight. It was almost dawn before he finally went to bed. I saw him tuck the satchel under his cot.

"Walter's up to something," I told Neil the next morning. He stayed up almost all night, reading."

"Yeah, the men have been having some kind of debate. I heard my father and yours talking about West Virginia."

"West Virginia? We aren't going to West Virginia!"

"We might be. Keep your ears open."

· · · · · · · · · · · · · · · ·

That evening we had a steak fry at the campsite. Doc went to town and bought New York Strip steaks for everyone – a payback from the pool hall incident. It probably cost him a small fortune. He must have hustled a lot of money that night, I thought; if he could afford staying in motels and buying steaks.

He and Charlie built up a large fire pit out of cinderblocks and wire grating. "Nothing like a thick steak cooked over a wood fire," Charlie kept saying. They sent us boys into the woods to get more firewood. When we got back, a spirited debate was in progress about the best way to cook a steak.

"Well-done," my father said. He said it with finality, as if there could be no argument with such a sage pronouncement.

"Pffft!" Walter exclaimed. "You might as well eat shoe leather! Rare is the only way to go with a steak. You get the best flavor."

"Medium rare," Pete said. "You need a little crust on it to hold the juices in."

The men went back and forth with their comments, as usual. I dropped a big armload of wood next to the fire.

"Hey Tommy," Doc said. "What are you doing gathering wood?"

I looked at him quizzically.

"I thought that you'd be down at the pool with Karen, she was looking for you."

"She went for a swim," Charlie said. "Guess she wanted a lifeguard."

I felt my face go red.

"She didn't say anything to me," I said. Somehow it felt like the statement was a lie, even though what I had said was true.

"Here she comes now," Charlie said, looking towards the trail.

Karen was walking up the trail at a leisurely pace, a towel over her shoulder. Her hair was still wet from her swim.

"How do you like your steak done?" Doc asked as Karen got closer.

"Pittsburgh style," she said.

"What's that?" I heard myself ask.

"Charred on the outside, raw on the inside," Doc answered for her. "It's not for the faint of heart."

"Hey Tommy," Karen said. "Where were you earlier? I thought you might like to go a few laps with me. She jumped playfully onto Doc's lap and took a sip of his beer.

"I was bored," she said. "All Doc does is sit around all day and drink beer."

"Guilty," he announced, raising his beer bottle in a mock salute. "Somebody's got to hold down the fort," he added.

"Tommy was out gathering wood," Charlie said. He made it sound like I had done something stupid. I just shrugged. I was getting inured to all the teasing anyway.

Dinner was potatoes and corn roasted in the fire, beans baked in a Dutch oven, lemonade and Carling Black Label for the men. And steak cooked to order over the wood fire. There were also a dozen trout, which Neil and I had gotten after lunch. We had driven twenty miles to a trout stream and fished for a couple of hours.

"Surf and turf, it doesn't get any better than this!" Doc proclaimed, tilting back his head and draining a bottle of beer. "What do you think, Karen? Better than any five star restaurant!"

"Really good," she said, slicing into her bloody steak with gusto. "And these trout are better than any lobster I've ever had."

I had boldly ordered my steak Pittsburgh style too. Doc looked at me with a wink and tossed it onto the hottest part of the fire. He stepped back, took a sip of beer, and flipped it. Another sip of beer and he tossed it onto my plate. I have to admit, steak Pittsburgh style is an unforgettable experience.

That night I waited impatiently for Walter to go to bed. I wanted to find out why it was so important that we go to West Virginia, and why it was so important that they obtain Pop's journal in the first place.

I stole a car and began wending my way west, using back roads,
I knew that the railroad would not be safe for me: the Detectives

would be scouring every train, looking for miners on the run, miners who had killed one of their own.

At a small town to the east I bought new clothes and scrubbed away as much of the accumulated coal dust as I could. But I knew how easy it was to spot a miner: he had a stooped walk from working in rooms shorter than he was tall, red-rimmed eyes from the coal dust, black fingernails, pale skin, and a cough that never went away.

I continued eastward for a while; then turned south. At every little town I expected to be detained by the local cops or, worse, a group of Detectives. My pistol was loaded and ready – I wasn't going to be taken alive.

My destination was the coalfields of West Virginia where a miner's strike was entering its third month. Sam, Don and the boys would be waiting for me there. Our plan was to hide in plain sight among the miners and families camped out in the hills – the Detectives wouldn't dare go into those camps. We would use our particular talents to help the miners in their struggle.

When I arrived, I found that the miners and their families were suffering. There was very little food, the tents were drafty and leaked when it rained and they had to wander farther and deeper into the surrounding woods to find usable firewood. It had been a rainy month and the main trails around and through the camp were a sea of mud. But there was a certain sense of shared struggle among the strikers. Everyone was willing, even eager, to help one another. The women did laundry together, cooked meals with the meager rations they had and watched each other's children. The men, when they weren't on the picket line, hunted in the hills, bringing back rabbits, squirrels, woodchucks, birds and even the occasional deer. Women and children scoured the woods for wild vegetables, nuts and berries. Everything went into common stew pots.

Some food, purchased with strike fund money, was brought in by the union: flour, sugar, salt, bacon and coffee. But the Detectives seized a lot of it at blockades on the dirt roads that led to the camp and by patrolling the trails that led up through the woods to the camps. Despite everyone's best efforts, the camp was slowly starving.

As soon as I could, I slipped down to the mines. That's where I knew I would find Sam, Don and the boys; and our Blodwyn contact, Lloyd.

Don, Neil and Thomas were working as strikebreakers. As such, they would be a valuable resource for the espionage Sam and I would likely be performing. They would be known to the Blodwyns and therefore under our protection. They would be away from the filthy strike camp. And they would be making money, which they would need when it was time to leave.

Sam and I would be posing as German immigrant strikebreakers. I was fluent and Sam had become reasonably so during the war. We were confident that company detectives wouldn't be expecting Welsh Blodwyns among the Germans.

I found Sam in the company bar where a large group of German miners were drinking after their shift. He was having a tipple with a dusty miner who turned out to be Lloyd, our Blodwyn contact. A man of medium build and steely eyes, he had the look of a man who had spent time in the trenches. After an introduction and exchange of required Blodwyn codes, I asked him.

"15th[th] Regiment, Red Dragons," he said. I recognized the unit. The 15th had been isolated by a German counter-attack at Mametz

Wood. Only seven men managed to fight their way out of the trap.

"I was wounded and captured," Lloyd told me. I spent the rest of the war in a German hospital and then a POW camp. Sam tells me you two were over there too."

I nodded and looked around the room at the Germans. "I wonder how many of these lads were in the trenches against us."

"Quite a few I'd wager," he said.

We raised our glasses to a toast for our fallen comrades; in Welsh, of course.

A little while and a few drinks later I heard a voice behind me. It whispered loudly in my ear.

"So, you made it back, Dylan," the voice said. I recognized it immediately as Gerald's. I turned and greeted him with a smile and a handshake.

"You too," I said. I motioned to the bartender for another round.

"Too bad about Corgi," Gerald said with a knowing smile. "The last I heard, he was hanging around with some of our lads."

We raised our glasses once again, this time to Evan, Marwyn, and Bowen.

We soon found out that the company was getting desperate. Production was down and the sabotage campaign of the Blodwyns, blowing mines in between shifts and destroying railroad lines with explosives, impeded mining and shipping. The strike was working.

Desperation leads to desperate measures. The Company brought in more Detectives.

The new detectives were of a different sort. The original detectives were mostly former beat cops, looking to make a little more money than they could on the street. They were bullies, to be sure, *and they weren't above beatings, torture and even murder. But these new guys had a look about them that I'd seen before, in the trenches. Life meant nothing to them and they knew no fear. They were killers, and they enjoyed their work.*

We vowed that for every miner killed by the Company there would be an equal number of detectives taken out. Soon, the bodies of detectives could be found every morning, their throats slit and a white flower on each of their corpses.

It wasn't long before there was a big reward on our heads. We knew that it was only a question of time before the promise of money or the threat of torture would convince someone to give us up to the detectives. Sam and I felt that it was time to develop an exit plan.

The Company paid it's miners in Company scrip, but the detectives would have none of that: they were paid in silver and gold, hard, cold cash. From our espionage, we knew when the detectives got paid and knew when the cash would be brought in. And we knew its precise location: the basement of the Company bank, in the Company safe, located in the central Company offices, and guarded by barbed wire fences, guard dogs, and several layers of security lines, manned by detectives. Impregnable, except to us. We were miners.

We planned to tunnel to the bank from one of the old abandoned mines that were near the offices. No one bothered with the old mines: there was nothing in them, and they were dangerous. The mine we chose was about four hundred yards from the bank. It would take us a while to tunnel that distance. The distance, depth and length of the tunnel would have to be precise; as precise as the tunnels our Welsh engineers dug under the German trenches during the war.

The entrance to the mine was welded shut with iron bars and had become overgrown with brush and brambles; perfect concealment for our operation. We filched a welding torch from one of the company storerooms, along with picks, shovels, headlamps and a quantity of explosives. We knew the company wouldn't miss the items: we knew where the inventory was kept and altered it. That night we began working.

We worked in shifts, two digging, two hauling and one standing lookout. I hated working the boys so hard, but time was of the essence. We dug day and night, only taking breaks to grab a few hours of sleep and some food. Sam and I also kept up our activities with the Blodwyns; we didn't want them to suspect our little side job.

The plan for the robbery itself was fairly simple: we would tunnel under the Company bank, break through the floor the night of the payroll delivery and blow the safe. We would then extract the payroll and exit through the tunnel. To cover our tracks, we would set charges on the support beams of the bank, causing it to cave in. The detectives wouldn't suspect a tunnel and would assume that the robbers had gotten in and out above ground.

We also needed a diversion, an explosion somewhere else to draw the guards away from the bank and to cover the sound of the blast that would open the safe. Coincidentally, it was the Blodwyns who provided us with just such a diversion.

Gerald came to us one night.

"We need to shake the company up," he said. "We need something big; something that will send shudders through their ranks; something that will show them that we can touch them anywhere."

"Like what?" Sam said.

Gerald didn't say anything for a little while, he just sat there, *hand rolling a cigarette. He lit it with a stick match and inhaled deeply, letting the smoke out in a slow, steady stream.*

"The arsenal," he said finally. "Send the whole thing up." He took another draw on his cigarette. "You're the only two that we have who can pull it off," he added.

"We can get in," Sam said. "That's not the problem. The problem is getting out."

"We've got that covered," Gerald said. He leaned forward in his chair.

"You'll wear guards uniforms," he said. "The common ones that nobody will notice.

"When the charges go off, everyone will be running. You run too. Look for me; I'll be driving a company truck, dressed as a guard."

"Sounds simple enough," Sam said. "But I don't like it."

Gerald gave him a hard look but said nothing.

"We can't go back to the camps," he explained. "There's no way in the world that word wouldn't spread. The reward for information on the raid would be enormous – enough that a man could leave the coalfields forever."

Gerald rolled another cigarette and considered our position. "You're right, of course," he said finally. "You'll have to leave the area."

I looked at Sam and saw the faintest twinkle in his eye: the second part of our problem had just been solved for us.

"We'll drop you off near the camps and drive out of here," Sam said. "We'll drop the car and the uniforms after a while and go underground. You'll never see or hear from us again," he added with a smile.

Gerald nodded. "It could work," he said. "We certainly don't want them getting their hands on you – you know too much."

"Right," I said. "We'll need money too, enough to keep us alive while we're on the run."

"You'll get it," Gerald said. He mentioned a number. I looked at Sam and he nodded.

"That should do it," I said. I looked hard at our old compatriot. We'd been together a long time.

"Come with us," I said.

Gerald took a long pull on his cigarette and exhaled audibly. "Don't you think that I'd like to?" He asked. He looked at me wistfully. "But that would be impossible," he said finally. "I'm needed here, to help organize the resistance. I would be running out on my comrades. Plus, the Union would never endorse it."

"Will they endorse our leaving?" Sam asked.

"They already have," Gerald said.

Our plan was now complete. As soon as we dropped Gerald off, we'd drive up the road that runs behind the old mine and pick up Don, the boys and the payroll. If stopped, we would be guards transporting prisoners. The company men wouldn't know that the payroll had been taken until they dug through the rubble. It would take them a couple of days to do that and by that time we'd be long gone.

We redoubled our efforts in the tunnel and reached the bank in less than a week. My brother Don pushed a small homemade periscope though a space in the rough plank floorboards. Although the room was dark, the shiny iron safe could clearly be seen. Now all we had to do was wait for Thursday night, the night before payday for the detectives.

It was an excellent plan, and everyone did his part. Don, Neil and Thomas broke into the bank, set the charges on the safe and support beams and waited for our diversion. At precisely midnight Sam and I touched off the charges that we had set in the ammunition locker in the armory and ambled out towards the gate. Dressed in guards uniforms, no one gave us a second look.

The ammunition went off like fireworks on the Fourth of July. We could see detectives running desperately every which-way, some trying to put out the fires, others just trying to run away from the carnage. Many were cut down by shrapnel. I knew that here would be hell to pay later; the detectives wouldn't take this attack lightly. But that was the union's plan anyway: the strikers were starving; the strike needed to be brought to an end.

We quickly tore at our uniforms and smudged our faces in order to fit in with the rest of the panicked guards. As we got farther away, a company car suddenly roared up to us. It was Gerald, dressed in a guard's uniform. The car skidded to a halt in a cloud of dust.

"Get in the front," Gerald ordered tersely. He jumped over the seat and lay down on the back seat.

"Drive to the gate," he said. "Tell them that I'm a wounded man and that you're taking me to the hospital." He took a vial out of his pocket and smeared the contents on his face and neck. It was blood.

I did as he said, my urgency real. I rounded a bend amidst running figures, some fleeing the conflagration, some, firefighters and cops, running towards it. I honked the horn and shouted, braking suddenly here and there to avoid hitting anyone. As I approached the gate, I saw a group of guards, armed with shotguns and Tommy guns, checking the IDs of those attempting to leave. I got my forged ID out of my pocket and got ready to flash it. A man in plain clothes, a detective no doubt, approached me and signaled me to stop. I complied. He stepped up to the car with a lantern in one hand and a pistol in the other.

"Wounded man in the back," I said. "He's pretty bad – we need to get him to the hospital.

The detective shined the lantern in my face, then in Sam's, glancing at our IDs. Then he looked in the back.

"Jesus," he exclaimed at seeing Gerald's blood soaked face and tunic. "The bastards!"

"Stand down and clear the way!" He shouted to the guards. He motioned for me to move through the gate.

We sped down the road and made a sharp left towards the main highway. At a darkened section of road we let Gerald out.

"Safe travels lads," he said with a wave. "And good luck!"

"Hwyl fawr," I said in Welsh. Goodbye.

"Gwelwch yn uffern," Gerald said as he slipped away into the darkness. See you in hell.

I drove fast down the darkened road. I knew that, very soon, police cars and ambulances would be heading our way, heading up to the mines. Without a wounded man in the backseat, we had no reason for speeding away from the mines. We would look like what we were: a getaway car. We needed to get to the old mine access road where we would pick up Don and the boys and the payroll; then our story would be that we were heading towards the police station with three prisoners if stopped by the police. But, just as we were nearing the access road, our plan was thwarted.

Two police cars, their lights on and their sirens blaring, came racing up the road towards us. When the police saw our car head-

ing towards them they quickly formed a 'V' roadblock and got out of their cars, their guns drawn. I looked over at Sam and he nodded grimly. He drew his pistol and I stepped on the gas.

The collision with the police cars was so jarring that I rammed my head into the steering wheel. Sam cracked the windshield with his head and was almost thrown out. But, somehow, we cleared the roadblock. I sat back, wrestling with the careening car and ducking the shots fired at us from the police. I managed to keep the car on the road and we were soon out of range and speeding away. I wiped the blood from my gashed forehead with my sleeve and looked over at Sam. He had a wan look on his face and was stuffing a wadded piece of cloth into his jacket, trying vainly to staunch the flow of blood from a chest wound.

I turned onto a side road and traveled a good distance down it before pulling over. I was counting on having damaged the police cars enough to prevent them from pursuing us.

I had seen plenty of wounds during the war and knew when one was bad. This one was.

I ripped away Sam's shirt and soaked up as much of the blood as I could. To my horror, I saw pink bubbles coming out of the wound.

"Sucking chest wound," Sam said. "The bullet hit my lung, didn't it?"

"Just sit tight," I said. "I'll get you to a hospital. There'll be other wounded guards there. We'll have you treated and out of there in no time."

Sam laughed and coughed. A splotch of blood ran out of the corner of his mouth. He smiled wanly and I dabbed at the blood with a piece of cloth.

"You always were a bit of an optimist," Sam said weakly. He coughed a few more times and died, gripping my hand.

I had no time for emotion; I'd have the rest of my life for that. I drove down the road until I came to an embankment. Pulling Sam's body over to the driver's seat, I threw my uniform jacket and hat into the car. I stuffed a rag into the gas tank and lit it. After a short prayer, I pushed the car over the embankment and slipped into the surrounding woods. I could hear sirens blaring as the car burst into a huge orange fireball.

Using all of the skills I had learned during the war, I made my way north, away from the coalfields. Our contingency plan, in case we couldn't make the meeting with Don, the boys and the payroll, was for them to hide the payroll and then slip back into the mines and work until things cooled off. Eventually they would make their way north. Don was resourceful and the boys were tough. I knew that somehow they would make it. We wouldn't have the payroll, but we would have our lives. One day, when things calmed down, we'd return for the money.

"What?" I thought. I set the journal down in my lap, sat up and looked around at the darkened campsite. "What?" I wanted to shout. "So that's what this trip is really about," I thought. "This is why we went to so much trouble to get the journal. This is why the furtive meetings at night among the men. They were searching for buried treasure! Wait 'till I tell Neil, I thought. I put the journal away, crawled back to my sleeping bag and got a good night's rest for a change, dreaming of gold doubloons in a big sea chest. Arrr!

CHAPTER ELEVEN

"What?" Neil said when I told him. We were at the fish pond the next morning, fishing with Walter. Walter had just gone off to the toilet; which was the woods.

Neil had stopped retrieving his lure and was staring at me, his mouth agape.

"Yeah," I said, "That's exactly what I thought when I read it."

"They can't possibly think that there is a stolen payroll still out there somewhere, after all these years," Neil said.

"Do you have another explanation for all of this?" I said. "Why else would they have gone to so much trouble to get that stupid journal?"

"Screw it," Neil said. "Let's ask Walter."

Just then Walter came walking up from the woods, his satchel over his shoulder. He gave us both a funny look.

"Well?" He said as he sat his satchel down and pulled out his pipe. "The two of you look like the cat that ate the canary."

He waited for a response.

That was so like Walter. He liked to keep people hanging. "Sandbagging," my father called it. As far as I know, the phrase was a military term for building a defensive position and inviting your opponent to make the first move.

Walter was a consummate sandbagger. Neil and I stood there, kicking at the dirt and staring at the ground nervously. I got the feeling that he knew that I'd been reading the journal and that Neil and I had been discussing it. I got the feeling that he was enjoying watching us squirm.

"How far have you gotten," Walter asked abruptly. I looked up. He was staring directly at me, a mild expression on his face.

No use pretending now, I thought. The cat was out of the bag and, apparently, he'd eaten a canary.

"The part where Pop sets the car on fire with Sam's body in it," I said. "Where he leaves Don and the boys behind; along with the payroll."

Walter nodded, repacking his pipe thoughtfully.

"Pop made it to Littleport eventually and moved in with us. He told Gram that Don and the boys wanted to stay and work in the mines, now that the strike was over. She believed him.

"He worked for a while as a carpenter, but then the Depression hit and there was no more work."

"That's when Pop left," Neil said.

"That's when he left, but not why he left," Walter said.

We both looked at Walter with puzzled expressions.

"Pop didn't leave," Walter said. "Gram sent him away."

He fiddled with his pipe a little, staring off into the morning, the memory obviously painful to him.

"It was because of a photograph," he continued, his voice a little shaky. "It was in a magazine article about coal mining. There were several pictures of miners, mines, carts full of coal, and a memorial to miners who had died in mining accidents. You could see the names on the memorial if you looked closely. Among them were Don, Neil, Thomas and Sam Edwards. But there was a fifth: John Edwards— Pop."

"Why would Pop's name be on the memorial?" I asked.

"Gram didn't know at the time, and Pop wouldn't say. According to the journal, Gram never forgave him. She told him to leave, and he did. The last thing he said to me was: "Take care of the family, Walter." And he walked out the door. I didn't see him again 'till after the war."

The three of us stood there for a long while, saying nothing. Red-Winged Blackbirds trilled and insects buzzed. It was a beautiful morning. Finally, I broke the silence.

"I have questions," I said.

"Me too," Neil said. There was a little edge to his voice.

"All right," Walter said. "I guess you're both owed an explanation. We both nodded.

"Betty and Yvonne visited him regularly during his later years. They told me that he always carried his journal around with him, making notations in it and flipping through the pages, reading to himself.

"This journal holds the key to my past – and your future," he told them. "You must read it after I'm gone."

"We used to joke about it," Walter said. We all suspected that Pop had something to hide. After he remarried, he became a recluse; he rarely went out in public, according to Margaret, his wife. She told Betty and Yvonne that he used to peek out the windows all the time, watching any stranger who happened to be walking by. We thought that there might be a secret bank account, or a life insurance policy. Maybe a safety deposit box full of stolen money. The family legend grew until we all thought that there must be *something* to it.

"When Henry Motors announced that it was closing, we thought that maybe there was something in the journal that would help us keep the family together. We decided to get it, just to see."

"And you found a stolen payroll," Neil said. "And some dead uncles."

"Right," Walter said. "Gram never told anyone about the memorial and the names on it, so we never knew that they were dead. Everybody just thought that they were living in West Virginia, still working in the mines. Except for me," he added.

"Except for you?" I asked. How would he know? Did Gram tell him?

Walter read my mind. "Gram didn't tell me," he said. "As far as she's concerned, that's a secret that she'll take to the grave."

"Then how…" I started. Walter stopped me with a hand gesture.

"I went down there," he said. "I never told anyone, but I had to know. Don and Sam were my uncles, and Neil and Thomas were my brothers. The fact that we hadn't heard a thing from them or about them weighed heavy on me.

"I went to West Virginia and took a job in the mines. While I was there I asked around a little, but carefully. I knew that something had happened that sent Pop up to Littleport and I didn't want to attract any attention.

"There are many mine companies in West Virginia and each one runs a number of mines. I would work for one company for a time and then move on to another. What I hoped to find was my long–lost uncles and brothers. What I found instead was their names on a memorial at the site of the Fieldstone Mining Company. After that I drew my pay and came home. I never told anyone about it until we decided to get the journal."

"If you know the mine company that was robbed, why didn't you guys just drive down there and get the hidden payroll?" Neil asked. "Why this charade of a fishing trip?"

Walter gave Neil a hard look. It was clear that he had crossed a line. Walter was funny like that. He could laugh and joke around all day long, but he didn't take criticism well. He knocked the ashes out of his pipe and put it in his pocket. What he said next was in measured tones, like a teacher explaining a concept for the last time to a couple of under achieving students.

"We took our time to see if we were being followed," he said. "Fishing and camping are good ways to expose a tail. Sudden stops, random changes in direction and jaunts off to remote and isolated fishing spots would force anyone following us to tip his hand at some point. Don and the boys could have taken the payroll away from the mines and hidden it anywhere."

"But you think the payroll is somewhere at the Fieldstone Mining Company," I said.

"Right," Walter said. He relaxed his tone a little, satisfied that he had made his point. "Don had no car. There was no way that he could have gotten the payroll away from the mine. Besides, if he had, he would have fled north with the boys. No, the payroll is somewhere near the tunnel that they dug to get it; most likely in the tunnel itself. They would have had to pull the supports to hide the tunnel anyway, so why not bury the payroll in it?"

"Well, when do we go get it?" Neil asked, suddenly enthused. "If someone was following us, he would have shown himself by now."

Walter laughed. "Not so fast," he said. "The closer we get, the more likely it will be that someone who knows the legend of the missing payroll will be watching. But, more importantly, we don't know which mine they used for the tunnel. We can't be rooting around an old abandoned mining company for very long without being noticed. We need to get in and get out quickly."

"Pop doesn't say which mine?" I asked.

"No, he doesn't," Walter said. "That's where you come in."

"Me?" I said.

"You," Walter said.

CHAPTER TWELVE

Neil blanched when he saw Walter pull the journal from his satchel. Unlike me, he hadn't seen it since that rainy night last December. As Walter opened it, Neil started gagging. He had to walk away for a bit. I didn't like seeing it either, but I'd been reading it for the last few nights. I looked down at the passage Walter was pointing to. It was in Welsh.

"Bydd Thomas yn Dngos I chi y fford," it read. I looked to Walter for explanation.

"Thomas will show you the way," he said.

I was taken aback. "Thomas will show you the way?" I thought. "How would I know? I wasn't even born when the payroll was stolen and only a kid when my Grandfather died. I looked to Walter for answer to my unspoken question.

"It's pretty clear," Walter said. "Pop wrote that you would show us the way. You're the only living Thomas in the family."

"You think that there's a clue in the journal?" I asked." Something that I would find that you guys couldn't?"

"I know it sounds strange," Walter said. "But that's the only thing we have to go on. Somehow you have to figure out which mine was used for the tunnel. I've got a map. There are several, clustered around the Company offices. They're the first mines, numbers 1 – 6. All of them had been mined out by the time of the robbery. It would take us way too long to try each one."

"Why didn't you come to me sooner?" I asked.

"Your fathers didn't want you involved in any of this," Walter said. "We took you two with us that night to serve as lookouts. You left your posts and saw what you saw.

"Pretending secrecy was the only way we could get you to read the journal," he said with a laugh. "Answer me honestly, would you have read the journal if we had asked you to?"

I looked over at Neil, who was still standing off at a distance, looking rather pale. I shook my head 'no.'

"Curiosity is a powerful motivator," Walter said.

"Right," I said. "But it did kill the cat."

"That it did," Walter said with a laugh. He put the journal away, much to Neil's relief.

"Who would be looking for the payroll, after all these years?" Neil asked.

"The Company detectives," I said. "They knew that the payroll had been stolen. The Company would want the money back."

"And the Blodwyns," Walter said. "They knew that Pop and Sam had robbed the Company bank."

"How?" I said.

"The second explosion," Walter said. "It wasn't part of the planned attack on the armory. They wouldn't stand for two of their own going rogue."

"Jesus," I said. "Vengeance?"

Walter nodded. "Maybe nobody has been waiting and watching, but we have to *assume* that someone has and take precautions."

I could see that Neil was processing the news, working his jaw. Walter puffed patiently on his pipe.

"So," Neil said in measured tones. "When Pop got to Litteport, he thought that he was being watched. That's why he didn't go back to the mines."

"Right," Walter said. "Later in the journal he mentions seeing some stranger or another showing up in town and asking questions. He was suspicious of everyone. He would slip away, sometimes for months at a time, telling no one where he was going."

"The Blodwyns were resourceful men," Walter said. "And so were the detectives. I wouldn't be surprised if there weren't several men on Pop's trail, Blodwyns and detectives."

"That explains a lot," Neil said. "But we don't have to worry; those men have to be too old to do anything now."

"Don't underestimate their persistence," Walter said. "And don't think that they might not have told some younger ones; maybe their own sons and nephews. Pop warned of that in the margin notes."

We stood quietly for a while, each lost in his thoughts. Finally, Walter broke the silence.

"Pop left us with nothing," he said wistfully. "Mom never complained, but I could see how she struggled to keep us fed and clothed. She is a proud woman who wouldn't accept charity or tolerate pity." He laughed, remembering. "We lived on stewed tomatoes for a month once," he added.

"I'm all in," I said. "Whatever you need."

"Me too," Neil said.

"Good," Walter said. He emptied the ashes from his pipe, re-packed it and lit it. Finally he spoke in a soft voice that trembled just a little bit.

"Sam, Don, Neil and Thomas are buried in a mass grave in West Virginia. They died because Pop's plan to rob the company went bad. They stayed behind, waiting for him, while he was busy hiding out. That's why I hate him. It's not because he left Mom, she was glad that he left. But he left Don and the boys there, and they were killed because of it."

Walter went back to fishing, struggling with his emotions and his memories. Finally, when he turned back around, he was all business.

"We made reservations at campsites across the state, all the way to Wilkes-Barre, where Pop lived for a while, working in the mines there. If someone is following us, we'll get him to head there; throw him off at least long enough for us to get to the mine in West Virginia and find the payroll."

"So we're not going to Harrisburg," Neil said.

"That's right," Walter said. "We've got reservations at a campsite in West Virginia under a phony name. We'll spend a couple of days there and then, if no one suspicious shows up, we'll head to the mine."

Later that day, after lunch, my father loudly announced that we were packing up and heading towards Harrisburg. I thought it was strange that he would make the announcement so loudly until I saw an old couple who happened to be camped nearby. They were cooking hot dogs over a fire and idly watching us. Their little dog was yapping at us as we went about our business.

As I rolled my sleeping bag up and stuffed my backpack, I noticed how efficiently the men were about breaking camp. Equipment was packed into army surplus bins and taken to the trailer, tents were dropped and folded and packed away. Neil, Joe, Calvin, Donnie and I were put to the task of policing the area. "Pick up anything that isn't nailed down or painted," my father told us. Soon, the site was as clean and empty as the day we had arrived.

It occurred to me that the whole trip had been conducted like a military mission. Every stage of the operation had been planned and carried out with military precision. They were all veterans and to them the mission was everything. Whatever the objective, or reason for it, the mission had to be carried out to a 'T.' The possibility that the Company had recovered the payroll, or that a couple of enterprising detectives had found it and kept it for themselves, or that Don and the boys had failed to get the payroll out of the bank in the first place was immaterial. It was the mission that mattered.

I began to see the fishing trip and the search for the payroll for what it really was: one last adventure for the Sleeper Street Gang.

CHAPTER THIRTEEN

The cars left the campsite caravan-style, my father's car in the lead. I was riding with Neil and Walter again. We followed the other cars to the interstate and traveled for an hour or so.

"Prepare to turn off at the next exit," Walter told Neil.

"Roger," Neil said. I wondered if he was joking or had picked up some military jargon from a movie.

"Keep a keen eye behind us Thomas," Walter said. "See if a car follows us."

I did, but no one followed. We pulled up to a gas pump at an Esso station. Walter told the attendant to fill it up.

"Can we get to the next exit from here?" Walter asked the man as he paid him. "We need a break from the Interstate."

"I know what you mean," the man said. "I prefer blue highways myself."

He pointed to the road adjacent to the filling station. "Turn left on that road, drive to the next light and turn left again. Stay on that road 'til you get to the exit, about twenty miles."

"Thanks," Walter said with a smile.

Neil pulled out and followed the attendant's directions. He had a puzzled look on his face.

"In about three miles, turn right onto Seymore Road," Walter said. "I'll tell you when we get close. Thomas, you keep looking out the back."

We found Seymore Road exactly where Walter had said it would be.

We turned onto it, drove south for an hour and then turned west.

"Each car is taking a different route to the campsite," Walter explained. "We'll all arrive at different times; that way we should be able to see anyone who is trying to follow us. Doc is already there," he added.

The whole ride I had the journal in my lap, flipping through the pages and looking for some clue as to which mine had been used for the tunnel. I found nothing.

"Why not start digging around the Company bank? Neil suggested. "We'd eventually find the tunnel."

"We thought of that," Walter said. "But Don was supposed to set a charge to obliterate any trace of a tunnel. We'd have to dig in an ever-widening circle to find it. It could take days. Besides that the building's out in the open; someone might notice all the activity and investigate. We don't want some rich, distant relative of the owners of the company to get the payroll."

"How were you so certain that there would be something to find in the first place?" Neil asked. "Before you got the journal."

"We didn't," Walter said. "As I said before, Pop always told the girls how sorry he was about what happened. He told them that, when he died, they should look through his journal, that it would help them understand why he had done what he did. He told them that there was information in it that might help the family. Said it would help pay us back for what he'd done."

"It became like a holy grail for all of us. We guessed at what it might contain: secret bank accounts, hidden caches of money, buried treasure. We knew that Pop had been up to something down in the coal-field, something that had sent him running for cover. There was someone he was trying to hide from – and something he was trying to hide."

"But we didn't get the journal when he died," Walter said. "Margaret— his new wife— kept it. None of us boys went to the funeral, but Betty and Yvonne did. We wanted them to get the journal, but they were unable. You know the rest."

Walter grew quiet, smoking his pipe thoughtfully. Neil stared down the road, lost in his own thoughts. I fell asleep.

As I slept I dreamt. The dream was a vivid recollection that night last December— the night that haunts my dreams to this day.

It was a cold, rainy night and the men were sitting around the kitchen table at our house, smoking, drinking beer and playing cards. The women were going Christmas shopping with the younger kids. My father and Frank wanted Neal and me to go with them, but we managed to weasel out of it. Our mothers thought that we were old enough to stay with the men. Besides, there wouldn't be room for us in the cars anyway.

The women and kids had no sooner left than the men stood up and put on their coats and hats.

"You boys might as well come with us," my father finally said. "We could use a couple of lookouts."

Lookouts? I thought. Lookouts for what?

As we waited to pile into the cars, my Uncle Charlie took the two of us aside.

"Can you two keep a secret?" he asked.

We both nodded.

"What we're about to do can't ever be mentioned to anybody," he said, a serious look on his face. "Understand?"

We both nodded again.

"You stay where we put you. Don't come down to where we are. Don't even look."

We agreed, both of us exchanging puzzled looks.

As we drove, a small caravan of three cars, the atmosphere was as grim as was the rainy night. We took back roads, the windshield wipers beating away the rain that made navigating the narrow lanes difficult.

Finally we crossed a rickety wooden bridge over a railroad track and then turned onto a muddy two-wheel lane. We stopped at a rusty gate that read Ridgewood Cemetery. There was a chain and lock on the iron bars.

Doc walked up to the gate, a cigarette dangling from his mouth. He had a big pair of bolt cutters in his hand. He looked around once in an exaggerated manner, then snipped the chain and opened the gate.

We drove through the gate with our lights out and parked in a secluded area.

"Tom, I want you to keep watch on the gate we just came through," my father said. "If you see lights, give a long whistle – and hide. Stay put, we'll come get you later"

I nodded and pulled my coat collar up around my neck.

"Neil, you follow this road 'till you can see the main gate," Frank said. "You see lights, give a shout." Neil couldn't whistle.

I was shocked when the men unpacked picks and shovels from the car trunks. With no explanation, they walked down the winding lane, slipping and sliding on the slick mud. The beams of their flashlights danced over the headstones of the graveyard, giving the stone monuments a strange life. They seemed to be searching for something; I could hear their loud whispers in the distance.

"Over here," one of them said. "I think it's over here."

"No, that's not it," another voice said. "It's farther down the lane."

"I thought you knew where it was, you moron," a third voice said.

"Shut up, it's not like I come here often to pay my respects!"

At that comment there was nervous laughter.

"You mean you didn't bring flowers?" This time the voice was full and I recognized it as my Uncle Charlie's.

"Keep it quiet," I heard my father say. "You'll wake the dead!"

More laughter ensued, this time a little louder. It seemed that the men were getting bolder. All I could do was stare down the hill at the dancing flashlights and wonder what in the world the men were doing in a graveyard at night with picks and shovels. There was only one thing that I could think of, and it wasn't a pleasant thought.

Finally I heard someone say: "Here it is!" The beams of the flashlights converged on a single headstone, it gleamed bone-white in the light.

"That's it!" Someone exclaimed. There was a collective murmur of approval and the distinct clink of bottles: a toast?

"Who wants to go first?" I heard my father say. He sounded nervous.

"I will," Walter said. There was the distinctive gravelly chink of a shovel breaking ground, it was soon followed by others. I remembered my promise and turned to look towards the road, but there was nothing but darkness, rain and headstones. No one traveled the Ridgewood road at this time of night.

"I hit something!" Doc exclaimed as I heard a shovel strike something hard.

"Get down in there and clear away the dirt," Charlie ordered.

"You get in there and clear away the dirt," Doc countered.

"Ah, what the hell," Pete said. "Get out of the way and help me down."

I could hear the scraping of metal on wood as someone cleared the dirt from the top of a coffin. Drawn to the clustered lights like a moth to a flame, I found myself abandoning my post and drifting towards the open grave. As I got closer, I strained to read the name on the headstone. I blinked my eyes and rubbed them in disbelief. The name read: John Edwards. Pop, I thought. They were digging up my grandfather's grave.

I stepped back and shook my head to clear it. Why were they digging up Pop's grave, I wondered. My heart pounded at the thought. I knew that

I should go back to my lookout post, but I couldn't resist the lure of the eerie action taking place in front of me. I moved closer.

"Don't try to get the whole lid off," Charlie said to Pete. I craned my neck and saw Pete deep in the grave, his hair wet with sweat and the rain. He looked up.

"Go ahead," Uncle Frank said. "Give it hell."

Pete raised his shoulders and brought the edge of the shovel down hard onto the pine coffin lid. It cracked slightly. He did it again, and again, until there was a sizeable hole in the general chest area.

"Pull those edges up," Charlie ordered. He put a handkerchief over his nose. "Jesus, that stench!"

"I haven't smelled that since the War," Pete said. "Bodies rotted quickly in the tropics."

I heard someone vomiting. A light was put on him. It was Neil.

"Neil!" Frank said. "What the hell are you doing here? You're supposed to be on the hill, keeping watch! Get back up there!"

"Sorry," Neil said, still gagging. He began moving back up the hill, doubled over.

The wind was blowing away from me and I hadn't yet smelled what the others had. I continued to watch, unnoticed for the moment.

There was a wrenching sound as Pete lifted at the plywood edges of the hole he had made in the coffin. Suddenly the entire upper half of the lid came up, sending Pete backwards into a sitting position. There, in the eerie light of the flashlights, suffused by the rain, lay the corpse of my Grandfather.

His wizened skin was drawn back, exposing his teeth in a macabre grin. His eyes, glued shut, were deeply sunken, leaving two black holes that seemed somehow to stare, sightless, into the depths of my soul. I closed my eyes, but the image wouldn't leave me.

"He's looked better," Pete commented. There was a murmur of nervous laughter. Just then the wind shifted and I was hit in the face with the powerful and cloying stench of death. It stung my eyes and robbed my breath. I staggered backwards, vomiting all over myself as I fell onto the slick ground. I rolled over and came up onto my knees, retching violently. The beam of a flashlight blinded me.

"Jesus," someone said. "Tommy's here too!"

"Goddamn it!" I heard my father say. "What the hell are you doing down here Thomas? I told you to stay up on the hill! Someone help him up. Pete, grab that goddamn book and get out of there! We need to get this hole filled in!"

Someone grabbed my elbow and helped me to my feet. It was my Uncle Charlie.

"Don't think about it," He said helpfully. "You shouldn't have come down here. We never should have brought you boys along at all!"

I nodded weakly and let him help me up the lane. By the time we got to the cars I had recovered enough to stand up on my own. "I've never smelled anything like that in my life," I said.

Charlie put his arm around my shoulders. "Just pray that you never do again. Now clean yourself up," he said. He handed me his handkerchief.

CHAPTER FOURTEEN

I woke in the car with a start. I blinked and looked around: we were driving down a bumpy back road and the bouncing had brought me out of my tortured slumber.

"You OK Thomas?" Walter asked.

"Yeah," I nodded. "Bad dream."

"Again?

I nodded, wiping my brow.

"I get 'em too," Neil said. "All the time."

Walter shook his head sadly, lighting his pipe. He blew a stream of smoke out the open window. "Never should have brought you boys along," he said. He suddenly turned and smiled his teasing smile. "Of course, you weren't supposed to come down there in the first place. You were supposed to be lookouts! If there'd been Japs or Germans around, we'd have all been in the ground!"

At that he reached down and grabbed my leg in a horse bite. I jumped and bumped my head, just like the other day. You'd think I'd learn.

After Neil got through laughing at me, he turned to Walter.

"Maybe we shouldn't have been at the grave, but we were," he said, a grim look on his face. "That makes us part of it, like or not."

"Right," Walter said. "You always have been; we just couldn't tell you."

I thought about the first night that I picked up the journal and shuddered. It was as unforgettable as the night in the graveyard.

Neil continued following Walter's circuitous route south and I continued trying to find the elusive clue. But I was only nine when Pop died, and I only saw him once a year at that; at Christmastime. How could he possibly have given me the location of a mine somewhere in West Virginia? He was a melancholy old man when I knew him, always reciting poems about his homeland in Wales.

Then, like clouds parting to reveal a bright spring day, it hit me.

I put the journal down and looked at Walter. "Do you still have that book of poems by Thomas Galvin?" I said.

Walter looked at me quizzically. "Thomas Galvin?" He said. "Do you think he is the Thomas that will show us the way?"

"You remember his famous poem, "The Way?" I said.

"Of course," Walter said. "Pop used to read it to me when I was a boy. Before he left."

He opened his satchel, pulled out the tattered book and began flipping through the pages.

"He gave me the book shortly before he died," Walter explained. "I had stopped by to visit him, knowing that his end was near. I told him that I had been to West Virginia; that I had seen the names on the memorial. He gave me this book and told me to keep it and read it in his memory. It was the only thing he ever gave me."

"I guess Pop was convinced that he was being followed," Neal said. "Even if someone got ahold of the journal, he wouldn't be able to find the key clues."

"He was a Blodwyn," Walter said. "The Blodwyns live by a code. Pop and Sam violated that code by going rogue. They didn't have permission to rob the payroll. There's a good chance that they sent a man after them. It's not about the money, it's about the code."

"Here," he said, stopping on a particular page.

"The Way," he said, announcing the title. "Let's see if he's left us any clues."

As he began reading, Walter's normally strong voice softened, catching now and then with emotion:

> "*Then when I was only six I wandered off one day*
> *Behind an ancient fieldstone fence, crumbled now with age*
> *Beyond the wall a foreign land, filled with bugs and birds*
> *They buzzed and whirred and questioned me, a harmony in thirds*
> *The barn was old and it loomed large, set in a copse of trees*
> *It beckoned with its creaking doors and begged for me to see*
> *A hundred shiny penny rounds, scattered on the floor*
> *Their colors lit by un-caulked walls, a hidden royal hoard*
> *I pocketed the trove of jewels and wandered on my way*
> *Traveling from room to room and using up the day*
> *I found a maze of darkened rooms where hazy spirits dwell*
> *Drawing me in deeper 'till my way was lost as well*
> *I rued the treasure stolen now, growing large and heavy*
> *Slowing down my progress, and making me unsteady*
> *Feeling judged and sentenced, I dumped my stolen gems*
> *I ran a darkened hallway, muttering amends*
> *Calling on the spirits to loose their cloying hold*
> *And free me from this prison, so dark and dank and old*
> *Then stumbling down a corridor, chased by fear and guilt*
> *I burst through a cluttered room, filled with trash and silt*
> *Then on the left a flicker, a tiny beam of light*
> *Offering me salvation, just before the night*
> *My path was clear, I knew it now, my sentence had been stayed*
> *Forgiven from my mortal sin, I'd been shown The Way*
> *- Thomas Galvin*

Walter set the book down for a moment, staring out the window. Then he turned and addressed us.

"Pop underlined passages throughout the book," Walter said. "And he wrote plenty in the margins. Here he underlined 'six', 'fieldstone' and 'on the left.' Next to 'on the left' he wrote: '43 feet."

He smiled. "Well, there it is," he said. "Thomas has shown us the way."

CHAPTER FIFTEEN

The two-track dirt lane to the next campground wound up a thickly forested hill. As we approached the hilltop, I could hear loud music and the babble of voices. The sound reminded me of a college frat party that a couple of my friends and I had snuck into earlier in the spring. A large sign proclaimed "New River Whitewater Campground." Rustic wooden cabins were nestled in the surrounding woods. There were kayaks and paddles leaning against the walls. Life vests, helmets and wet suits were scattered everywhere. Several of the cabins sported tie dyed flags with peace symbols and Grateful Dead logos. Old worn-out station wagons, VW vans, pick-up trucks and jeeps were parked at the cabins. Everywhere fit looking people milled about carrying coolers and six packs. They had made their last whitewater run of the day and now it was time to party.

We pulled up to the administration building which was a converted cabin. A sign above the door said: "You Are Entering Whitewater Heaven." Piles of life jackets, helmets, paddles and wet suits crowded the porch under a sign that said: "Rentals". We walked in.

A man behind the counter named Steve smiled and said hello. He was deeply tanned and had that lean, weathered look that people who spend their lives in the sun and wind and rain have; surfers, sailors and river rats. He looked older than most of the other kayakers, but it was impossible to gauge his age.

"A friend of ours was supposed to reserve some campsites," Walter said.

"Big guy with a pretty girl?' Steve said.

Walter nodded. "His name is Doc," he said.

"Right," Steve said. "Doc and Karen. They're down at the tiki bar right now."

Steve opened a tattered registration book and ran his finger down a column. "Sites 52, 53 and 54," he said. "Right on top of the hill. Best view in the camp."

Walter took out his wallet.

Steve raised his hand. "Already taken care of," he said with a smile. "Doc said to meet him at the bar before you get situated."

We walked out of the building and looked across the grounds. There, at the far end of the compound, was the source of the loud music. It was called "Eskimo Joes Rock and Roll Bar." An old weathered kayak hung above it.

As we walked I could see Doc sitting at the Tiki bar just to the left of the main entrance. Although there was a large crowd, Doc was easy to spot: he was a head taller than everyone else, even while sitting down. Karen was nowhere to be seen.

"Ladies and gentlemen!" Doc announced. "It is my esteemed honor to present three of the finest men who ever walked the Earth!" A cheer went up from the patrons. Uh oh, I thought. Doc must be buying.

"Barkeep!" Doc shouted, slapping a large bill down on the bar. "Three flagons of your best ale for my compadres!"

The bartender, a tall read-headed man they called "Big John," looked at me a little dubiously. "Is he old enough?" He asked Doc.

"Hell yeah," Doc said with a grin. "He's my nephew – I'll vouch for him."

"Good enough for me," Big John said. "What'll it be?"

I quickly glanced at the beer bottle in Doc's hand. "Iron City," I said. Neil ordered the same and Walter ordered a Coke – he didn't drink.

Big John brought the drinks. Doc slapped another bill on the bar and circled his hand in the air – the signal for another round. Another cheer went up. Doc was getting right popular, I thought.

Doc clinked bottles with us. "Here's to West Virginia," He said. "May it prove to be worth the trip!"

"Cheers," we all said in unison.

Walter and Neil finished their drinks and headed up to the campsite. I decided to stay behind with Doc, ostensibly to wait for the rest of the group to show up. The real reason, well, she hadn't shown up yet.

I looked around at all the kayakers and rafters standing near the cabana. Some were, like me, novices; tourists who had come to take their first raft trip down a real whitewater river. They grinned a little too much, filling themselves with false courage and beer. Others – the young fit and tanned ones – had the look of college kids staying for the summer, maybe picking up tuition or a little beer money guiding. Then there were the weather-beaten permanents – they'd come for a season and stayed. They might work as guides, groundskeepers, bartenders, or in one of the rental shops. But everyone seemed to have one thing in common: an adrenaline glint in their eyes. I'd seen it before – in skiers, moto-cross riders and sky-divers— they liked the rush that came with fast and dangerous sports.

Doc, as usual, was the center of attention at the Tiki bar, and not just because he was buying drinks: people in general and girls in particular were drawn to his easy smile and carefree attitude. My father said it came from his experience in Korea. "When you've seen the kinds of things a combat medic has, everyday worries don't matter," he told me once. "Doc is one of those people who just walks the Earth, happy to be alive."

My mother had a different opinion. "Doc has an eye for the ladies," she said. "He can't help himself— and neither can they. The Grandfather Walpole was like that— you've got cousins all over the county from his adventures, I expect."

The funny thing was that other men didn't seem bothered by Doc's popularity with the women – he wasn't trying to steal anyone's girlfriend, he was just being friendly. I guess that's how he ended up with a girl on each knee that day at Eskimo Joe's.

The girls were named Bonnie and Sue. Bonnie was tall, with blonde hair and a dimple in her chin. Sue was shorter and had light brown hair, tied back. They were both very tan and very fit. On Doc's lap they looked small.

"Hey Tommy," Doc said, gesturing towards me. "Come meet my new friends."

I walked over and said "hi" – a little nervously. I wasn't used to meeting girls in a bar. They jumped off of Doc's lap and began lightly teasing me, tousling my hair and playing with the buttons on my shirt. I guess they picked up on my nervousness and it worked: my face turned red and I stammered out nervous answers to their quick questions about what my name was and where I was from and how long was I staying and did I like whitewater paddling. Doc seemed to be enjoying himself immensely.

"Watch out Tommy," he said. "These girls will burn you down."

Everyone laughed at his comment.

"You girls get your hands off him," I heard someone say. It was Karen. She had walked up to the group with a kayak paddle in her hand and a guide named Johnny at her side. She was wearing a short-sleeved wetsuit and her hair was wet.

She looked around at the laughing group. "This is Neptune, I found him in a river with a fish skewered on a trident. I brought him home and Doc said I could keep him."

"Aw," Sue said. "Can I borrow him?"

"No way!" Karen said.

Johnny stepped up to the bar. He was wearing weathered surfer shorts and a snaggle-toothed grin. Big John handed him a beer. He turned and smiled.

"Any friend of Doc's is a friend of mine," he said. He shook my hand. "I'm Johnny, but everyone calls me Johnny."

"Nice to meet you Johnny," I said. I could feel power in his grip, but he didn't push it.

"Johnny's one of the guides on our raft trip tomorrow," Karen explained. She hopped up onto Doc's lap and stole a sip from his beer. "He just gave me a private lesson."

"How's she doing?" Doc asked.

"Good," Johnny said. "Quick learner." He turned to me.

"You kayak?" he asked.

I shook my head. "Canoed a little," I said, immediately sorry that I had. A canoe is to a river kayak as a grocery-getting station wagon is to a Porsche. At least I hadn't said "in the Scouts."

"Cool," Johnny said. "You'll like kayaks, they're very…liberating. It's like you're flying in the foam."

I nodded and sipped my beer.

"I just took Karen on a few runs," he continued. "We're right on a river bend here. You take your kayak down the east trail and run the river around the bend – about a mile and a half. There's five sets of class three and two sets of class four. Rapids, I mean. You come back up the west trail and do it all over again if you want."

"I think we're taking rafts tomorrow," I said.

"Yeah," Johnny said. "Karen told me. I'll be one of the guides. But if you stick around for a few more days, I'll teach you how to kayak. It's pretty simple, really."

"Cool," I said.

Bonnie— Johnny's girlfriend, it turned out, came over with a tray of shot glasses filled with a golden amber fluid, a salt shaker and a bowl of cut limes. "Tequila?" She said to the group with a grin. Everyone took a shot glass and a lime. I took one too.

"Know how to do it?" Karen asked me.

I shook my head no.

She licked the skin between her thumb and forefinger and sprinkled salt on it. She licked the salt, put the shot glass to her lower lip and tilted her head back, downing the tequila in a single gulp. She immediately bit into the lime wedge.

"Lick it, slam it, suck it!" Someone shouted. Everyone cheered and did the same.

The salt seemed to open up my taste buds. I was expecting the tequila to taste like turpentine but it was surprisingly smooth after the salt. The lime made me wince and took away any unpleasant after-taste. As it went down, I felt a sudden warm sensation rising up through my body. It made me shudder and caused my eyes to water.

"First shot of Cuervo?" Johnny asked, noticing my reaction.

I nodded.

"It won't be your last," he said with a grin.

Doc handed me another beer. "Take it easy with that stuff," he said. "Your mother would kill me if she found out I let you get drunk."

"Don't worry, I'm fine!" I said. The tequila had somehow energized me. I plunged into the crowd of my new friends, ready for anything.

I woke in the back of the station wagon, a horrible taste in my mouth, a screaming headache and the stench of vomit in my nostrils. The dome light blinded me.

"Get up, you sot!" Neil commanded from the open door. "Jesus, you better get cleaned up before your father wakes up!"

I sat up and stared at him, blinking to bring my eyes into focus. "What happened?" I managed.

Neil handed me a cup of lukewarm black coffee and a couple of aspirin. "What happened was that your friends brought you back last night, singing at the top of your lungs."

Oh yeah, I thought; the rugby songs. Johnny and some of his friends played rugby for the Morgantown Maulers. They thought I'd make a good Lock, whatever that was.

"You're lucky your father had to park down here," Neil said. "You'd have woken the whole camp if the car was closer."

I took the aspirin tablets and washed them down with the coffee.

"Are you going on the raft trip?" Neil asked.

"Yeah," I said, shaking my head to clear it

"Well, if you're going with us, you'd better get ready."

"Going with you?"

"I talked the guides into letting the four of us – you, me, Calvin and Joey— take a four man raft on our own. But we have to get down to the river an hour early for training."

"Calvin?" I said dubiously.

"We need four," Neil said. He hesitated for a moment. "He'll be OK. We'll put him up front."

"Yeah," I said. "He'll be OK up front." I banished my negative thoughts and suddenly felt a surge of excitement. A four-man raft! Everybody else would be riding in the big rafts paddled by guides, totally safe. We'd be on our own, free to choose our own path through the rapids! I jumped up, cleaned up, grabbed my swim-suit and headed over to Neil's car. Calvin was sitting shotgun.

"Where you been?" He asked me. "We been waiting."

"Move," I said.

"I ain't movin'" Calvin said. "I got shotgun."

"You have to move, or I can't get in," I said, indicating the back seat. I was too tired to fight with Calvin. Besides, it was where I usually sat anyway. Joe was sitting there behind Neil, smoking a cigarette.

"Let him in, stupid," he said to Calvin. He blew a stream of smoke at him.

Calvin leaned forward and made enough room for me to squeeze through. But as I did, he shoved back on the seat, trapping me briefly. I shoved forward, causing Calvin to bump his face on the dashboard.

"Hey! What're ya doin?" Calvin exclaimed, holding his nose

"You two idiots break my seat and I'll kick both of your asses," Neil said. Neil was very protective of his car.

As we pulled into the staging area parking lot, I could see a beehive of activity by the docks that jutted out into the eddy. People were gathering in three general areas: kayaks, four-man rafts and the big twelve-man boats. I noticed Karen at the kayak site. She waved. We selected full and partial wet suits, helmets, lifejackets and paddles and drifted over to the area where the instruction was to take place. To my surprise, our head guide indeed was Johnny. He looked amazingly chipper for someone who had partied so late into the night. He flashed his snaggle-toothed grin at me and jumped up onto a granite boulder with a flat top.

"Gather round crazies!" He announced. Everyone moved closer, although his voice carried well in the crisp morning air.

"You wear this and this…and you don't lose this!" He said, tapping his helmet, pulling at his lifejacket and holding his paddle high in the air. Everyone did the same, except for Calvin, who was working on his pipe again.

"What do you have in that pipe, Dude?" Johnny asked. "Anything good?"

There was a smattering of laughter from the group as Calvin looked up. "Huh?" he said.

"Never mind," Johnny said. He went over safety basics first: "Keep the bow of your raft pointed downstream. Aim for the orange ropes that hang over the tricky sections. Listen to your guides; we'll be kayaking near you, and there'll be other guides up on the bank. If you get turned around, just ride it out – don't try to turn back around, that's where you'll get in trouble. If you fall out sit facing forward, your legs extended and your arms crossed over your chest. Again, just ride it out 'till you get to the next eddy." Johnny sat down to demonstrate the proper form. "Like this. Just watch out for Castration Rock."

Everyone laughed, except for Calvin. "What's that?" he asked Neil in a whisper.

"Jesus you're lame Calvin!" Neil said swatting him on the back of the head. "It's where a rock rips your balls off."

"Jesus!" Calvin said. "Where is it at?"

"Ahhh!" Neil exclaimed in mock desperation. People who had heard the exchange began snickering and shaking their heads.

Johnny laughed. "We'll let you know just before you hit it."

Calvin tried to ignore the laughing by fiddling with his pipe.

"One more thing; and this is serious," Johnny said after the laughter died down. "The guys in the back— the stern— steer the raft in open water, but in a tight spot in whitewater, it's the guys in front— the bow— that are responsible for getting around rocks and away from the rock walls. If you hit an obstruction, it'll turn you around— or even flip you. And if the obstruction is big enough, you can get pinned. You – we – don't want that. The bowman closest has to push off immediately and the guys in the stern have to bring the ass-end over in the opposite direction of the obstruction. Capice?"

We all nodded.

"You'll have plenty of time to practice in the first section. It's only class two. But later, in the class threes and fours farther downstream, that skill will be important."

Johnny looked the group over critically. "Look, if things get weird, hang tight. Don't panic. We'll be there to get you." He waited a few moments for his words to sink in. "Any questions?"

No one said anything. Neil elbowed Calvin. "Ask him about castration rock," he whispered.

"Shuddup," Calvin said.

• • • • • • • • • • • • • • • • •

As we carried our raft down to the eddy, I noticed that the kayakers were already in the water, circling around, working on their paddling skills and practicing their rolls. I stood mesmerized as the guides played: they rolled, turned and stood their kayaks on their tails. They dropped their paddles and rolled their kayaks with their hands.

We dragged our ponderous balloon boat down to the water and paddled out into the Eddy. Neil and I were in the stern, with him on the left. Calvin and Joe were in the bow, with Calvin on the left. Johnny paddled over and began coaching us.

"When you come up to a rock, you two guys in the stern have to decide which way to go around it. If you're on a bend, pick inside. If you're going left, yell out 'left!' to the bowmen. The bowman on the right paddles hard and the bowman on the left steers left by sticking his paddle into the water at an angle." He showed us. "It's called a cross bow draw. In the stern, the guy on the right paddles and the guy on the left rudders or uses a forward sweep." Again, he showed us. "You do the reverse if you're going to the right. Remember, if you come up against a rock wall, the guy closest has to push off, quick."

We all nodded and began circling the eddy, practicing our techniques. When we got it right, the boat responded surprisingly well. When we got it wrong the boat floundered helplessly.

"See those guys over there?" Johnny said, pointing at another raft. "They've done this a few times. Follow them and do what they do."

The kayaks left first. They made one last circle and then, with much whooping, cheering and paddle banging, filed out of the eddy and into the first set of rapids. The four-man rafts were next.

We waited in line as the first few boats paddled out into the current. I felt the nervous anticipation in the pit of my stomach that came when I was on the starting block at a swim meet. I gripped my paddle tightly and looked over at Neil. He tried to affect a nonchalant smile, but I could see that his knuckles were as white as mine. Calvin turned around and with a nervous grin said: "Let's go!"

We paddled madly out into the rushing current. The river was deeper and more powerful than it seemed from the eddy and it quickly had us in its grip. Try as we might, we couldn't get the bow pointed downstream. First we went sideways and then backwards.

"Guys on the left, paddle backwards! Guys on the right paddle forwards," a voice commanded over the roar of the river. It was Johnny and he was paddling back up through the current. We did as he said and suddenly found our boat pointed in the right direction. "That's better! Keep it pointed downstream!" He yelled as he continued upstream, coaching the other boats.

After a few bumps and turnarounds, we managed to keep the boat relatively straight. Lucky for us, the first rapids was only class II: fast water with a few riffles and no major obstructions. By the time we got to the next eddy, we felt like we almost had the hang of it.

"The next set of rapids is a little stronger," a guide announced from a rock at the edge of the eddy. "Still mostly class II, but a few twists and turns. It gets pretty wide for a while, and there's a small eddy on the left where you can take a break for a couple minutes. Watch for the guides on the rocks and banks and do as they say." We all gave a little cheer and filed out into the current again.

The guide was right; there were several tricky sections that put our newfound skills to the test. On one long run, we got turned around and had to ride it out going backwards. Fortunately it ended at the little eddy that the guide had mentioned. We paddled into the shallows and beached the boat onto the shore in order to bail out some of the water that had splashed into the boat.

"Lookit that," Calvin said, pointing downstream. "Somebody lost their kayak."

I looked and saw a yellow kayak upside down, pinned against two boulders. It was jerking and shaking, as if trying to escape the hold that the current had on it. I realized immediately that there was a paddler trapped in it. I took off on a dead sprint across the rocky shallows between me and the trapped kayaker. Out of the corner of my eye I could see that Neil was running next to me. We grabbed the cowling of the kayak's seat, pulling with all our might. At first it didn't budge at all; the current was too strong. I looked at Neil and he nodded. We gave it one more desperate effort. Suddenly, surprisingly, I felt the kayak pop upright. We both fell backwards into sitting positions, still holding the kayak upright. The kayaker appeared unconscious, maybe dead. Blood streamed down his face from a gash in his forehead and his head and body lolled about like a rag doll.

"Hold him up!" A voice shouted. "Don't let him roll again!"

Johnny and two other guides had paddled up to us and jumped out of their kayaks. They gave the limp kayaker a serious look. "I think he's still alive," Johnny said. There was an unsettling note of hopefulness to his voice.

They gently grabbed the man under his armpits and pulled him out of his boat. As they did he came to with a gasp. He puked a fountain of river water out as he flailed desperately with his hands, not sure where he was or why these guys were restraining him.

"Take it easy Ralph," Johnny said. "You're OK."

They got him onto the shore and pulled a first aid kit out of a wet bag and began working on the gash on his forehead. We pulled the kayak out of the water and walked over to see how he was doing.

Ralph was sitting up now, a thick bandage tied around his head.

"He's OK, Johnny said. "No broken bones, no concussion and the gash on his forehead isn't as bad as it looked at first. Lucky."

"Are these the guys that rolled me over?" Ralph asked.

"Yep," Johnny said. "Quick thinking."

The man put his hand out. "Ralph Lyman," he said. "I owe you big time."

We shook hands and Johnny said that they'd have to get Ralph up to the road so that he could be taken to the hospital, just to be on the safe side.

"You guys be safe," he said. "I won't be around to get you out of a jam." We all laughed and wished Ralph well.

"I'll buy you each a shot of tequila at the after party tonight," he said.

Tequila, I thought. I shuddered.

At the next eddy it was decided to mix the kayaks and four man rafts because the raft guides were still busy getting Ralph off the river.

"Everybody helps everybody on the river." a guide named Alex announced. "You people in the rafts stay tight, pay attention to what the guides tell you. We're about to enter "The Surprise." It starts slow and easy but, when you come to a big rock there'll be a hole below it – that's the surprise. There's a big hydraulic below it. Don't take it head-on. To the left is a little safer, to the right, well, that can be a little hairy. Decide which one you want on your way down and follow the guides on the rocks. They'll dangle orange ropes for you to aim for."

Everybody cheered. We were psyched. Class IV!

As we began filing out into the current, Karen paddled up to us.

"Nice job on the rescue guys," she said. "Everyone on the river's talking about it. You probably saved Ralph's life."

She back paddled, letting us out into the current ahead of her.

Our experience on the earlier rapids had given us a sense of confidence that we hadn't had before. Joe and Calvin were aggressive up front, pointing to hidden rocks and obstructions and steering away from them. Neil and I had learned how to read the river – how the current moved in and among the boulders and rocks of the small canyon the river had carved over hundreds of years. Like a living, breathing thing, the river seemed to have a mind of its own. If you showed respect to her, she would reward you with a thrilling ride. But if you tried to fight her, she could turn vicious and mean.

We struggled during the first run: it was steeper and faster than it looked and we bounced around like a pinball in the narrow passage. We got turned around several times and finished the run going backwards. But, where I had felt nervous and even a little bit scared earlier, I now felt exhilarated – we had made it through the run and had fun doing it. Even Calvin was cheering as we drifted out into the calm of a large eddy. Kayaks and four-man rubber boats were circling as a guide standing on a large boulder explained the next run. As our turn came and we approached the chute at the beginning of the run, I noticed a large sign that had a hand painted skull and crossbones in black. It read: "Caution! Dangerous rapids! Proceed at your own risk!"

"It's a long straight run," the guide on the boulder shouted over the roar of the rushing water. "At the bottom, there's a very large hydraulic. Take the left path marked by the orange ropes. Guides on the boulders will coach you. If you get off course and can't make the left turn, then go right. *Do not* attempt to take it head-on!"

Neil and I signaled that we understood and began paddling towards the chute.

"Ahoo!" Calvin yelled at the top of his lungs.

Neil and I exchanged nervous looks. Calvin rarely showed any kind of excitement about anything – he usually followed everyone else's lead in showing any emotion. He rarely got jokes and we often caught him laughing along without understanding the punch line. We even planted phony jokes on him with nonsense punchlines and then got him tell the joke to someone else.

"Let's go!" Calvin yelled as we entered the chute. He looked over at Joe and the two began paddling madly. Neil and I ruddered desperately, trying to keep the raft headed straight as the combination of the rushing current and Calvin and Joe's paddling sent us shooting forward, like some kind of amusement park ride gone crazy.

As we neared the bottom of the run, we could see the towering hydraulic. A guide on a huge boulder motioned to us to start steering left towards an orange rope. "Left! Left!" We could hear him scream above the roar of the river. But Calvin and Joe kept paddling straight. I suddenly realized that they must have made a secret pact to take the hydraulic head on. I glanced again at Neil who was yelling: "Left! You goddamn idiots!" at the top of his lungs.

We missed our chance to go left. The guide was now frantically signaling and yelling for us to go right. Neil and I both ruddered hard towards the right, but Calvin and Joe were determined and all we managed to do was get the boat sideways. "Shit!" Neil and I both yelled at once. We had no choice but to straighten the boat and take the hydraulic head on.

"Go ahead and kill yourselves!" The guide yelled.

A hydraulic is a standing wave in a river, caused by some underlying rocks or change in the river bed. This one towered ten or fifteen feet above us, with a plume of mist above it. As we approached it, the hydraulic seemed more of a wall of water than a sloping wave. The surging current carried us straight up and into the cloud of spray above it. I felt that strange sick feeling in my stomach that I always get at the top of a roller coaster. We teetered at the peak for just a brief moment before tipping forward and plunging towards the big trough behind the hydraulic. When we hit the bottom, we shot up the other side of the trough and flipped end over end. I saw paddles, feet, arms and legs flying every which way, discombobulated by the spray and the spinning. I hit the water, my momentum carrying me straight to the bottom. Pushing off, I surfaced, but to my surprise, I found myself under the raft, alone in the powerful current, heading downstream at a rapid rate.

I knew I had to get out from under the boat and get my feet pointed downstream in order to ride out the rest of the run, but before I could do anything the raft was pushed up against a flat rock wall. In an instant I was pinned against the wall by the rubber raft, the current pushing the soft bottom around me like shrink wrapping. I couldn't move, and I couldn't catch a breath. I began to panic, struggling desperately against the cloying rubber, but all that did was deplete the little oxygen I had left.

But, as I felt my consciousness rapidly slipping away, the raft began to move – someone was tugging at it. The raft came off the wall and the current, just a moment ago my enemy, suddenly became my friend. It flipped the raft over with me in it and I found myself riding down through the last section of the run, gulping in huge lungfuls of air. Just ahead of me was a kayaker – the one who had pulled the raft free. As I approached the eddy at the end of the run, the kayaker turned – it was Karen, a scolding look on her face.

Joe, Calvin and Neil were standing in the waist deep water of the eddy as my raft, circling around and around, drifted into it. Karen paddled over to us.

"What made you guys decide to take that hydraulic head on?" She said as we gathered our paddles from the unhappy guides.

I shrugged my shoulders and recited the punchline of the old joke about a guy who took off all his clothes and jumped into a patch of cactus. Somebody asked him why he did it. He replied: "Seemed like a good idea at the time."

The guides weren't amused.

"You guys stay in line for the rest of the trip," Alex said sternly. "One more stunt like that and I'll have you walk out on the trail."

We all nodded contritely. As Alex paddled away Neil cracked Calvin on the helmet with the flat of his hand.

"Idiot!" He said.

The whitewater company put on a steak fry and bonfire after the trip and everyone talked excitedly about their individual experiences. Guides on the big boulder above the big hydraulic had taken pictures of the passing rafts and kayaks and had them available for purchase. Neil was laughing as he pulled out his wallet.

"I'll take a couple of these," he said.

I looked over his shoulder. There were two pictures: one was the standard going- down-the-chute-with- eyes-wide picture of the four of us, but the second one showed our raft shooting straight up into the spray below the hydraulic. There was a jumble of feet, hands, arms and loose paddles. In the center of it all, clear and plain, was Calvin's face – a mask of shock and bewilderment.

"Lookit Calvin!" Neil exclaimed. "He looks like Lenny in "Of Mice and Men" when he found out his mouse was dead!"

People gathered round, laughing at the picture. Calvin tried to push through the crowd saying: "Lemme see, lemme see," but everyone playfully kept him away.

I walked over to the tiki bar to see what was going on there. Karen was sitting on Doc's lap, sucking on a lime, an empty shot glass in her hand. She smiled. "Hi Neptune," she said. "Tequila?"

I shuddered. "No thanks."

Doc had spent the morning at the Tiki bar. Extreme sports didn't interest him. "Basketball, football, baseball and pool are my sports," he had said earlier. "Drowning or getting my head bashed in by a rock isn't my cup of tea."

"From what I've seen, pool is a lot more dangerous for you than river rafting," Karen said wryly.

"You're right," Doc said. "But you can't hustle the river."

"You guys are the talk of the town, Tommy," Doc said. "Whose idea was it to take that hydraulic head on."

"Calvin's," I said. "He and Joe decided to go for it. Neil and I couldn't steer us out of it."

"That's what I figured," Doc said.

"You could have gotten yourselves killed," Karen said. There was a strange seriousness to her voice— almost motherly.

"Yeah," I said. "Bye the way, thanks for pulling the raft off of my back; it was starting to get a little weird underneath it."

Karen looked shocked. "I didn't know anyone was in it," she said. "I saw a raft pinned against the rock and pulled it off— thought I'd save the guides the task."

"That's not what I heard," Doc said. "I heard from Neil that you paddled back up through the current and pulled the raft off Tommy."

Karen blushed. "Just trying to help," she said.

"You probably saved this young man's life," Doc said. He ruffled my hair and handed me a beer. "Don't tell your father I gave you this," he said as I took a long swig.

"Hey! There he is!" A voice boomed. We all turned to see who it was. It was Ralph Lyman, a big bandage on his forehead, and he was talking to me.

"Here's one of the guys who saved my life!" he announced to everyone. I suddenly realized that he was a very big man, one of Johnnie's rugby buddies. His nickname was Scooter and he had a flattened nose, puffy ears and was missing one of his upper front teeth. He approached me and put a big arm around my shoulders. "I've been on this river for years, taken every rapid dozens of times; never had an accident. But today, I screwed up – rookie mistake. I let myself get turned sideways in some strong riffles and decided to do a roll to get straightened out. But the river is too shallow there – and I'm too tall. I got wedged. I was running out of air when Tommy and Neil pulled me over – just in time!" He grabbed my hand and raised it over my head, like a referee raising a boxer's hand.

"Speech, speech, speech," everyone chanted playfully.

I was embarrassed to be the center of attention, embarrassed at the exaggeration, and embarrassed that Neil wasn't there. But mostly I was embarrassed that the real hero of the day, at least for me, was sitting on Doc's lap, cheering along with everyone else. Scooter stepped back and gave me room. The bar went silent.

"Go ahead," he said.

Crap! I thought. I was never good at public speaking and hated even being put on the spot for an answer in a classroom. Oh well, I thought: Here goes. I hoped that I wouldn't say anything stupid.

"I learned two things today on the river," I began, my voice shaking. "One is that we're all brothers and sisters and that we all have each other's backs. Neil and I saw a kayaker in trouble and did what anyone else in this room would have done. The second thing is that you have to respect the river – and the guides that know her. We didn't. We ignored the guides and took a hydraulic head on. We didn't just put ourselves at risk – we put the guides that had to fish us out at risk too."

There was a murmur of approval. I looked over at Karen. She shook her head "no" and put her finger to her mouth, saying "ssshhh" silently. I smiled and shrugged.

"After the hydraulic, I let myself get trapped under my raft. I was pinned against a rock and out of air. Somebody pulled the boat off me – just in time."

The guides all looked at each other and shrugged.

"What color was the kayak?" Johnny asked.

"Red." I said.

"What about the helmet and lifejacket?"

"Purple helmet, yellow jacket."

Everyone turned to look at Karen. On the river, everyone knew everyone else's colors. Karen raised her hand. "Guilty," she said. "But I didn't know anyone was in the raft, so it doesn't count as a rescue."

Everyone laughed.

Later, Johnny spoke to me. "You did good today," he said. "Everyone knows that it was your two idiot cousins that steered you into the hydraulic, but you didn't give them up. And you didn't act like you did something special in rescuing Scooter – glory hounds don't belong on the river." He stopped for a moment and took a thoughtful sip of beer. "Your words were good – they rang true."

I nodded. I was getting the sense that kayakers didn't hand out compliments easily.

"Come around tomorrow morning," he said. "I'll show you a few things."

"Cool," I said. "What time?"

"First light," he said.

I hung around for a little while longer and then ambled up to the campsite. Neil was walking around, making sure that everyone saw the picture of Calvin in the rapids and commenting loudly about how stupid Calvin and Joe were to steer into the hydraulic.

"The guides steered us right around that big wave," Donnie said. "It was huge. Why would anyone want to go right into it?"

"Because they're *stupid*!" Neil said.

"Shuddup Neil," Calvin said weakly. "No one got hurt."

Neil walked over and slapped Calvin lightly on the back of his head. "We could have been!" Neil said. "Plus, all the guides were pissed and think we're a bunch of idiots!"

The slap caused Calvin to exhale through his lit pipe, sending a shower of sparks into the air. "Hey!" He exclaimed.

"Leave him alone Neil," Pete said. "He knows he screwed up. You don't have to rub it in."

"Yeah," Calvin said, standing and brushing himself off. "Don't rub it in." He began refilling his pipe, a self-righteous look on his face.

• • • • • • • • • • • • • • •

Later, when we usually had our campfire, the men clustered around a large picnic table laid out with maps. They held grease pencils in their hands and drank tepid coffee from tin cups. Some chomped cigar butts, others smoked nervously. The whole scene had the look of a military planning operation.

"Hey, there you are," my father said when he saw me. "Get over here and take a look at these maps for a minute." His tone was all business.

The men cleared a space for me as I approached.

"You can read a topo map, right?" Pete asked, a little pointedly. "Learned it in the scouts, didn't you?"

I gave him a hard look and bent over the map. It seemed to me that all the men were a little testy, Pete in particular. I looked up briefly at Neil, standing at the back of the small crowd. He shook his head and rolled his eyes. I realized that Neil had the same opinion of the whole operation as I did: the men were chasing after fool's gold in a quixotic attempt to bring things back to the way they used to be. It wasn't just the factory closing either; they'd seen adversity before: the Depression, the War, raising families, making ends meet. It occurred to me that what they were really after was the reclamation of their youth. They wanted to recapture that vibrant energy that they had when they were up against it all. One last mission, that's what this was all about,

The trouble was, I didn't really believe in the mission, and I didn't think that Neil did either. We'd both been traumatized by that night in the graveyard, something that the men hadn't considered when they brought us along. They had all seen death in the war, and dead bodies were not an uncommon sight. Come to think of it, they were our age when all that happened. But that was their experience, not mine and I was beginning to get a little tired of the whole charade. I didn't think that there was any hidden payroll. It stood to reason that if the company bank had been robbed, the company would have done everything to recover its property. Pop said that it had been hidden in a secret tunnel in an abandoned mine, but the thought that company detectives hadn't scoured every possible hiding place and found it was highly doubtful to me. And not only company detectives would be searching for it: word of a robbery like that would have spread – every miner and his brother would have been searching the hills for it. I found myself wishing that I could just step away from it all. I longed to be back at the tiki bar with my new friends, talking about the river. But I knew that I couldn't. I knew that it would be wrong to deny the old men their dream. I studied the map.

"Here's Number Six," I said, having located the abandoned mine. I noticed that there already was a grease pencil mark at the spot. I located the main company complex and saw another mark. I measured the distance between the two marks. "Looks to be about 400 yards in a straight line," I said, looking up.

"Brilliant," Pete said sarcastically. "We already determined that."

"We're looking for a rear access road to the complex," my father explained. "There's not one marked but Pop mentions one."

I looked at the key one the lower left-hand corner of the map. "1952," I said. "That's when the aerial photograph was taken. The topo map is based on that."

"We figure that, after the explosions, the company probably closed the road," Walter said. "We need to determine where that road was."

"Why?" I asked.

"We're not going in through the front door," Pete said impatiently.

I looked at him, biting my tongue, but saying nothing.

"Anybody keeping an eye on the complex would see us," my father said. "Don't forget, an unsolved robbery like this would become legend in these parts. And treasure hunters are very persistent and patient people."

I nodded and scanned the map for a while. Finally I saw a pattern that might indicate an abandoned roadbed. I lightly traced along it with a grease pencil.

"It meets a functioning dirt road right here," I said, marking the spot with an "X."

"But it's probably overgrown. I doubt you could get a car down it."

"We didn't plan on it," Pete said. His tone had changed slightly, an admission that he felt that I had made a contribution after all. "We're going to hoof it," he said.

"Prickers and brambles usually grow in first," I said. "It might be tough going."

"We brought machetes," Pete said. "It can't be any thicker than the jungle in the Philippines."

"Looks to be about a two mile hike," I added. No one said anything, but I saw Neil roll his eyes again. He cleared his throat for attention.

"When do you anticipate carrying out this operation, Generals?" He said. "When is D-Day?"

"I told you we shouldn't bring these pups along!" Pete said angrily. "They're still wet behind the ears. No telling what they'll do if things get hairy!"

My father held up his hand to hush him. "We need a couple of extra hands," he said. "Besides, they've been in it from the start."

I looked intently at the topo map and something caught my eye

"Right here," I said, pointing to the spot with my grease pencil. "There's an old access gate right here."

My father leaned over the map and squinted – he needed glasses but was too proud to wear them. "It's across the entire complex," he said. "But it looks clear. It's on a side road and we can drive across the complex with our lights out." He stood up and patted me on the shoulder.

"You just saved us a long walk," he said with a smile.

"We'll recon the area tomorrow morning," he continued, addressing everyone in his commander's voice. "Just a couple of us. The rest will fish or raft or whatever; nothing out of the ordinary. We'll decide then when to go."

Everyone nodded solemnly.

"Get some rest," my father said as he rolled up the maps.

That night I had a hard time getting to sleep. I kept thinking about the upcoming mission and about Johnny's offer to show me a few things on the river. My father had told me that it was OK for me to go rafting the next morning— I didn't mention kayaks. But I was nervous about making a fool of myself again.

When I finally did get to sleep I had a vivid dream of paddling a kayak down a pristine river, confident and happy. Then, suddenly, the river turned angry. I was tossed and turned and slammed into hidden rocks. The river had me in her grip and she wasn't about to let go. I fought and struggled, trying to gain control of my bouncing craft. But the current got stronger and the rapids more intense. I found myself in a chute that got steeper and steeper until it turned into a waterfall. I plunged downward, leaving my stomach and breath behind. The waterfall stretched out before me, lengthening until it seemed as if I were flying high above the distant pool at the bottom. The pool suddenly rushed towards me, a whirlpool in the center widening to engulf me like some kind of wild animal's maw. As I entered the whirlpool, I found that I was in a tunnel; the walls were shiny black anthracite. I saw my grandfather's face at the end of it, laughing maniacally and calling my name.

I awoke to find Walter shaking me. "Thomas," he said. "Wake up. You'll miss your training on the river."

I blinked and rubbed my eyes. "I was having a nightmare," I stammered.

"I know," Walter said. "Your screaming woke me. Are you OK?"

"Sure," I said, a little dubiously. "Did I wake anyone else?"

"I don't think so," Walter said. "Come and get some breakfast. We're the first ones up."

He handed me a plate of burned, crumbled bacon, scrambled eggs that had bacon bits, ashes and bits of burnt wood chips in them, and some burnt toast – Water wasn't known for his cooking. But I appreciated the effort and ate, washing the food down with some tepid coffee.

"You don't believe much in this mission," Walter said. It was a statement, not a question.

I looked over at him, my mouth full of food. He was peacefully smoking his pipe, looking up at the trees.

I started to say something, but Walter held up his hand to stop me.

"Neil doesn't either," he said. "He didn't say anything, but I can tell, just as I can with you."

He sat silently for a minute, letting his observation sink in.

"Truth be told, most of us don't either," he said. He tapped the ashes out of his pipe and stood up. "But it's something we have to do. It's not about the money; none of us has ever had any real money, and it's likely that we never will. This whole thing, well it's something that we had to try, just to do it, you understand?

I nodded; my mouth full of ashy eggs and bacon. Walter rarely explained himself this way; none of the men did. I got the sense that they somehow missed the constant fight for survival that had defined them during their youth. Now, in their middle ages, they were tilting at windmills, looking for that last glorious battle. I thought of all the quotes I had heard from them since I was just a little kid: "Any job worth doing is worth doing right," "Success comes to those who are ready when their opportunity knocks," "A man who wastes one hour of time has not discovered the value of life," Pete's simple Marine Corps slogan: "Semper Fi," and, everyone's favorite, Walter's: "Do unto others, before they do unto you."

I remembered the books I had been given to read by my father: "The Iliad and the Odyssey," Cooper's "Leatherstocking Tales," "The Frontiersmen," and Crane's "The Red Badge of Courage." All were stories about perseverance against great odds; heroism. Growing up, I'd watched "Gunsmoke" and seen Marshal Matt Dillon up against a dozen bad guys every week. I'd seen Audie Murphy hold off Germans with a machine gun while standing on a burning tank, John Wayne fighting Indians in the West and Japanese in the Pacific, Gregory Peck standing on top of Pork Chop Hill in Korea. That was the culture I had grown up in and it was the culture that was slipping away – the culture that the men were trying, one last time, to revive. I decided then and there that I was all in.

Walter stood put his pipe in his pocket. He didn't say anything, but I had the sense that he knew what I was thinking. Finally, he smiled.

"Go down there and show the river who's boss," he said. "We'll be leaving later, so take your time. And don't let Karen out of your sight; you never know when she might need your help."

I was too tired to be embarrassed. I knocked the scraps from my breakfast into the fire and stood up, wiping my hands on my jeans.

"Nothing gets past you, does it Walter," I said.

He chuckled.

• • • • • • • • • • • • • • • •

It was still dark when I got to the staging area. No one was there yet. I sat down on a rock and listened to the river as it bubbled and gurgled its way past me. I remembered Walter telling me about a Greek philosopher who said that you couldn't step in the same river twice. "Everything flows," he said. "Nothing stays stagnant, except what is dead."

As the light of dawn crept reluctantly into the river gorge, I began to see the ghostly hulks of the rafts and kayaks, the piles of lifejackets and stacks of paddles and helmets. I heard voices in the distance and turned to see the beams of flashlights dancing among the trees along the path that wound down the steep hill.

"Hey, you made it after all!" Johnny exclaimed as he emerged from the dark of the woods. "I knew you would." He walked up to me and shook my hand.

"A whole new world is about to open up for you my friend."

He walked me over to the pile of lifejackets, wetsuits and helmets and helped me get kitted up for the day.

A dozen or so people entered the area, chattering amongst themselves. I noticed Karen among them. She gave me a wave. I decided to be bold and walked over to her.

"Anybody else coming?" She said as I approached.

"Are you kidding," I said. "After yesterday, I don't think any of them, except Neil, would ever go on the river again."

"I thought he'd be down here with you," she said, looking around.

"Me too," I lied. I knew that Neil was on the little recon mission the men had planned for the morning. I didn't want to get caught up in some elaborate explanation that was certain to be full of contradictions. I was never much good at making up stories.

Karen shrugged. "Maybe he went fishing. He and Walter and your father took off pretty early."

"Most likely," I said, glad that I hadn't said anything.

"Those guys have been pretty secretive lately," Karen said. "They're always talking in hushed tones and arguing."

I feigned indifference and fiddled with the buckles on my PFD.

"Those guys are like that," I said after a bit. "They scheme and argue everything. Where to eat, which route to take, where to fish; my father and Walter got into an argument once over gorgonzola cheese."

Karen laughed. She picked up her helmet and walked off towards the stacked kayaks.

Once we had our equipment, the guides took us to a large, calm, shallow section of the eddy, roped off for swimming. "The pool," they called it. We stood around, uncomfortable standing in our full river kit: wet suits, lifejackets, helmets and the strange neoprene contraption called a spray skirt. It was meant to seal a paddler into the kayak so that it wouldn't ship water. It was put on like a pair of pants and tightened over the waist with compression straps. The skirt was designed to stretch over the cockpit and was held in place on the cockpit's lip by a hoop of stretch cord sewn into the fabric. Sitting in a kayak with it stretched over the cockpit gave a sleek compact look that melded the paddler and kayak into a single unit. But, standing around with them hanging from our waists, they looked like some kind of strange appendages that didn't belong.

There were a couple of guides in kayaks and several more standing around in the waist deep water, ready to demonstrate and assist. A tall guide named Sully stood on a large boulder holding a paddle and surveying the crowd. He held up two fingers, index and pinkie, like a baseball player. "We had two rescues yesterday. Either one – or both – could have ended badly. Quick thinking and quicker action saved two lives." He let his words sink in for a moment.

"We have taken people out of the gorge in body bags," he added.

Sobered, we listened to Sully's presentation intently. He had the guides demonstrate how to paddle forward, turn, and back paddle. They showed us the high brace, the low brace and the side draw and side push. Finally came the part we were all waiting for and dreading: the Eskimo Roll.

"Eskimo Roll is a generic term," Sully announced. "There are actually several rolls, all developed for specific situations. The kayakers demonstrated a bewildering number of rolls as Sully announced the purpose of each. The Storm Roll, the Screw Roll, the C to C, and the Back Deck Roll. Amazingly the guides tossed their paddles away and rolled using just their hands. "The hand roll is important to know if you lose your paddle." Sully said. "But you won't need it, because you won't lose your paddle, right?"

"Right!" We all answered in unison.

"And now my favorite," Sully said with a mischievous grin on his face. He reached down and fished a can of beer from a small cooler and tossed it down to one of the guides, a guy called Derf. He opened the can and rolled his kayak, transferring the can from one hand to the other across the bottom of the boat without it touching the water. As he sat up, Derf raised the can in a toast and chugged it. We all cheered.

I found my impatience growing, the guides made the paddling and rolls look easy and, since I had a fair amount of experience paddling canoes, I was anxious to apply those skills to the kayak. When it was my turn, I wriggled myself into the kayak, slipped the spray skirt over the cowling, put my feet on the foot pegs and braced my knees against the hull. I was ready.

I shook off a guide's offer to help me into the water and, using my hands and scootching down the ramp, I pushed forward and into the pool. The kayak seemed to come alive as it floated on the soft current of the eddy. I applied my paddle on the right and felt the kayak respond. I brought the double bladed paddle around and dipped the left blade into the water. To my surprise, instead of catching the water on the blade's surface, it sliced through the water. I'd forgotten that the paddle was feathered: the blades were at right angles to each other. I was thrown off balance and, in an instant, found myself upside down in the water.

It's a strange sensation, being upside down in water. Your nose fills, your eyes blur and sting and the urge to breathe becomes overwhelming. I tried to remain calm and remember how the guides had effortlessly rolled back up after capsizing. I positioned my paddle as they had, made a sweep and flicked my hips. It felt for a moment that I had done it right, but, just as it seemed as if the kayak was going to right itself, the roll failed and I was back upside down. Now the question was whether to try again or pull the spray skirt and bail out. I decided to try again.

I let out some air and repositioned. I swept the paddle and flicked my hips. This time, to my immense surprise, and relief, I popped right up. But before I even had a chance to settle myself, I rolled over again. I hadn't had a chance to take much of a breath and was about to pop the skirt when the kayak suddenly righted itself. I took a breath and came face to face with Sully, who was holding the kayak steady.

"Thought you could use some help," he said.

"Thanks," I managed.

"You had it," Sully said. "But you forgot to go into a high brace when you came up. "Try it again."

Before I could say anything, Sully flipped the kayak over. I positioned myself as before, swept the paddle and flicked my hips. I popped right up and went into a high brace.

"Good," Sully said. "Again." Once more he flipped the kayak. This time I only came partway up before I started to roll back. Sully pulled me the rest of the way up. "Don't bring your head up so soon, it spoils the hip flick." Over I went again.

After a dozen or so tries and a half-dozen failures, I began to get the hang of it. Sully then had me work on the other side and stayed with me until I'd managed a few good rolls.

"Keep at it Kid," he said. "Practice until you don't have to think about it."

I thanked him and paddled off to work on my new skills.

I paddled forwards, backwards, turned and rolled. I drew and skulled and spun around in circles. I practiced the high brace and the low brace. Occasionally a guide would swim or paddle over and coach me on some fine point. Finally, my arms and body aching from my efforts, I took a short break, letting the current take me around the pool in a large, irregular circle.

As I sat, my paddle resting easily across the cockpit, I watched the others working on their skills. Karen could have been a guide herself, she was so good. She carved delicate turns, rolled effortlessly and sprinted forwards and backwards with amazing speed.

A few minutes later, Sully paddled out into the pool. "Follow the leader!" He shouted with a grin. He deftly executed a series of turns and rolls. Kayakers and guides fell in line and attempted to do what Sully was doing. I joined the procession behind Johnny.

"C'mon!" He said, waving to me with his paddle. "Let's show 'em what we got!"

Sully led us on a winding course in the big eddy, venturing out briefly into the main river where the stronger current presented different challenges to our fledgling skills. As I tried to turn in the swirling current, I overbalanced and rolled. My attempt to roll back up failed twice and I was completely out of air when I finally succeeded on the third try. I found myself out of line and some distance downstream when I recovered. Embarrassed, I paddled furiously in order to rejoin the group.

I noticed that others were having difficulties too, and the guides had a chance to practice their skill at water rescues. I saw Johnny towing a bedraggled paddler towards shore as another guide helped with the man's kayak and paddle. To his credit the paddler, a man named Marc, climbed back into his kayak and paddled gamely back into the line.

Karen seemed to have no problems at all. She was paddling with Bonnie and Sue.

"Look at that!" Johnny exclaimed. "They're like a pod of dolphins playing in the waves!"

We watched for a while, marveling at their skill.

"Your uncle's a lucky guy," Johnnie said. "Every guy here has a thing for Karen."

"Yeah, I noticed," I said. "Everybody's tripping over themselves to be near her."

"She's only got eyes for one guy, though," Johnny said. "Everybody knows that too."

"Yeah," I said. "She is my uncle's girlfriend."

"Yeah," Johnny said. "I know." He laughed over his shoulder and paddled off.

When Sully finally called for a lunch break, my arms, back and shoulders were as grateful as my aching stomach. I was exhausted and ravenous. I felt a little light headed as I squirmed out of my kayak and pulled it up onto the shore.

"You OK Neptune?" Karen said walking by. "You drank a lot of tequila the other night."

"I'm fine," I lied. In truth, I knew that I had worked too hard on an empty stomach. I also hadn't had anything to drink since the night before and felt dehydrated.

"We're at a table over there," Karen said. "Come join us."

I stripped out of my life jacket and spray skirt and walked over to the table. Johnny, Karen, Bonnie, Sue, Scooter and a short, balding guy named Derf - the guide from the beer-roll - were seated, working on their lunches. "Grab a seat Neptune," Johnny said.

"How'd you get that name?" Derf asked, an open grin on his face. Nicknames, I was finding, were part of the river culture. I guess I now had mine.

"I gave it to him," Karen said. "I caught him poaching some trout with a trident. Neptune seemed to fit."

"Poached trout?" Derf said. "I love poached trout. Healthy way to eat."

"Not cooked," Johnny said. "Illegally taken. You're not supposed to fish with a spear."

"Oh," Derf said. "Can you get us some tomorrow? I love trout."

Johnny and Scooter both laughed. "You get hit in the head a lot when you play Hooker," Scooter said. He playfully rubbed Derf's bald head. Karen looked at him in surprise.

"Hooker?" She said, a surprised look on her face.

"Hooker's a position in Rugby," Johnny explained. "You're right in the middle of the scrum, trying to hook the ball away from the opposing hooker. You're suspended from the shoulders of the two biggest guys on the team, the props. You get banged around a lot."

"Support your local Hooker," Derf said with a grin. I'd seen a bumper sticker with that slogan on a car parked at the camp. I also noticed that, like Big John, he was missing a front tooth.

Lunch was assorted lunchmeat sandwiches in a paper sack, along with a two-pack of Twinkies and a piece of fruit – an apple or a banana. To drink there was a large galvanized steel container with a spigot, filled with various flavors of Kool Aid. It was a sweet concoction of indeterminate flavor and was a strange, reddish-purple color. Everyone called it 'bug juice'. I drank about a gallon.

"You're going to be sorry you drank so much of that bug juice later," Johnny said.

"Getting out to pee on the river is a challenge."

"Whaddya mean?" Scooter said. "Just pee in your wetsuit. Warms you up."

"Eww," Bonnie said. "You do that?"

Everyone laughed as Scooter tried to backpedal: "Well, no, not me exactly," he stammered. "But I know a lot of guys who do."

"You know a lot of guys who tell you they do so that you'll do it," Johnny said.

"Really?" Scooter said, looking around at the crowd with a hurt look. "That was a prank on me? You guys are assholes!"

"C'mon you guys," Karen said after the laughter died down. "Everybody pees in their wetsuit. You ever see surfers coming off a break and stripping off their wetsuits to line up at the Johnny-on-the-spot? The water washes it right out. Scuba divers do it when they're in cold water."

Scooter looked around at his friends again. This time his expression was accusatory. "You guys really *are* assholes!" He paused for a moment, considering something. He suddenly burst out laughing. "A double prank!" He exclaimed. "Beautiful!"

Derf was looking in awe at Karen. "You surf?"

She nodded. "I spent a year in Malibu, living with my Aunt." She stopped for a moment and then broke into a wide grin. "Right on the beach!"

"Woo hoo!" Everyone exclaimed.

"I've heard those surfers are a crazy bunch," Johnny said.

"No crazier than you," Karen said. "And they don't have big rocks to worry about."

"Yeah, just sharks," Scooter said. "I don't like sharks."

"You never been near any sharks," Derf said.

"So? That doesn't mean I can't not like 'em!"

Everyone just looked at him and shook their heads.

The conversation turned to general banter. I just sat there, pretending I was listening. But I wasn't. I was thinking what an inadequate fool I was for entertaining any thoughts about Karen at all. She was a college swimmer, a surfer from Malibu, a skilled equestrian, and now a kayaker. And she was dating my Uncle.

As I sat, stewing in my foolishness, I noticed that Karen staring at me. It was a strange look, almost as if she were assessing me. She looked like she wanted me to say something to her, but I could think of nothing. Moments later she got up, ran down to the staging area and began busying herself gearing up for the afternoon run. Strange behavior, I thought absently.

Just then, Sully's voice rang out, calling the guides to a meeting.

"See you on the river," Johnny said with a grin.

I walked down to the staging area and kitted up. The banter among the paddlers soon lifted my spirits and I forgot about my worries as I began to anticipate the run. It was one thing to practice paddling skills in the pool, but it was another thing to put those skills to use in some real rapids. With a surge of adrenaline, I paddled out into the pool. I flicked my hips from side to side, worked the paddle blades in a series of skulls, draws and forward and backward strokes. I practiced my roll on each side. Everyone else was doing the same.

"Gather round, paddlers!" Sully shouted, maneuvering his kayak expertly so as to face us all. "It's follow the leader. Do what I do, do what the guides do. And don't maverick." This last comment was for me, and everyone knew it. I gave a little perfunctory salute.

"Let's do it then!" Sully shouted. We all raised our paddles and cheered.

Sully paddled hard out into the main current and then aggressively charged downstream. A guide stood on a rock, directing traffic. "Next! You!" He'd shout, pointing at a paddler and indicating that he should paddle out into the stream with a sweep of his arm. "Don't bunch up," he cautioned. "Keep moving."

When it came my turn, I paddled out and into the surging current. It seemed to bring life to my kayak, and I felt like a cowboy on a spirited but unbroken horse. I used my hips and paddle to control the bucking craft and shot down through the first run, a sluiceway nestled between a jumble of boulders.

"Yeah," a guide shouted from one of the big rocks. "You got it! Keep it going straight!"

I realized that going straight was the only option: if I got turned sideways, one end or the other of the kayak would catch on a rock and flip me. I didn't want to ride the run out on my back with the kayak on top of me. I needed to remain calm – panic and over compensation were my two worst enemies, and they lay in wait for me like a couple of schoolyard bullies grinning in the shadows.

The last part of the run was steep and obscured by a wall of mist. I couldn't see to steer, so I pointed my kayak forward, lay back and slid into it, shifting my hips slightly from side to side. I had the sense of weight-lessness for a moment as I dropped straight down. It took me a moment to realize that I was in a waterfall.

I hit the pool at the bottom of the falls and submerged completely. For an instant the kayak went dead in the water before the bow rose up and popped through the surface. I followed, breaking the surface like a rising submarine. I quickly went into a high brace, stabilized the kayak and paddled forward. As I emerged from the roar of the falls I could hear cheering. I looked around to see the paddlers who had gone ahead of me, arrayed in a semi-circle. "Nice job," Johnny said as I joined them.

"You didn't tell me this was a falls," I said.

"Only a small one," Johnny said. "We didn't want to worry anyone."

"Yeah," I said as I turned my kayak and joined the crowd. Moments later another kayak shot down the sluice and entered the cloud of mist. I could just barely see its shape behind the wall of water cascading down the last few feet. The kayak popped up, rolled once and then stabilized. We all cheered. The paddler, a big guy named Swenn Sanderson, paddled over to us.

"You didn't say there was a falls," he said.

"We didn't want to worry you, Swede," Johnny replied.

Not everyone made it down so neatly. One guy came down backwards, another went sideways, flipped when he hit the water and came out of his kayak. Sully paddled forward and deftly pulled the man back just as the next kayak came down.

"That was hairy," Johnny commented. "People get hurt when a kayak lands on them from a distance above."

I read somewhere that Mark Twain said: 'a man who carries a cat by the tail learns something he can learn in no other way'. I think that same principle applies to whitewater kayaking. Practice all you want in a pool a pond or an eddy, but once you get into the current you're in the world of the river. You learn to read its currents and its flow. You see submerged rocks hiding just below the surface, waiting to send your kayak sideways with just a subtle touch on the bow. You see the sweepers, the most feared thing on the river: a downed tree with its branches aligned along the river bottom like the iron bars of a jail cell. The current flows freely through them, but a kayak becomes pinned below the surface with no way out for the paddler. You see inviting false paths that lead off into some shallow flats where you have to get out and drag your kayak, forlorn and alone. Or, worse, into a set of dangerous rapids where you get knocked, banged and rolled through a jumble of boulders and you're lucky to land on a flat rock and get out and carry your kayak back to the main stream.

Above all, you learn that the river is a living, breathing thing – a siren beckoning to you with her silver flowing currents, her glistening pools and her towering cliffs. Her roaring waters call to you, beg you to come along on a journey that you'll never forget. And it's all true, except that she can turn on you in an instant, transforming herself from a soft, gentle beauty into a raging bitch that would like nothing more than to dash your pathetic little body on her boulders and suck the life from you in her cloying currents.

But, when it's all over, you look back upstream and want to do it all over again.

At the pull-out we all gathered, swapping stories and congratulating each other on a nice run. Sully walked around, checking names off on a list to make sure that no one was still up river. When he was done, he allowed himself a smile and nodded to one of the guides, who broke open a cooler of iced beer and began tossing the cold cans around to everyone. The cans, shaken somehow in the travel or the tossing, shot geysers of foam into our faces and mouths.

After a while we loaded up on a small bus and made the trip back to the camp.

When we arrived at the camp, Neil was leaning on his car, waiting, chewing on a toothpick.

"Looks like I gotta go," I said to Johnny as I waved to Neil.

"See you on the river," Johnny said.

I waved to everyone and jogged over to Neil's car.

"Get in," Neil said. "We've been waiting for you."

He seemed a little tense. But then Neil could be like that: confident and in charge most of the time, but then, when something came up that challenged that confidence, he drew inward, wrestling with some insecurity. He never talked about it much. Neil usually kept his own counsel.

"What's up?" I asked, settling into the empty passenger seat.

"We're going tonight," he said. "To the mine."

I swallowed hard. After all the discussion and planning, the time was finally here. Now I understood Neil's tension, I felt it myself. The feeling ran deep, down into the pit of my stomach: butterflies. The memory of that cold rainy night in the cemetery flooded back into my mind. I felt a chill, even though it was a hot summer afternoon. I nodded without speaking.

It was dusk in the mountains as the small convoy of overloaded cars left the interstate and wound its way over a series of back roads. Each car towed the rented trailers that we used for our camping gear. We left the gear back at the campsite and went to different lumber yards, loading up piles of timber for bracing the tunnel. Individually, we doubled back from the interstate and rendezvoused at a large truck stop. Then we headed for the mine.

We were in the lead in Neil's Chevy. Walter sat with a map in his lap and a flashlight clenched between his teeth. "Left here," he'd say, and Neil would turn onto another overgrown and crumbling road. We surprised a few deer, several raccoons and dozens of squirrels who were unused to traffic in their neck-of-the-woods. Trees loomed above us in the gloomy dusk and branches grabbed and scraped at the sides of the car. The headlights of the cars behind us danced crazily in the woods as the drivers negotiated the rough road, causing strange, threatening shadows to appear, feinting towards the car like some native spearmen looking for a chance to attack.

"Shit!" Neil said as the chassis of the Chevy bounced on its axle. "This road is ruining my car! Are you sure this is the right way?"

"Should be up here on the right," Walter said. His words were almost unintelligible because of the flashlight still clenched between his teeth. As I watched him consult the map and then squint up the road, I imagined Walter during the war, guiding his plane on some mission deep in enemy territory.

It had just turned full dark when the narrow road ended at a large rusty fence with a gate and a dilapidated, crumbling gatehouse. Neil stopped and Walter got out and shined his flashlight up at a faded sign. "Fieldstone Mines" it read.

"This is it," Walter said as he reached into the back seat of the car and pulled out a large pair of bolt cutters. He walked up the gate and cut the ancient lock that held a rusty chain in place around the two parts of the gate. As the chain dropped he began to pull at one of the sides of the big gate, but it hung up on some weeds and some chunks of crumbled pavement. He turned and looked at Neil and me.

"Well, are you going to help or sit there?" he said.

The three of us managed to dislodge the gate and open it enough to admit the caravan, which roared through without waiting for us. I noticed that Doc was riding with Charlie; someone said that he had sent Karen to their hotel with his car.

It seemed to me that my father and uncles had reverted to their younger years, when they fought a war against a determined enemy. The entire operation had taken on a distinctly military aspect.

After we drove through the entrance, Walter told Neil to drive a ways and then stop. He led us back through the gate on foot, where we used pine branches to swipe away the tire tracks and footprints around the entrance. We closed the gate and re-wrapped the chain. Walter pulled a big padlock out of his satchel and clasped it onto the chain. "Just in case someone gets curious," he said. We cleared the road all the way to Neil's car and then drove into the old mine grounds.

Machines, carts and piles of rubble, abandoned decades ago, littered the mine grounds. Dilapidated buildings with broken windows and doors hanging from their hinges loomed above us. Everywhere weeds, bushes and small trees struggled to reclaim their natural place, forcing their way through broken buildings and crumbling pavement. We followed the faint tire tracks made by the convoy through the grounds and up a hill to a large landing beneath the gaping maw of a mine. An old sign identified it as "Number 6."

Flashlight beams danced around the landing as the cars were un-loaded and the gear taken to the mine. Uncle Frank appeared out of the gloom.

"Unload here and then park over there with the rest of the cars," he said, pointing towards an area shielded from sight by the wall of an old building.

I lugged two heavy duffels up the roadway, their clanking contents bouncing against my legs. Neil came up next to me. He was doing the same.

"What's in these things?" he asked. I noticed that he was a little out of breath. Good, I thought, so am I.

"Pick and shovel heads," I said. "I saw them in the trailer's storage compartment about a week ago. I wondered what they were for. Now we know."

"Why so many?" Neil said, shifting his load. "The tunnel can't be that big."

"I don't know," I said, shifting my own load. In truth, I hadn't con-sidered the size of the tunnel, nor had I thought about actually working in it. Would it be like one of those prisoner of war escape tunnels in the movies? Narrow and short – more of a crawl space than a real tunnel. I remembered the frequent cave-ins where guys had to be pulled out by ropes attached to their ankles, spitting dirt and gasping for air. I didn't like the idea of being buried alive and hoped that the tunnel would be big enough for me to stand or at least crouch.

I noticed a strange, flickering blue glow as we approached the mine entrance. I saw my father and uncles standing around in a semi-circle, watching whatever it was that was going on, their faces made ghoulish by the light. Neil and I let our burdens drop and approached the group.

"Don't look directly at the arc," my father said.

I immediately looked at the arc and then, slightly blinded, shielded my eyes and closed them. I could still see the blue arc. Looking away, I opened my eyes again and glanced towards the activity. I recognized Joe, wearing a big welder's helmet. He was burning his way through one of the rusted iron bars that covered the mine entrance. Calvin was standing by, as if to assist, working on his pipe and offering advice from time to time.

"Shut up Calvin," Neil said. "He knows what he's doing."

"I know a lot more about welding than you do," Calvin said. He puffed angrily at his pipe.

"Well, there, Calvin," Neil said. "Right there you've shown what you don't know, because Joe's not welding, he's cutting."

"I know he's cutting, Bonehead," Calvin commented. "But he's using a welding torch – that makes it welding."

The bar that Joe was cutting clattered to the pavement. He stepped back and looked at the width of the space he had made. "One more?" he said, looking at Walter.

"One more should do it," Walter said. He turned to Calvin. "Why don't you amble down towards the gatehouse with Donnie and keep watch."

"Why me?" Calvin asked, obviously outraged at being sent off on an errand when he had important advice to impart to Joe. Plus, he and Joe usually did things together. Now Walter wanted to send him off, leaving Joe to do the welding without him.

"I think I'll just stay here," he said, a defiant tone to his voice.

"Calvin, you heard Walter," Frank said sharply. "Now get your ass down to where you can see the gatehouse."

I could see that Calvin was struggling with the situation. Did he dare defy his father too, or should he cut his losses and comply. In the end, Calvin knocked his pipe out on the heel of his shoe, stuck it in his pocket and began walking. "I don't know why it has to be me," he muttered as he walked away.

"Pffft!" Neil snickered into his hand. Frank heard it.

"You set up a position to watch the back gate, the one we came in on Neil," he said. "And take Joe with you when he's done cutting," he added.

I remembered the night that Neil and I kept watch at the cemetery while my father and uncles dug up my Grandfather's grave. Curiosity had led me to leave my post. What I saw that night would haunt my dreams forever. Now we were about to begin digging again. Another iron bar clattered to the ground, startling me.

"That should do it," Joe said, rising and flipping his helmet up.

"Let's get to it," Walter said. He stepped past Joe and into the black hole that was the mine entrance.

As I slipped through the passage that Joe had cut, I wished that I were on lookout duty with my cousins. Large timbers — whole trees, it appeared, lined the interior of the shaft. Walter, my father and the others were carrying lanterns and moving swiftly down the old rusty tracks, two sets, side by side, meant for the big metal carts that carried miners down into the mine and coal up from it. The shaft itself was maybe eight-by-eight, just large enough to handle the carts and coal. I tried to imagine being a miner and spending my life in the bowels of the earth, subject to flooding, cave-ins and gas, working with a pick and shovel and breathing coal dust.

After a while the men stopped and shined their lanterns on something in the side of the shaft. A jumble of rocks and shattered beams covered what looked like a depression in the side of the main mine shaft.

"This is it," Walter said. "Forty three feet on the left."

After removing some of the bigger pieces of rubble, the entrance to a much smaller tunnel was revealed. It was much shorter and narrower than the main shaft, maybe four feet tall and four feet wide. There was just enough room for two men to work side by side crouching. I shuddered at the thought of going in there.

"It looks like they took the overburden a ways down the shaft," my father said, shining his lantern toward a pile of rubble fifty yards away.

"Well, let's get to it Owen," Walter said. He put on a miner's helmet and clicked the light on. My father did the same. They threw picks and shovels into a wheelbarrow and prepared to enter the tunnel. My father turned and faced my uncles.

"Wish us luck," he said.

Everyone nodded. Charlie and Doc crossed themselves. It was then that my father noticed me. He looked surprised.

"What are you doing in here Thomas?"

I didn't answer. It was obvious that I wasn't supposed to be in the mine shaft, but no one had told me not to come along.

"You go out with Joe and Neil," he said. "We'll let you know if we need anything, but none of you boys are to be in this mine."

I was tempted to ask him why not, but I had already figured it out. I felt a sinking feeling in the pit of my stomach. What my father and uncles were doing was extremely dangerous. The type of tunnel they were clearing had already caved in once – it could easily happen again. I crossed myself and walked out of the mine.

The men worked in shifts, two digging and bracing, two hauling the debris out and dumping it, and two coming out to take a break and get some food and water. Joe, Neil and I perched ourselves on a rock next to the mine entrance that gave us a vantage point for watching the back entrance and the mine entrance at the same time.

"Do you really think there's a payroll in there?" Joe asked skeptically. He had only just been told about the mission that afternoon.

"The men are convinced, and that's all I need," I said.

Joe shrugged and lit a cigarette.

"Cup that," I said nervously. "If we can see the back entrance, anybody there will be able to see the glow of your cigarette. And keep down a little more; you're sitting up too tall."

"Jesus!" Joe exclaimed. But he did crouch down a little. He didn't cup his cigarette, but he did keep it low.

He looked nervously down at the back entrance. "Do you think someone is following us?" He said. "It's been a lot of years," he added, squinting up at me from some smoke that had gotten in his eyes.

I laughed and relaxed a little. I realized that I was acting more and more like the men, glancing over my shoulder every few minutes.

"No," I said. Probably not, and there's probably no payroll. And even if they find one, inflation will have made it worth so little that it probably wouldn't even pay for this trip. Or worse, it could be company script. If that's the case, it'll be worthless."

Joe took another drag on his cigarette. "Dig you guys really dig up your grandfather to get his journal?"

"Yep," I said. "I didn't do any digging, but I was there. So was Neil."

"Jeez," Joe said. He sat quietly for a few moments, mulling over the news.

"What did he look like, your grandfather?" He said.

I shuddered at the memory. "Like a skeleton with grey-green skin stretched over it; big hollow eyes and sunken cheeks. And a grin, a crazy grin. I'll never forget it."

Joe shuddered. "I don't think I would have looked," he said.

"I had to," I said. "It was like I was drawn to it— the grave. I was supposed to be on lookout, but something made me go down there. My father was pissed when he saw me," I added.

Joe shook his head in disbelief.

"But that wasn't the worst of it," Neil said. "It was the smell. You know how a dead animal smells? Well this was ten times worse."

Joe started to turn a pale shade of green. He flicked his cigarette away.

"I feel like I'm going to puke," he said.

"On top of that, I read the journal, to help look for clues," I said. I was feeling a little peaked myself at the memory. "It still has that smell!" I added.

Joe stood up and walked away, his hands on his hips. "Enough!" He managed to say weakly.

• • • • • • • • • • • • • • • •

Much later, Doc and Charlie emerged from the mine, soaked with sweat and covered with dirt and dust. They were breathing heavily.

"Whew, I could use a beer," Doc said. He reached into a cooler and fished two cans out. He tossed one to Charlie.

"I could use two," Charlie said. He took a church key out of his pocket and opened the can. It foamed from the throw, but he drank it anyway.

"How's it going?" I asked.

"Slow," Charlie said. "Most of the tunnel is caved in. We have to dig and brace, dig and brace. Even the sections that are still intact have to be braced. The collapsed sections are full of rock – mostly shale – and clay. They went deep enough to avoid topsoil."

"It's narrow and hot in there," Doc added. "I'm sweating like a pig."

"When did you ever see a pig, except on a plate cut up into chops," Charlie said.

"You dated a few, if memory serves," Doc said.

I laughed but Joe didn't. He loved his mother and didn't like the idea that Doc might be referring to her. Doc noticed.

"Not your mom," he said, punching Joe playfully on the shoulder. "Your mom was the best thing that ever happened to Charlie, he was just too stupid to know it. She was smart, classy, and beautiful."

Doc was right, I thought. Joe's mom, Patty, was a beautiful woman. There was a picture of her on the mantle at our house, taken a couple of years before her death. Joe never talked about her much, but sometimes I'd catch Joe looking at her picture when he was at our house. I asked my mother once how she had died.

"Car accident," my mother said. She provided no details and asked me to never ask her again. It wasn't until years later that I learned the truth. Aunt Betty told me— she felt that I should know, for some reason.

"She ran off," Betty said. "One day she was just gone. No note or any-thing. I heard that she got a letter from her old high school boyfriend who lived out of state. Just up and left."

"Jeez," I said. "How come everyone says that she had so much class— doesn't sound classy to me."

"Patty and Charlie were very young when they married. They had only been going out for a few months when Patty came up pregnant. They thought that they could make things work, but Charlie was gone a lot— a reporter is on the road almost every night of the week. We all blamed

Charlie when she left. Patty was a nice girl and Charlie should have gotten another job so he could be home more. But he's stubborn and that stubbornness was what drove her away. At least in my opinion," she added.

Patty's departure left Joe to be raised by Charlie and Doc and my mother on weekends. She even tried to get Charlie to let Joe move in with us, but Charlie wouldn't hear of it. I guess that Charlie missed Patty and that Joe was a connection with her that he wouldn't let go of. At least that's what Betty told me. I always wondered why Patty never tried to get in touch with Joe as he got older. I asked Betty once.

"She feels guilty for abandoning him," Betty said. "She's afraid that Joe would hate her for it."

Doc and Charlie took a fifteen minute break and then went back into the mine. A few minutes later, Pete and Frank emerged, they were as sweaty, dirty and dusty as Doc and Charlie had been.

"Two dig, while two haul away the overburden," Frank explained after he caught his breath. "The third pair takes a break. It's hard going," he added.

"I thought the payroll was supposed to be just past the entrance," I said. "That's what Walter said, from the Welsh clues in the journal."

"Walter thinks it could be farther down the tunnel," Pete said. "He figures that, when they didn't get picked up by Pop and Sam, Don worried that the tunnel would be discovered before they could come back for the payroll. His theory is that Don and the boys took it way down the tunnel and then blew the whole thing.

As the night stretched out towards the morning, I began to realize the enormity of the task. The five of us boys worked out our own shifts: one watched the gatehouse, another kept watch at the mine entrance while the others brought up supplies— food, water and bracing lumber from the cars. Soon we knew the paths well enough to turn off our flashlights. The darkness was eerie. Ghosts of miners killed in accidents or shot by detectives populated the corners of my eyes. Calvin was especially spooked.

"What took you so long?" he said when I came to relieve him at the gatehouse watch. He was tense and, not being able to smoke his pipe, a little jumpy. "I think I seen something down there," he added, pointing into the darkness.

His nervousness was catching and I squinted towards where he was pointing. Just then, an owl hooted.

"I'm out of here," Calvin said. He scrambled up the road, stumbling over rocks and debris on his way and leaving me to figure out what he had seen down by the gate.

I was tired from carrying bundles of bracing lumber up the hill, but there, at least, I was working. Here I had nothing to do but imagine creepy things sneaking up on me. Of course, I knew that there was no real threat to me. If someone was going to investigate our activity, we would have seen headlights, then searchlights. Someone might have even gotten on a megaphone, demanding to know our business. But there in the dark, alone, my imagination ran wild.

It reminded me of a time when I was younger and decided to sleep outside in our backyard to watch the Perseid meteor shower. There was a new moon and I hoped to see some spectacular shooting stars.

I watched the night skies for hours and saw dozens of meteors burning their way across the sky. Some were especially large, proudly arcing across the sky and stealing the light from the stars. I could see why the ancients spoke of flaming chariots, fiery dragons and balls of fire hurled by the gods.

At some point I fell asleep, dreaming of piloting a space ship through the Milky Way and dodging asteroids and comets.

I awoke with a start, not sure of where I was, but knowing somehow that something unusual had awakened me. Instead of the sea of stars that I had gone to sleep with, my vision was filled with a man's face, just inches from my own. It had black stubbly whiskers, yellow broken teeth stretched wide in a macabre grin and evil red-rimmed eyes. I tried to scream but couldn't. I shut my eyes, expecting at any moment to feel a choking hand on my throat. But nothing happened. Gingerly, I opened my eyes again. The face was gone and the stars were back. Had it been a dream? But when I sat up I saw a man in a trench coat and battered fedora climbing over our picket fence. He stopped for a moment, looked back at me and laughed.

• • • • • • • • • • • • • • • •

Dawn comes grudgingly to the West Virginia Mountains. Its arrival is delayed by a thick fog that blankets the countryside and clings to the valleys and gorges like a gauze blanket. As the fog began to lift from the old mine grounds, a suffused light revealed the broken buildings and piles of debris I had seen the night before by the light of bouncing headlights. In the middle of the yard was the crumbling brick building that had once served as the Company headquarters and bank. According to Walter, it had been rebuilt after the explosion but now, decades after the mine had closed, it was in a state of sad disrepair.

I looked at the distance between the mine and the building and wondered how far my father and uncles had gotten. It seemed like a long way to dig, but Pop and his brothers and sons, working part-time, had made it in just less than two weeks. I found myself beginning to doubt our chances. Could we make it to the bank? Would we ever find the elusive payroll? Did it even exist? I shook my head, blinked my eyes and tried to push those doubts from my head and concentrate on watching the gatehouse.

Joe relieved me later. His shirt was soaked through from carrying bundles of bracing timbers up to the mine. He was carrying a canteen and a sandwich, obviously too tired to eat quite yet. He sat down heavily and wiped his face with his wet shirttail.

"How's it going up there?" I asked.

"Slow," he said. "The guys say it's worse than digging a new tunnel from scratch because the rocks and clay above the caved-in sections were loosened by the explosion that caused the tunnel to collapse. They dig out a section, only to have it cave in again. They have to use twice the bracing."

"How far have they gotten?" I asked. I looked again at the distance between the mine and the bank and felt the sense of anxiety that had gripped me earlier return.

"Don't know," Joe said, drinking deeply from his canteen. "They haven't said. But they keep measuring the distance with a length of rope."

Walter and my father were on the break part of their shift when I arrived at the mine entrance. They looked exhausted. Their clothes were soaked and dirty, their faces were smudged and their eyes red-rimmed and vacant. I was reminded of the old black and white photographs I'd seen of miners coming off their shift. I felt guilty about not doing my part down in the tunnel even though the men had made it plain that none of us boys could go into it. I decided not to ask any questions and walked down to the trailers to help Neil bring up more bracing lumber.

The sun was fully up and beginning to heat the dusty mine yard. It glinted off the pieces of metal and shards of glass that littered the area. Today was shaping up to be a hot one.

Neil was pulling lumber out of one of the rental trailers and making a small pile to carry. His shirt was soaked through too.

"We're running low on lumber," he said. "If we have to make a run for more, we'll have to shut the whole operation down for a day." He threw some more lumber on the pile. "You know those guys will want to go at night and travel to get it."

"I've got more slivers in my hands that I've ever had," he said as he shouldered the lumber.

I nodded and began making my own pile as he trudged up the hill. It was true, the trailer was more than half-empty and it was the last one.

"Leave it right here," Walter said as I tried to go into the mine with my load. He pointed to the pile that Neil had just dropped. "We'll get it from here."

I wanted to protest, to tell him that we were all in this together and should be sharing the work and the risk. After all, Pop had used his sons, younger than any of us boys, to dig the original tunnel. But I knew that it would be fruitless and probably draw a sharp rebuke from my father, who was absorbed with some calculations he was making on a scrap of paper with the stub of a pencil.

"We're about halfway," he said. He gave Walter a hard look.

"How much lumber is left?" Walter asked, looking at me. I told him. He looked at my father. "We'll have to go for more lumber tonight."

My father nodded and got up, wiping his face with his sleeve. "Better get back at it," he said. The tone of his voice was not encouraging.

As I walked down to the trailers, I noticed Calvin sauntering across the mine yard, carrying a couple of pieces of lumber on his shoulder—about half the load that Neil and I were used to carrying. His shirt was dry and he had his unlit pipe clenched between his teeth.

"Where the hell have you been?" Neil asked when Calvin walked up to us.

"Lookin' around," Calvin said as he nonchalantly dropped the lumber at our feet. "I found these," he added.

Neil looked at the lumber. It was old but firm looking. "Where did you find it?" He asked.

"Over there," Calvin said, pointing towards a dilapidated building. "There's a big pile of lumber in it."

"Well Calvin," Neil said grinning. "You finally saved the day."

Calvin did not respond. He was trying to light his pipe.

Calvin's new source of lumber allowed us to work the rest of the hot day and through the starry night. Although we wouldn't run out of lumber for a while, I was worried that we would run out of energy. I myself was exhausted from carrying wood and I could see that Neil was too. Although Calvin had saved the day by finding the lumber, he was put on permanent guard duty because he refused to carry more than a few pieces at a time. "I've got a bad back," he said when Neil criticized him for being lazy. Joe had tried to carry too much and stumbled over a rock, twisting his ankle in the process. That left all the carrying up to Neil and me.

As tired as I was, I couldn't imagine how fatigued the men were who were doing the digging. When they came out on brief breaks, two at a time, I could see their energy and resolve was flagging. Charlie began to mumble about a "wild goose chase." Doc bitterly resented the lack of any more cold beer on the job site. Pete had hurt his arm in one of the many small cave-ins but was still gamely taking his shift. Frank, who wore a pacemaker for a heart condition, had turned a frightening shade of pale grey.

Only Walter, the oldest of the men, and my father, the youngest, had managed to maintain their drive. Walter still joked and argued and my father still bristled and argued back. The fact that they were still arguing was encouraging. There was a sort of normality to those arguments: it let everyone know that everything was all right, that everything was as it should be. So, Neil and I kept on carrying bundles of lumber up to the mine, Joe and Donnie kept guarding the gatehouse, Calvin kept trying to light his pipe and the men kept on digging.

Dawn came for the second time to the mine yard in the mountains. A crow called to announce it; it echoed eerily across the empty yard and bounced off the facing hills. From where I stood, next to the old lumber building, I could see Joe, still on guard. He waved. We had run out of food sometime during the night and were getting dangerously low on fresh water. My stomach rumbled.

"How much longer, do you suppose?" Neil asked. It was a rhetorical question: he knew that I didn't know any more than he did.

I shrugged. "Until it's done, I guess," I said.

Neil laughed. It was a family joke: whenever anyone would ask Gram about one of her recipes she would always answer vaguely: "How much salt?" "Enough." "How much flour?" "Enough." "How long do you cook it?" "Until it's done." She never followed a recipe. From many years of cooking, she knew instinctively just how much of every ingredient to use, which spices and herbs to add, what cooking temperature to set the oven, and how long to leave it in.

Sharing a laugh, we trudged up the hill for what seemed to be the millionth time. But as we arrived we saw a strange and troubling sight: all six men were standing around together, looks of dismay on their faces. Neil and I dropped our burdens and stood, saying nothing.

"They hit water," Calvin said. He said it in a nonchalant manner, as if he were looking at the sky and predicting rain. He lit his pipe and tossed the match off to the side.

"There's no getting through," my father explained. "The tunnel is intact but completely flooded. Doc tried to swim it, but it was too far."

I looked at Doc. He was soaked from head to toe. He had a defeated look on his face— something that I had never seen before.

"I swam as far as I could, but I'm not a good swimmer," he said. "I ran out of air and barely made it back."

"I'll swim it," I said. Everyone looked at me in surprise, but I was the one who was most surprised. I hadn't thought it out, hadn't considered the length of the tunnel, and hadn't considered the danger. But, once I said it, I was committed.

My father shook his head. "Absolutely not," he said. "Doc tried…"

"If I can do one thing well, its swim," I said. "And I can hold my breath forever. You know that."

"Let the kid give it a try," Doc said. "I smoke and drink too much. I don't have any wind any more. He can make it a lot farther than I did."

"What are you going to do if you don't get to the other side of the water?" My father asked. I could tell that he was starting to waver – there was never any quit in my father; or anyone in my family, for that matter.

"I'll bring a rope," I said, thinking on my feet. "I'll tie it to my ankle. I'll tug twice when I get clear of the water. If I find the payroll, I'll tie the rope to a handle and tug three times; you can pull it back. I'll follow."

"And if you get past your point of no return and can't swim any farther?" My father asked pointedly, a hard look on his face.

"Keep feeding the line out," I said. "If I stop swimming and don't tug, pull me back."

My father crossed himself, a rare and strange thing.

"Let's do it," he said.

The ceiling of the tunnel was short, maybe five feet, and narrow; I had to crouch as I walked its length. It soon became very steep and I slipped and slid down the slick mixture of crumbled shale and clay that formed its floor. I had the sense that we were going down the hillside towards the yard, keeping a few feet from the surface. I was amazed at the skill of Pop and his crew. They had dug the tunnel with great precision, using dead reckoning for direction and depth – and they had done it in their spare time, keeping it a secret from both their friends and the detectives. And the risks: cave-ins, floods, gas; not to mention the detectives, who would have certainly shot them. It was sad that they had come so close but had not succeeded in retrieving the payroll. It must have tortured Pop, to have lost so much in the effort. It reminded me of Icarus, the ancient Greek who had flown too close to the sun with his wings made of wax. The sun had melted the wax and he fell to his death in the sea.

As the tunnel leveled, I had the opportunity to notice the work the men had done with the lumber I had carried, shoring it up. Bigger pieces of lumber served as the framework, while smaller scraps, along with flat pieces of shale, were wedged behind the framework in order to keep the loose dirt and rock at bay. Still, there were piles of debris everywhere, oozing out from between the bracings. I shuddered to think of what would happen to us all if the thing decided to just give way.

After what seemed like a long time, we finally came to the flooded section of the tunnel. I stopped and stared at it with apprehension. The tunnel dipped down again, probably to get below the large drainage ditch that ran across the mine yard. I reasoned that when the explosion had occurred, the standing water in the ditch had flooded the tunnel. Rainwater had leaked in there ever since. The problem was how far the dip in the tunnel went. It was now my job to find out.

I stripped down to my shorts and bare feet— the better to flutter kick on my swim, which I hoped would be a short one. I tied the end of a long rope around my left ankle. "Two short pulls on the rope means that I reached the other side," I repeated nervously. "Three long pulls means that I've tied the rope to the strong box. You can start pulling it back. I'll follow."

"You don't have to do this, Thomas," my father said. There was a strong tone of apprehension in his voice. I realized that he was allowing me to gamble with my life and, if anything went wrong, he would blame himself for the rest of his life. It also occurred to me that it would be a hard thing to explain to my mother and the rest of the family.

"Don't worry, I may be dumb, but I'm not stupid," I said, quoting one of Walter's favorite sayings. I turned and began walking down the decline and into the water.

The first thing that I noticed was that the water was a lot colder than I had anticipated. In fact, it was downright freezing. I started shivering before I even got in up to my thighs. Girding my resolve, I waded in until the water reached my waist. Boxers, when they are overheated, will dump ice down their shorts to cool themselves; evidently, blood vessels are close to the surface in that area and the coolness quickly spreads to the rest of the body. The water in the tunnel had the same effect on me, but, in this case, the effect was undesirable. I started shivering uncontrollably and felt my lips going blue. But gradually my body acclimated to the temperature. I took a few deep breaths to purge my lungs of carbon dioxide and plunged down into the submerged tunnel.

I had a waterproof headlamp to guide me down the dark passageway; the wet walls shimmered in its light. I hoped that the dip in the tunnel was not too long; I could swim a good distance underwater in a pool or warm lake, but the chill water of the tunnel caused my heart to beat like a rabbit's in order to warm my blood; it was using oxygen at a rate I hadn't expected and producing carbon dioxide in the process. The desire to breathe came very quickly and I became anxious that I would have to turn back before I reached the other side.

I swam hard, hoping to warm my body. It worked, at least to a certain extent, and my progress was good. I had hyperventilated before diving in and I let out short bursts of air at regular intervals to keep the carbon dioxide from building up in my system. I had a good sense of how far I had gone, and knew almost exactly where my point of no return would be. I also knew that, if I turned and swam back, I would be sacrificing the mission. There would be no second try.

I had seen the drainage ditch that Pop had tunneled under, and knew that, even though the path of the tunnel crossed it diagonally, the distance wasn't prohibitively great. When I reached what I thought was my point of no return, I decided to go for it.

Pride can spur a person on to super-human effort, and it can bring victory over overwhelming odds. Pride, coupled with the fear of failure is a powerful thing. But it can be a dangerous thing too: it can over-ride com mon sense. Like the fabled Icarus, who flew too close to the sun with his waxed wings, it can cause a person to over-reach and plunge into failure. That combination of pride and fear of failure caused me to swim on.

Once, when I first learned that I could swim a long way underwater, I decided to test myself. I spent a lot of time at a place called Bedford Beach, an old quarry turned into a private swimming facility. Spring fed, it had beautiful clear water that was green hued in the deeper spots. One side had a beach of pure white sand, trucked in every year at the beginning of the season. There was a snack shack, locker room and recreation center. On the other side rock cliffs, formed by the quarry excavation, stood at varying heights. Swimmers climbed up the cliffs and dived into a deep pool; some of the divers had been on high school and college swim teams and put on a show for the spectators sitting at picnic tables or on blankets on the beach.

A tall lifeguard tower stood in the center of the lake. Lifeguards usually took a rowboat out and back but some, to be cocky, would swim it. I decided to do it under water.

I hyperventilated and dove in, swimming hard. Big quarries like Bedford Beach have underwater currents, caused by subterranean springs; they're powerful, and cold. I struggled against several on my way to the lifeguard stand. It was taking me longer than I had guessed. I reached a point where the urge to breathe stopped and my lungs ceased burning; I felt like I could swim forever. The water suddenly turned iridescent, swirling around me in beautiful patterns, like a living kaleidoscope. Shallow water blackout is caused by a lack of oxygen in a swimmer's system. It causes the swimmer to pass out. He then breathes involuntarily, filling his lungs with water. That's called drowning.

That day, at Bedford Beach, I should have drowned. But, quite by chance, I ran into the substructure of the lifeguard tower and slid up onto the wooden pad where the rescue rowboat was stored. When I breathed, it was air.

The lifeguard on the tower, a guy whose name was Clarence Wellington but who everyone called "Duke", told me later that he heard a thump, looked down and saw me on the pad.

"You swam all the way out here underwater?" Duke asked me.

"Yeah," I managed, still gulping air and trying to get my bearings.

"Awesome," he said. "You OK?" He added, a little dubiously.

"Fine," I lied.

Now I felt myself heading towards another shallow water blackout, but this time it was in a mine tunnel with no lifeguard stand at the end of it. I had an additional worry: if the men decided to start pulling me back on the rope, I would use the last of my energy – and air – fighting them. I did not have enough air to make it all the way back, even if pulled. I let out the last of the air in my lungs and swam on.

I knew that I was moments away from blacking out when I saw a strange shimmering above me, reflected off the walls by my headlamp. At first I thought it was the beginning of shallow water blackout and a surge of panic engulfed me. I squeezed my eyes shut, trying to banish the oncoming hallucination, but when I reopened them the shimmering was still there. I suddenly realized that it wasn't a hallucination at all. It was the surface of a pool in an air pocket. I swam upwards towards it.

Desperate to get air, I swam too hard and banged my head into the ceiling of the tunnel as I surfaced; I was only able to get a small gulp of air before sinking back into the pool. My head swam from the concussion and the long period of oxygen deprivation. As I started to head for the surface again, more carefully this time, I suddenly felt a strong pull on the rope around my ankle. The men, thinking that I had stopped before reaching the end of the tunnel, were going to pull me back. I swam hard, trying to resist the powerful force that was dragging me away from my precious air supply, but the men, thinking me unconscious, were pulling fiercely. I tucked, turned and swam at the rope, causing it to go slack for a moment. I grabbed the rope and tugged twice on it. Thankfully, I felt it go slack again.

I swam back to the air pocket and filled my lungs. Shining my headlamp down the tunnel, I could see that the pool ended at a clear and dry section of the tunnel. I had made it. I climbed out of the pool and, ducking under the short ceiling, began walking, the rock and debris on the tunnel floor cutting my feet painfully. Training my headlamp on the floor in order to avoid shards of rock, I walked on for a dozen or so yards. I stopped for a moment and fixed the headlight beam on the tunnel ahead of me. What I saw shocked me: it was another pile of debris, completely closing off the tunnel. I walked up to it, hoping that it was just a small blockage, but as I examined it, I could see shattered beams. It was completely closed. It would be impossible to get equipment and men through the flooded tunnel in order to dig through. It looked like our quest was at an end.

I felt deflated. Like an athlete who gives the game his all and still loses, I slumped down, my head on my knees. I hated the idea of swimming back through the tunnel, only to deliver the bad news. How is it, I wondered, that I would be the one to end the adventure that had taken so much work, that had cost everyone so much effort. I bitterly regretted volunteering to swim the tunnel; regretted coming along on the mission in the first place. I should have been sitting back at the campground, toasting marshmallows over the fire. Like a field goal kicker who misses the winning kick, I felt that the failure of the whole operation was my fault alone.

Finally, with no other options open to me, I stood up and prepared for the swim back, this time aided by the rope. I took one last look at the debris behind me, wondering if I should try to pull away the rocks and soil by hand. However, I realized that, without tools and bracing, it would be a futile and dangerous effort. Plus, I knew that if I stayed overlong, someone would try to make the swim in an attempt to rescue me.

As I turned away from the debris pile, something glinted off to my left in a little alcove. I shined my headlamp directly on the area and got a shock that haunts my dreams to this day.

There, sitting side by side, were two dead miners. I fell to my knees, unable to wrench my eyes away from them. They were small, just boys and I knew exactly who they were right away. They were Pop's sons Thomas and Neil, my lost uncles. They were holding hands; the smaller of the two had his head resting on the other one's shoulder. The rare atmosphere of the tunnel had mummified them. I saw that they were sitting on a large strongbox with "Property of Fieldstone Mines" stenciled on the side.

The thought occurred to me to leave the brothers where they were, undisturbed, as they had been for so many decades. Just swim back, tell everyone that the tunnel was impassible, and leave that god-forsaken pay roll behind. But the sense of mission had infected me. During the war the men had all gone on missions that they thought were futile, or even pointless. But they carried them out anyway. I had the same sense about this mission: I had volunteered to get the strongbox, and get it I would. Whether I could bring myself to tell them about the two boys was an open question.

I gave the rope two slow tugs to indicate that I was still OK and then began the onerous task of removing the bodies of the boys from atop the strongbox.

They were desiccated, light and fragile, like marionettes without their strings. I tried not to think that these were once humans; that these were my missing uncles. I laid the first one out next to the strongbox and straightened out his body, crossing his hands over his chest and placing his miner's helmet over them. I did the same with the second brother, but when I came to cross his hands, I noticed a scrap of paper clenched in one of them. Carefully, I removed it and unfolded it. It was dried out and crumbly but the writing was still legible.

> *We are Neil and Thomas Edwards, two brothers caught up in a fool's errand and now dead because of it. Make no mistake: we volunteered for the mission. Our father was against it, but we insisted.*

> *The plan was to rob the detective's payroll. We did it – it's in the strongbox we're sitting on. I don't think it'll do us much good now.*

> *We tunneled for days to get under the company headquarters where they kept the payroll. While our father and uncle Sam set off an explosion in the armory as a diversion, we, along with our uncle Don, broke through the floor of the headquarters building and got the strongbox.*

> *While we carried the strongbox out through the tunnel, uncle*

Don set a charge to cover the deed. It must have gone off when he was setting it. He must be dead too. The tunnel caved in behind us and flooded ahead of us. Neither of us can swim very far and we have no tools to dig out. The detectives would shoot us if we got out anyway – after they tortured us.

So it is for us to sit here and gradually run out of air. But, at least we're together.

I folded the paper back up and put it in a plastic bag that I had in the pocket of my shorts for carrying my wallet. I pulled the heavy strongbox, it was much bigger and heavier than I had expected, along the floor of the tunnel and to the edge of the water, tying the rope to one of the heavy metal handles with a clove hitch. I checked to make certain that the lid was secure and tugged on the rope three times. Almost immediately, the rope tightened. I pushed the heavy strongbox into the water and watched it bump and bounce along the floor of the tunnel until it disappeared into the water.

I walked over to the bodies of the two boys, knelt and said a prayer. I imagined what it must have been like for them, trapped in this little crypt, knowing that they were going to die there. Then I thought again about all of the miners who had suffered the same fate over the years, the coal companies refusing to put any real effort into a rescue. Well, at least the boys and Don had died trying to get something more for themselves than a few dollars a day and an early grave.

Turning, I hyperventilated and dove into the cold water once again.

I hadn't gotten halfway back when I encountered the strongbox, caught on a rock. I swam over top of it and tugged twice on the taut rope as a signal for the men to stop pulling. It immediately went slack. I squatted and heaved upwards on the handle, but the strongbox wouldn't budge. I was almost out of air, but thought I had enough for one last effort. This time the box came free, but, to my horror, the men, thinking that the tug on the rope was a signal to start pulling again, began to do just that. The big box, riding the big rock it had been trapped behind, loomed above me.

On my back, I cocked my legs against the rock and pushed off for all I was worth. I stretched out and kicked frantically, grabbing ahold of the rope as I did. A line from the Thomas Galvan poem occurred to me: "I rued the treasure stolen now, growing large and heavy." The box came down with a thud, barely missing my feet.

Trapped in the position I had gotten into, I had no choice but to brace my feet against the box and allow myself to be banged, bounced and dragged along the bottom of the tunnel. I had purged my system of CO_2 before I had entered the water and now I let out the last of my breath, hoping to get pulled out before I blacked out. But it was not to be. One moment I was cold and battered, my lungs screaming for air; the next my pain went away, replaced by a feeling of utter peace and serenity. Colors, warm, brilliant and inviting, filled my head. I felt my consciousness drifting peacefully up and away from that horrible flooded tunnel and my two dead uncles lying at the end of it, younger than me when they died.

• • • • • • • • • • • • • • • •

I awoke to a circle of faces above me. Strong hands pushed at my chest and I felt myself retching up quantities of fetid water and choking violently.

"He's alright," I heard Doc say. "He's breathing!"

There was a murmur from the faces and they were smiling. I tried to respond, but I gagged and threw up more water.

"What'd ya do kid, try to drink the tunnel dry?" It was my uncle Charlie. He reached out and tousled my hair. "Thought we'd lost you for a minute," he added somberly.

I saw my father's face, pale but relieved. He winked and nodded his head as if to say: "Glad you made it." But he didn't say anything.

Doc sat me up and someone handed me a towel while he swabbed at my cuts and gashes.

"Looks like you went through a meat grinder," Neil said.

"He's bleeding like a pig!" Calvin added, referring to the blood pouring out of a big cut on my scalp.

I began to feel dizzy and light headed. I thought I might pass out again.

"Easy kid," Doc said. "You're OK. Scalps bleed a lot but there's no danger." He put a second towel on my head and sat me up. "I've seen a lot worse than this," he said softly. "Don't worry."

"I'll be alright," I said gamely. Then I passed out again.

When I again awoke I was propped against the far wall in the main mineshaft, a blanket wrapped around me and another behind my head. Neil was sitting next to me, his hand on my shoulder.

"Can't get the lock off the strongbox," he said when he realized I was awake again.

I could see my father standing over the strongbox, banging at the heavy-duty lock with a hammer.

"We might have to use the torch," he said, looking at Joe. "This thing is built like a brick shithouse!"

"I'll go get the tank," Joe said. As he turned, the light beam from his headlamp fell on a figure standing in the entrance to the mineshaft. It was an old man, bent and wizened. He held what I recognized as a Thompson submachine gun in his hands, the barrel pointed at us.

"I'll be taking that strongbox," he said in a thick Welsh accent that reminded me of my grandfather. "Step away from it, and you might live through this night," he added.

My father and uncles stood transfixed, their mouths agape.

"I won't tell you a second time," the old man said. There was menace in his voice.

The men began to step slowly away from the strongbox, their eyes warily on the mysterious old man.

But then, out of the shadows behind him, stepped Walter. He put his Nambu to the old man's head.

"Lower the barrel and drop the gun," he said. He repeated his statement in Welsh. The old man did as Walter said. I expected at any moment that he would duck away from Walter's pistol and begin firing. I think the men thought so too as they crouched nervously, watching the scene play out.

"Take the barrel from my grandfather's head Walter," a voice commanded. It was female and familiar. I was shocked to see Karen step into the collective light of everyone's headlamps. She had a shotgun on her shoulder, aimed directly at Walter's head.

"Jesus!" I heard Doc say.

Walter lowered his pistol and stepped away, but his eyes weren't on Karen and the shotgun; they were on the old man. He said something to him in Welsh. The old man looked shocked. Walter rolled his sleeve up and showed him a tattoo on his upper arm. It was a white flower with the Blodwyn code: "Na ad I'th dafod dorri'th wddf"; let not your tongue cut your throat."

With a shock, I suddenly remembered that it was Walter's tattoo that I had seen once, while he was changing his shirt. It was the same white flower and inscription that was on Pop's journal. Walter was a Blodwyn!

"Lower the gun lass," the old man said to Karen. "He's a friend."

Karen gave him a quizzical look, but eased the safety on the shotgun and lowered it.

"Everyone stand easy," Walter said. He set his pistol on the floor of the mine. Karen did the same with her shotgun. The tension, so palpable only moments ago, melted away.

The old man fished a crumpled cigarette package out of his pocket, pulled a cigarette out, and lit it.

"I'm Gerald," he said. "I was your father's direct contact in the Blodwyns. I've been shadowing him and you for all of these years, hoping to find the whereabouts of this strongbox, the rightful property of the Blodwyns. And now I find that Walter here is one of us."

"Walter?" my father said, looking at his brother for an explanation.

"After the war I came down here," Walter explained. "I had to find out about Neil, Thomas, Don and Sam. I went to work in the mines.

"After a time the Blodwyns contacted me and I joined. I hoped that someone might know something. But all I could find out was that they had been killed by the detectives and buried in a mass grave. Their names and Pop's are on a plaque at the spot of the grave."

Walter paused for a moment, fighting a strong emotion. He visibly collected himself, lit his pipe, and continued.

"The Bodwyns were active during the war and were involved in the wartime miner's strikes. But after the war, union membership began to shrink. The leaders of the United Mine Workers turned away from strikes and violence and concentrated on gaining better terms and conditions at the negotiating table. A few years or so after I joined, the group disbanded. Not long after that I quit the mines and came home."

Gerald shook his head. "The boys aren't in that grave," He said. "And neither are your uncles."

Walter looked shocked. "I know that Sam isn't, he was killed during Pop's escape. But then…"

Gerald interrupted. "I didn't want the Company to suspect any of them of the theft. There was a huge demonstration at the mines that turned violent. Many were killed on both sides. I slipped their names onto the list of dead miners after the shooting.   Its news to me that Sam was killed, but what of Don and the boys? Where have they been hiding all these years? Why aren't they here now?"

The men looked at each other, shrugging and wearing questioning looks.

"They never got out of the tunnel," I said. My words seemed to echo in the dark damp mineshaft. Everyone looked at me in surprise.

"They were trapped in there," I explained. "Don's explosives must have gone off prematurely, at least that's what the boys said."

"You saw them?' Walter asked. His face had gone pale and he was struggling to control his emotions. No one understands the fear of being trapped in a mine better than a miner. I pulled the plastic bag out my pocket and took the note out. Shakily, I read it to the group. Walter made a sound I had never heard before; it was a cry of pure grief. He sank to his knees and buried his face in his hands. Gerald walked over to him and knelt, his hand on Walter's shoulder. He said something softly in Welsh that could only have been a prayer.

No one said anything for a really long time, each lost in his own thoughts. I stared at the floor of the mine trying to get the image of my two dead uncles out of my mind. At one point I saw Karen walk over to Doc and put her hand on his arm.

"I'm sorry," she said softly. Doc patted her hand lightly and then lifted it away from his arm.

"I know what you must be thinking," she said.

"Do you?" Doc said. He got up and walked out of the mine. Karen stood for a moment, a look of profound sadness on her face. Then she followed him. As she passed me she turned and did a strange thing, she mouthed the words 'I'm sorry.' Tears were streaming down her face. She broke into a run with an audible sob.

"Poor lass," Gerald said. "I raised her after her parents died in a car accident; put her through school, the best on money I'd taken from the Blodwyns when I left to find your grandfather. She moved away and was living her life when you lads decided to dig up your father's grave to get his journal. I had no one else and needed her help. I called her back."

"How did you know we got the journal?" my father asked.

"I was at his funeral and saw his wife throw the journal into his casket. I figured you guys might try to retrieve it someday, so I kept watch at the graveyard for a few hours every night. I had nothing better to do. I watched you dig him up."

I swallowed hard and looked down at my hands. I was supposed to be on watch that night.

"It was Karen's idea to befriend Doc," he continued. "She got him to invite her along on the fishing trip. She would call me every night with your location and I would follow, staying in local hotels along the way."

"Seems like a lot of effort for a week's payroll for the detectives," Neil said.

"You don't know what's in the strongbox?" Gerald said incredulously.

He looked round at everyone. The men shrugged.

Gerald laughed. "Do you think I would spend most of my adult life trying to find a weeks payroll? Pop knew exactly what was in it too, that's why he ran and hid for so long. He knew someone would be coming for him. The strongbox contains the mine company's gold reserves; gold ingots worth a fortune. Pop knew about them and knew that we planned to take them during his attack on the company arsenal. We had been planning it for weeks.

"I was surprised when John and Sam had volunteered for the diversion, we all thought that it was a suicide mission. I never thought that I would be able to get them out, but I did. It was only later that I learned that Don and the boys had gone in and got the strongbox – before our team could get in there. I never guessed that they were trapped in the tunnel. I always thought that they had gotten clean away. I was sent to find the the strongbox and kill John."

He looked around at the group, a sad look on his face. He walked over to the strongbox and sat down heavily, extracting another cigarette from the crumpled packet that he kept in his pocket.

"Coal killed John, as it is killing me," he said, inhaling his cigarette over a cough. "And here I sit, on the box that cost so many people their lives."

Walter, still shaken over the news about his two brothers, walked over and sat down next to him. I was struck by the irony of the image: two old men, re-creating the scene of the two young miners I had encountered in the tunnel, sitting on the same strongbox.

Walter shook his head sadly. "Don was an expert demolitions man," he said. "He never would have pre-maturely set off the charge under the bank. "He had to have done it on purpose."

Gerald looked at him quizzically.

"Don must have heard your team coming down the stairs and thought they were detectives. He cut the fuse short and, hoping that the boys had made it out, set off the charge to cover their escape."

"That explosion killed three of our lads," Gerald said sadly. "And it killed three of yours."

"Well," Walter said. He stood and brushed his pants off. "Here we are with two missions accomplished. "The last of the Blodwyns."

Gerald stood and shook Walter's hand. "Na ad I'th dafod dorri'th wddf," he said.

"Amen," Walter said. They turned and walked out of the mine. Strangely, the other men followed, seemingly disinterested in the strong-box and it's contents.

I looked at Neil, who was still at my side.

"Mission accomplished," I said.

"Roger," he said with a laugh.

Joe brought in his welding equipment and knelt next to the big strongbox. He lit his torch and applied the flame to the rusty padlock. An eerie blue light filled the mine, along with the loud hissing of the torch.

The End

About the Author

Marshall Seddon graduated from Fredonia State University in 1971. He served six years in the New York State National Guard, taught history at Brocton Central School for forty years and was a founding member of the Blackhorse Rugby Football Club. He enjoys fly fishing and playing jazz guitar. He and his wife Heidi live in Fredonia, New York. They have eight children, two golden retrievers and a cat named Twist.